RURIK: A ROYAL DRAGON ROMANCE

Brothers of Ash and Fire Book 3

LAUREN SMITH

This book is a work of fiction. Names, characters, places, and incidents are the product of the author's imagination or are used fictitiously. Any resemblance to actual events, locales, or persons, living or dead, is coincidental.

Copyright © 2018 by Lauren Smith

Excerpt from *Grigori: A Royal Dragon Romance* by Lauren Smith, Copyright © 2018

Cover art by Cover Couture

Photography by Wander Aguiar Photography

All rights reserved. In accordance with the U.S. Copyright Act of 1976, the scanning, uploading, and electronic sharing of any part of this book without the permission of the publisher constitutes unlawful piracy and theft of the author's intellectual property. If you would like to use material from the book (other than for review purposes), prior written permission must be obtained by contacting the publisher at lauren@laurensmithbooks.com. Thank you for your support of the author's rights.

The publisher is not responsible for websites (or their content) that are not owned by the publisher.

ISBN: 978-1-94206-22-9 (e-book edition)

ISBN: 978-1-94206-23-6 (trade paperback edition)

ISBN: 978-1-947206-30-4 (hardback edition)

PROLOGUE

GREAT HEROES NEED GREAT SORROWS AND BURDENS, OR HALF THEIR GREATNESS GOES UNNOTICED. IT IS ALL PART OF THE FAIRY TALE. —PETER S. BEAGLE, THE LAST UNICORN

Moscow, Russia

Rurik Barinov watched the men and women dance in his nightclub, Logovo—the Lair. Its dark interior was lit by flashing strobe lights and fog from the machines at the opposite ends of the dance floor. The entire club looked like a cross between a cave and a dungeon. The walls were rough stone, and dancers were showing off their moves in iron-barred cages.

While Rurik's older brother ran a sensible business, one that was built on technology in commerce, Rurik traded in something far older: pleasure. Dancing, drinking, and sex never went out of style. He was not buttoned-up and proper like Grigori. He enjoyed wild nights with wicked women, bodies straining and yearning for that headlong rush of mutual satisfaction. It never ceased to amaze him that Grigori had walked away from such things. But he'd heard that after a thousand years a dragon tended to lose his wildness, at least in part. Only when they found their mate did they experience a resurgence of that frenzied lust.

Rurik chuckled. He could not picture Grigori doing *anything* with a frenzy except slaughtering the competition in a boardroom. He was damned good at that. Scary as fuck too, always cool and controlled. Yet when Rurik had shown interest in the little mortal professor, Madelyn Haynes, Grigori's eyes had blazed and he'd growled a dark and dangerous warning. It was the first time he'd ever been afraid of his own brother. Dragons were possessive by nature, and as Russian Imperial shifters they were more covetous than others when it came to jewels and women.

Thinking about jewels reminded Rurik of his other brother, Mikhail. The brother who was lost to them. He'd failed to secure a hoard of jewels from a treaty they'd made with English dragons and had been exiled for his failure by their father. For one brief year when their father and mother had traveled the world, Grigori had called Mikhail home. For four seasons, Mikhail had been part of the family again. That had been two centuries ago.

He wished Mikhail were here now. Mikhail knew Grigori better in some ways, even though he hadn't been home since the nineteenth century. Mikhail would have known how to warn Grigori against the temptations mortal females presented.

"Rurik?" A sweet voice caught his attention and dragged him out of his ancient thoughts. A beautiful French woman with dark hair and green eyes watched him from across the bar. His best bartender, Nikita, wore a silver sequined dress and killer black heels that made every man in the room assume she was a customer and not the bartender. Whenever he looked at her, the hardness in his heart always softened. But she was human, and he could never be with a human. Not for long.

"How are the numbers tonight?" he asked as he joined her, leaning on the bar toward her. He couldn't help it—she pulled him in like the glint of a diamond just within reach. It made him practice his self-restraint.

She smiled warmly, a smile meant only for him, and he knew why. She was in love with him, but she was too much like him, a free spirit, unchained even by the forces of love. Any other woman he would have slept with and moved on, but he couldn't do that with Nikita. She had the potential to be a true mate. If he even dared to kiss her, it could destroy his family. Battle dragons couldn't risk love; their lives were dangerous. If they dared to mate a human, that human could be used against them. A fragile mortal life was easy to snuff out, and that would kill the dragon because mated dragons always died shortly after their mates.

"Good. We are at maximum capacity, but—" Her voice trailed off, and her eyes widened as she stared at something over his shoulder.

"Niki?" he queried.

Her green eyes cut to his, and she whispered one word.

"*Drakor.*"

He spun, instincts kicking in. Ruslan Drakor stood only a few feet away, grinning like the devil he was. As the eldest son of Dimitri Drakor, the head of the Drakor family, Ruslan was an arrogant bastard who believed he didn't have to abide by the terms of the treaty between the Barinov and Drakor families.

"Ruslan. What the fuck do you want?" Rurik made a grand show of leaning casually against the bar, even though every muscle in his body was tense.

He prayed that Ruslan wouldn't be so stupid as to attack him in a club full of humans. The Drakor family ran the eastern half of Russia, while the Barinovs controlled the west. The Yenisey River acted as the formal boundary between their territories because it split Russia almost cleanly in half.

The Barinovs had control of both Moscow and Saint Petersburg, and under Rurik's father in 1750, they had made a treaty that allowed the Drakors to enter and leave those two cities without incident so long as they did not interfere with Barinov business or cause trouble. This protected both of their families. Conflict between supernatural houses tended to attract the wrong kind of attention, such as the Brotherhood of the Blood Moon.

"I've come for a drink and women." Ruslan laughed, but there was a feral gleam in his eyes.

Rurik remained still, the picture of casual ease. They both knew that Rurik could knock Ruslan on his ass without breaking a sweat.

"Good for you, Ruslan, but find another club. *Not mine.*" Had they been outside the city, Rurik would have attacked, but the damned treaty kept him on his best behavior.

Ruslan brushed his dark hair out of his eyes and walked to the other end of the bar. His expression changed to one of hunger as he spied Nikita.

"You, female, bring me the best vodka in the house." He slapped his palm on the counter hard enough that the expensive glass layer over the wood fractured, tiny cracks fanning out around his hand like spiderwebs.

Son of a dog... Rurik growled softly, the dragon inside him stirring. He could feel the tattoo moving on his back. He'd never been very good at restraining the beast within him, even at the best of times. His father had said it was because he was built for battle.

"Ruslan, leave now," he warned.

The other man made a show of getting comfortable. Then he looked over at Nikita and licked his lips. That was it.

"Nikita, the alarm if you please." Rurik tried to stay calm, but he could feel the dragon surging to the surface.

His bartender ducked beneath the bar and slapped a red button. An alarm blared, cutting the music off. Dancers scrambled out of the cages and off the dance floors, rushing toward the exits in varying degrees of panic.

It was a shame to lose a good night of business, but better to have an empty club than risk human casualties. There was nothing like a spike in mortality rates to draw the Brotherhood into their business. They had no offices in Moscow that he knew of, but there were always agents about, and they could mobilize from Saint Petersburg in short order. The last thing either he or the Drakor family needed were supernatural hunters swarming the city.

"Such hostility," Ruslan said. "I was just here to talk business. I like your bar. I was thinking about buying it. How about...one ruble?"

Rurik growled. "One last chance, Ruslan. Walk away and I leave your pretty face intact."

The other man laughed. "I was about to tell you the same thing."

Rurik sensed Nikita close behind him. Not everyone had left when the alarm went off. "Nikita, get out of here."

"But—"

"Go!" he roared, his voice dropping to a low pitch as his vocal cords started to transform.

Nikita tried to flee, but Ruslan threw up a hand. Fire shot out of his palm, and a blazing beam cut off her escape. Ruslan's eyes morphed into red irises with slitted pupils. A hint of smoke puffed from his nostrils. Both men were fighting to stay in control and not fully transform. The club wouldn't be able to fit one full-grown dragon, let alone two.

"You would break your father's treaty?" Rurik bellowed, raising his own palm, unleashing a spray of fiery sparks. It was the closest thing to a warning shot he could manage without starting a fire in his club.

"I am not bound by *his* word!" Ruslan balled his other fist and slammed it down on the bar. The glass counter shattered into thousands of pieces, and the wood beneath exploded in a burst of massive splinters.

A six-inch piece of wood buried itself in Rurik's lower belly. *Fuck!* Pain set in like a dull ache, and he knew it was bad.

"Rurik!" Nikita screamed and ran toward him. He gripped the shard and ripped it out. Hot blood streamed down his shirt, and his belly throbbed. He would heal fine—the wound was already clotting—but the sight of it must have scared her. When Nikita reached him, he waved her away.

"You have to get out." He panted. "I can't fight him and worry about you."

She bit her lip and nodded. "Be safe," she said. She kissed his forehead and fled, but she never reached the door. Ruslan raised his hand and aimed a jet of fire at Nikita. She was knocked into the wall against a massive mirror just feet from the exit. The mirror shattered, and her limp body fell to the ground. Blood dripped from Nikita's lips, and the light in her green eyes faded like the light of a dying star.

Something inside Rurik broke, a piece of his heart.

A cold, harsh laugh escaped Ruslan's lips. "What's one more human, more or less?"

Shock and grief raged inside Rurik. His Nikita, *his Niki* was gone. A red mist descended over his vision. He didn't care about the club, the treaty, or the Brotherhood right now. He cared only for vengeance.

With a deafening roar, Rurik's clothes shredded as his body transformed into a fifteen-foot-tall black-scaled dragon. His frill fanned out around his neck as he opened his jaws and a stream of fire shot out, so hot it was nearly blue.

Ruslan tried to change into his own beast, but Rurik's jaws caught Ruslan's elongated neck mid-change and snapped shut. The heavy crack echoed in the room as Ruslan went limp beneath him. The battle was over before it even began.

Rurik released him, and the body changed back to a man, lying broken and bleeding at Rurik's feet. Rurik's eyes darted around the room, seeking out more threats, and then he saw Nikita's body. The beast recognized the loss of a woman he cared about, and he let out a mournful sound.

Rurik let go of the dragon side of him, and his body shrank back to its mortal shell. Rurik fell to his knees.

Nikita was dead, Ruslan was dead, and a three-century-old treaty had been broken.

He dug his hands into his hair, trying to stop them from shaking as emotions rolled through him like violent riptides. How was he going to tell Grigori that he had killed Dimitri Drakor's eldest son?

I've just started a war.

I

AMONG ALL THE KINDS OF SERPENTS, THERE IS NONE COMPARABLE TO THE DRAGON. - EDWARD TOPSELL, 1658

Moscow, Russia – *Three months later*

Charlotte MacQueen tugged the sweetheart neckline of her red satin cocktail dress up a few more centimeters. Despite the thick red velvet winter coat she wore, her exposed skin had drawn the cabdriver's eyes and made her shift restlessly until he'd had to focus back on the road. But then, she'd known her dress would have this effect. She was practically falling out of the damn thing, but she had a hunch this would be one of the few times having full breasts would be an advantage instead of a hindrance.

She'd spent most of her life hiding her curvy figure behind draping sweaters and lab coats. It was silly, but she'd never felt comfortable in sexy clothes.

Charlotte wasn't sure if it was how the slide of satin felt on her skin or the way every masculine eye fixed on the thigh-high cut of her dress or the lowered neckline, but tonight she was trying hard to ignore how exposed she felt. She couldn't be distracted because she was pulling a Mata Hari. She was going behind enemy lines—or rather, into dragon territory—to seduce a seriously dangerous dragon shifter.

How the hell did I get here? It wasn't the first time she'd asked herself that question.

Before tonight, the idea of chasing down a man who could shift into a dragon was ludicrous. Not because she didn't think they were real; she'd grown up her entire life knowing the truth about things that went bump in the night. Vampires, dragons, werewolves, shifters—all of it. Until now, she'd been kept safe by her overprotective older brothers, but she was done with that. She wanted to do something meaningful with her life, and tonight that meant quite literally walking into the dragon's den.

If my brothers figure out I'm here, they'll probably try to send me to some convent like it's the middle ages. The thought almost made Charlotte smile, despite the dangerous situation. Her brothers, Damien and Jason, were the experts at this sort of thing—well, not the seduction part, but the infiltration. They would know exactly how to handle something like a dragon shifter. But she'd never been a part of their secret supernatural hunter lifestyle. Until tonight.

If I bag this guy, they'll have to admit I'm not just their kid sister anymore. Maybe then they'll let me join the Brotherhood.

But if she were being honest with herself, coming all the way to Moscow hadn't just been about proving her brothers wrong. It began when she saw the man from the files she'd gotten from the Brotherhood's headquarters. The man she couldn't get out of her head. The man she planned to capture.

Her target was Rurik Barinov, youngest of the three remaining dragons in the Russian Imperial bloodline who controlled the western half of Russia. Pulling out her cell phone, she scanned the pictures she had of him, probably for the hundredth time. She'd been lucky enough to snap some shots of the surveillance photos they had of him on file.

He was gorgeous in a dangerous sort of way, with a strong jaw, bright green eyes, and wavy dark hair that was a little too long, making him look a bit like a pirate from those swoon-worthy romance novels she'd devoured as a teenager. Charlotte hadn't known men could look like that in real life, and she'd already had some seriously dirty thoughts about what he would be like in bed. He'd been her first choice out of the three brothers to try to capture, but that wasn't because of his looks.

Rurik tended to wear leather jackets, jeans, and biker boots, and there was a long scar down one side of his face, which only made him look that much more dangerous. Her sexy biker dragon was too much of *everything*, and she had to admit getting close to him tonight was going to be a heck of a thrill.

God, there has to be something wrong with me. He's not my sexy biker. He's my target. But she couldn't deny the fact that the idea of getting up close and personal with Rurik turned her on.

Keep your cool and focus on the mission. It was the tenth time she had to remind herself of that.

Tonight was strictly recon, though. She needed to get into Rurik's club, survey the scene, locate and observe him. Nothing more. She'd read the notes on the Brotherhood's dragon monitoring. These days they really just tried to keep an eye on the dragons' activities and not interfere, but a few months ago two dragons had fought in a nightclub and a woman had died. This sparked rumors of a coming dragon war between two families in Moscow, possibly drawing in support from other countries. It could easily spiral out of control, and the Brotherhood were desperate to figure out how to stop it before it happened. And it all came down to Rurik.

He'd been the dragon at the nightclub who'd survived. Her brother Damien had made a note in the file that Rurik might be the key to all this. If they could question him, they could determine how serious the situation really was and whether or not they would have to intervene.

So far no one had been able to get close to Rurik. Direct contact was useless. Shifters didn't trust the Brotherhood and always closed ranks the moment they appeared. They'd tried incognito female agents. It seemed logical, given his background and reputation, but he never let any of them get close enough to lure him to a secure location. He always seemed to sniff them out somehow. And bringing him in by force would only justify the distrust shifters had and make it even harder to get answers.

That's why I'm here alone. Rurik won't see me coming.

She grinned a little. She wore a light perfume she'd concocted that contained a bit of enhanced pheromones, a side project she'd been working on. If it worked, she would catch his interest and then go with him rather than try to lure him somewhere with her. That had been the tipoff, she assumed. The moment the female agents had tried to get Rurik someplace he wasn't familiar with, the warning flags went up.

But Charlotte had a better way in mind.

Once she had him alone in a place he felt comfortable, she'd use her secret weapon on him: a drug that could incapacitate him long enough to call in the Brotherhood to help her transport him to secure facility where he could be questioned safely without anyone getting hurt.

The cabdriver hit the brakes as a car ahead of them swerved into their lane. Charlotte winced as she jerked forward and collided with the cab's back seat.

"Sorry!" the driver muttered in heavily accented English. Then he flashed an obscene gesture at the driver ahead of them. At this rate, it would take them forever to reach the club where Rurik was supposed to be.

Charlotte slid back in her seat and tried to still her jittery nerves. She would have been back in her little lab in Detroit—safe and sound, instead of here dragon hunting—if it hadn't been for her friend Meg.

Meg Stratford, a hunter for the Brotherhood, had secretly called on her to analyze a serum Meg had found in London—a drug that could subdue a dragon's shifting abilities. Charlotte had unraveled the chemical composition in a matter of days. The product she'd synthesized essentially made them human for a period of time depending on the dose. She'd made samples that would last around twenty-four hours on an average-sized shifter.

But the drug was potentially dangerous. Not in terms of

directly harming the shifters, but because of how easily it could be misused. In the wrong hands, it would threaten the balance that existed between the various supernatural factions. Even certain members of the Brotherhood, known for their overzealous nature, couldn't be trusted with it. As a result, Meg had sworn her to secrecy, even from her own brothers.

A stab of guilt cut through Charlotte. She'd told Meg she needed more information on dragons to help her solve the mystery of the serum, but that hadn't been true. The real reason she needed to know about dragons was because she planned to prove she was a worthy hunter just like her brothers.

She'd created a batch of the dragon-dampening serum for herself, and she had the vials tucked away safely in her hotel minifridge. She went over the list of what she knew about dragons in her head as the taxi drove toward Rurik's nightclub, the Lair.

1. Dragons could grow old—like thousands of years—but for most of their lives they resembled men and women in their mid-thirties.
2. There were more than a dozen breeds, such as Russian Imperials and Nordic ice dragons. Rivalries were common between many of them.
3. Dragons could breathe fire as well as control it.
4. They had protective thick hides with scales. Those scales were often used in magical spells.
5. Dragons could shift between human and dragon forms in seconds.
6. They were obsessed with jewels.
7. For some reason they were sensitive to pure iron. It could both injure them and bind them. While they could be wounded by normal weapons, they healed fast, and only iron weapons could do lasting damage.

Charlotte studied the Moscow nightlife nervously as the taxicab came to a stop in front of the nightclub. Being out of

America for the first time in her life, she definitely wasn't used to the cultural differences. On the flight over she'd listened to some Russian language lessons on her smartphone, trying to learn some phrases, but it gave her a headache. It didn't help that Russian was a notoriously difficult language, requiring a greater range of vocabulary just to reach a basic understanding. Luckily, the majority of the hotel staff and taxi drivers spoke English, something she was incredibly grateful for. However, once she stepped into that nightclub, she was positive it was going to be all Russian. The driver had warned her that this was a Russian-only nightclub, not the sort of place for tourists.

"Here is okay?" the driver asked.

"Yes, thank you." She slipped him a few hundred rubles and then got out of the cab. There were several men lingering at the entrance of the club, one of whom whistled when he caught sight of her.

She clutched her cell, which contained an emergency number for the Brotherhood office in Saint Petersburg, hoping she wouldn't have to use it. If things went poorly, she'd have to face her brothers and listen to them tell her "I told you so" about staying in Michigan, where life was safe but boring.

Please don't let this be a bad idea.

One of the men by the door said something to her in Russian, but she didn't understand him. She smiled but kept her head down as she brushed past them. One of the men slapped her ass as she walked by. She tensed and almost tripped.

Just stay cool, her inner voice warned her. She might not be a hunter like her brothers, but she'd taken enough self-defense classes to know how to take care of herself. If this guy wasn't careful, she'd kick him in the balls so hard they'd snap up into his cheeks. But she couldn't afford to make a scene. She needed to stay calm and not call attention to herself.

Ignoring the harsh laughter of the men outside, she slipped into the dark club interior. The energetic dance music enveloped her, and the bass pounded so hard against the walls that she could feel them shake as she skirted the club's interior. It took a moment for her eyes to adjust, even with the flashing white lights and pulsing strobes. Fog filled the bottom of the club, hiding a clear view of the dance floor. Everywhere people were dancing, drinking, and laughing. It was a hedonistic gathering where pleasures ruled the night.

Charlotte clutched her slender purse and headed for the bar. A dark-haired man with an intricate neck tattoo of a wolf howling was flipping bottles and pouring drinks. He took one look at her and retrieved a large rounded glass, then poured a dark red wine in it. He slid it across the slick wood surface of the bar to her. He chuckled when she caught the glass, which glided smoothly into her waiting hand. Then she took a sip.

Wow. The red was soft and dark with a hint of oak and… cherry? Yes, that was it. She smiled at the man, who gave a roguish wink before he turned to see to his other customers. A bartender who guessed your style of drink…that was certainly interesting. A guy like that would rake in tips in America. She studied his wolf tattoo more closely. Was he a shifter? Meg had told her all sorts of things about shifters over the years. Tribal tattoos were pretty popular among the wolf clans. But what were the odds that a wolf shifter was working in a dragon-shifter-owned bar?

She watched the dancers on the floor for a while, scanning the room until she saw what she was looking for. A back door. It probably led to some offices. That might be where Rurik hung out when he wasn't working in the club. But she had no plans to barge in there and look. She would stay here and wait. Hopefully he would come out soon, and then she could start her reconnaissance.

The files she'd studied assured her that he always stuck close to Moscow and rarely went to his second residence, which was somewhere south in the country. She took another sip of wine and looked back to the dancers. Three of the men from outside the club stood in front of her, watching her with wicked grins. She froze. The man who had slapped her ass was talking to her again in Russian.

"I'm sorry—I don't speak very much Russian," she told him, one of the few Russian phrases she could manage, and tried to turn back to the bar. One of them grabbed her from behind and dragged away from her seat.

"Let go!" She swung her purse, smacking him in the face. The heavy gold clasps thunked as they made contact with the man's nose. He cursed, clutching his face as he waved his other hand at his friends, who rushed her.

Oh shit! She dropped into a fighting stance, praying she wouldn't break an ankle in her low heels when she tried to roundhouse whoever made the first move on her. A man tried to grab for her hair with a meaty hand. She pulled herself back and countered. The man was too close for a roundhouse, but not a solid knee to the breadbasket. He dropped with a gasp, and Charlotte backed away, waiting for the next. But there were too many of them, and she doubted they'd oblige her by coming one at a time after that.

A deep bellowing shout thundered through the room and sent the men scrambling away like rats.

Panting, she held her purse, which dangled on its chain from one of her hands. She felt someone's eyes upon her, a gaze as tangible as a caress along her skin, making her shiver. She looked around for whoever had scared the men off. Her heart thumped in a panicked beat against her ribs when she saw who had rescued her, standing behind her.

Rurik Barinov. He looked dangerous and sexy in jeans and a black T-shirt and especially those biker boots. If she was being honest with herself, those boots had always played quite a large role in her fantasies whenever she thought of him. Considering he was supposed to be her target, not the star of her most sensual daydreams, that wasn't a good sign.

"Are you all right?" he asked. His accent, a deep, rumbling, slightly growling tone, did funny things to her insides. For a second she couldn't speak—her brain had short-circuited.

"I..."

Rurik gently grasped her by the elbow. That got a reaction

from her, as her first instinct was to pull back. But his response to this surprised her; he looked at her and said, "Please," while holding out his hand. Something about his voice disarmed her, and she allowed herself to be led away. He took her into a dark, quiet alcove where the acoustics of the room couldn't reach them. His eyes, a beautiful green, swept over her from head to toe. He pressed her back against the wall and cupped her chin, lifting her face. She shivered as his thumb caressed her bottom lip.

"Are you hurt?" he asked.

She shook her head.

He tilted his head, still studying her in an intense manner. "American?"

"Y-yes."

"You shouldn't come to a club like this alone. It is too dangerous for a flower such as you." He let go of her face, but he leaned in a few inches, inhaling deeply before he murmured something to himself in Russian.

"I'm not that delicate," she replied stiffly. Sure, she wasn't a kick-ass supernatural hunter like her brothers, but she wasn't *totally* helpless.

His lips curved into a grin that made a storm of butterflies come to life in her stomach. "It is true. Some flowers have thorns, and you certainly showed yours." The dim lights and the way he stood half in shadow exposed a thin scar that swept down his face across his cheek. It had a distinctive shape to it, as if he'd been slashed by something. Was it from another dragon's claw? She had to admit she was fascinated. The Brotherhood files on the Barinov dragons were slim. She wished she knew more about him, and she had a feeling she was about to.

"Yet I think you are more delicate than you realize, little one." He reached up to brush the backs of his fingers over her cheek. She shivered as a wave of arousal buzzed through her. She opened her mouth, even though she had no idea what she was going to say, but he placed a finger over her lips.

"Why don't you leave your purse with my bartender and come

dance with me?" He was tugging her away from the wall before she could argue. He slid her purse off her shoulder and tossed it at the tattooed man, who caught it in one hand and tucked it beneath the bar.

"Hey—"

"Shhh." Rurik pulled her against him as music wrapped around them, pulsing and thumping. His hands curled around her hips, the tips of his fingers riding the edge of her ass as they began to dance. He moved smoothly with a rolling gait, and the slide of his feet felt like he'd had tons of practice. She'd always been a terrible dancer, but with his hands and body guiding hers, he made it seem so easy. It bordered on surreal, being here with him, the lights of the club spinning around them and music pouring into her soul.

Maybe I'm just dreaming about him again.

It wouldn't have been the first time since she'd seen his face in those files that she'd woken up in the dead of night, her heart racing and her body hungry for the touch of this man...this man who was also a beast.

Her plan to capture him was still on track. If anything, this could work to her advantage. But she could relax, enjoy herself for a few songs first, couldn't she? Dancing was one of the few ways a man and a woman could speak to each other without words. Well, that and kissing. But she couldn't let him kiss her, not after she'd heard Meg's lecture about dragon pheromones.

As a biochemist, she was well aware of the drugging influences of pheromones in some animals, and that had led to an idea: What if she could turn the tables on him? Shifters were still essentially human, and while human pheromones did not affect people the way they did other animals, some samples obtained from a rogue dragon shifter the Brotherhood had had to take down had resulted in a minor breakthrough. The pheromones they gave off were still human, but they were supercharged somehow, amplified in a way that no human could do naturally, but she could reproduce it artificially. She was wearing a sample of it now, a field test to see if it might make her more interesting to Rurik.

But she was also worried about the reverse happening. She didn't want to come under the influence of anything she couldn't control, biological or chemical. Part of her worried that he might have already exerted some kind of subtle influence over her. There were rumors that dragons could compel humans with a form of hypnotism.

"You are enjoying yourself?" he asked in her ear.

His hands drifted lower, cupping her ass. A new flash of arousal hit her, and she couldn't help but moan when he pressed closer to her. She was too aware of him, of his undeniable sexuality. At times like this it sucked being a virgin. She felt like a live volcano ready to blow whenever she got too close to someone with raw sexual chemistry like this.

"Yes, this is fun!" she shouted over the music.

What the hell, right? Life is too short not to enjoy yourself.

He spun her in his arms, grinding her backside against him. She watched the dancers around them. The club was modeled to resemble a cave, but it also had a hint of a dungeon about it, complete with women dancing inside cages. Iron-barred honest-to-God cages. For a second she pictured herself in one of them, Rurik outside the bars, hungry to reach her, unable to touch her, yet knowing he had caught her. It was... Holy hell, it was so hot just to think about it.

Rurik's hand slid up her body from behind, not quite cupping her breast, but coming close. "Want to give it a try?"

"Try what?"

"The dancing cages. I can see that you're tempted."

She tried to shake her head, not wanting him to know she'd been way too turned on at the idea of him putting her in a cage. "No..."

He chuckled, his lips feathering against her ear. "Yes, you are."

She ducked her head, hair falling in front of her face, trying to hide from him. But he brushed it back, tucking it behind her ear and over her shoulder.

"Come." He led her toward one of the cages where a blonde

girl was shaking to a dance rhythm that Charlotte would never be able to copy. He opened the cage door and jerked his head. The girl left immediately.

Rurik pushed her toward the cage. "Get in, little one." She stumbled, caught herself on the bars, and turned to face him as he closed the cage door behind her. Then he leaned against the door, his arm muscles flexing. He had *trapped* her in the cage.

"Now, dance for me, sweetheart." Rurik's green eyes met hers, and she seemed to spiral into them. Every worry, every self-conscious thought she'd ever had seemed to fade into the back of her mind.

"Dance for me. Show me your heart's desire." The words were his, but he hadn't spoken them. It was as though she'd heard the words inside her head. An irresistible compulsion to do what he said came over her, almost as though she was drunk—only on words instead of alcohol.

Charlotte rolled her hips, feeling the beat of the music and letting it run through her blood like a current. She moved, spun, leaned against the bars and threw her head back, sending her hair in a cascade as she gave in to the wild part of herself. A part she'd always denied, ignored, or repressed.

All the while he watched, satisfied, the dragon with dark brown hair and bewitching eyes. The green of his eyes was intense like emeralds. His lips were parted, and his hands were white-knuckled on the bars. Was he restraining himself? Holding himself back? That only made Charlotte bolder, wilder. Dimly, she was aware that she was being very reckless, but she couldn't seem to stop.

I'm playing with fire. She just prayed she wouldn't get burned.

2

STARS WOULD FALL TO THEIR KNEES AT HIS COMPELLING VISION. - RAINER MARIA RILKE

"Come in with me," she said, knowing he would hear her despite the pounding music. A dragon's hearing was keener than any human's.

They stared at each other, the bass of the music making her heart thud against her ribs. His gaze pulled a woman in and drowned her with its promise of dark, delicious things. Charlotte could feel every cell in her body humming with sexual tension. Would he join her? Would he touch her again in a way that made her forget her very name?

Please...please make me forget everything but you. It was dangerous, but she wanted it, wanted to lose herself in this moment, lose herself in him.

Rurik flung the cage door open and entered, clanging it shut behind him. She swallowed hard, realizing that what she'd just asked had come true. She was trapped in a cage with a dragon—ancient, powerful, accountable to none but themselves—and this one was making her legs shake as he kept looking at her as though he wanted to eat her.

He spun her around to face away from him. She gripped the bars, bracing herself. He pressed his body against hers from behind and nuzzled her neck. She moaned as he began to kiss her throat and bare shoulder. It was as though he knew just where her sensitive spots were, the ones that electrified her entire body. They still swayed to the music, but everything had changed. She wasn't focused on capturing him, not now—she could barely think straight. All she wanted was to stay close to him, to keep touching him wherever she could. She needed to feel his body caging hers and his mouth and hands on her body. She'd heard people talk about animal magnetism, but *holy shit*, this was beyond that.

They weren't dancing anymore—they were grinding against each other, the sensual movements almost too much to bear. She was so close to danger, so close to the one thing she knew she couldn't let happen.

I don't care. I should...but I don't. I want him...

His right hand touched her right knee, sliding up her leg beneath her skirt. When he reached her panties, he brushed a fingertip along her satin-covered slit. She whimpered at the explosive reaction her body had at that simple caress. Rurik bit her earlobe, and a zing of pleasure shot through her body. She knew people were all around them, probably watching them, and she couldn't find it in her to care, not when he was making her feel so wild, so out of control in the best possible way.

"Tell me your name," he whispered in her ear.

She struggled to focus. "Charlotte..." She wouldn't tell him her last name. Even through the fog of her desire, she knew that would be a mistake.

"Charlotte." Her name rolled off his tongue in that decadent accent, and she shivered. "My name is Rurik." He flicked his tongue into the shell of her ear, sending a new bolt of arousal through her.

"I'm going to kiss you now, little one," he warned, and she nodded, wanting, *needing* his mouth on hers. It didn't matter that it was breaking her promise or that she knew her brothers would kill her for kissing a dragon. She had to kiss him. Pheromones be damned. Something inside her demanded it with a force that she couldn't stop. He turned her around to face him, chest to chest, their bodies still pressed tight together. The bars of the cage dug into her back, but she didn't care. All that mattered was this slow, delicious burning moment leading up to his kiss.

He lowered his head and their lips brushed, and then he kissed her. *Hard*. It was the kind of kiss that made a rational, sensible person like Charlotte lose her mind. It was a kiss out of her darkest fantasies. He moved his lips over hers with a hint of roughness that kept her on her toes, as though at any moment he could take things to another level. It left her dancing on a razor's edge of fear and excitement. He curled her hair in his hand, fisting the strands while he held her captive. His other hand gripped her hip, his firm hold keeping her right where she was. *A dragon's prisoner*.

The music around them changed from one song to another, and then another, and yet neither she nor Rurik wanted to come up for air.

It was strange, but the more he kissed her, the more she had this funny feeling that she could hear whispers—soft, dark growling sounds deep inside her head. Like a man murmuring erotic words to her, but she couldn't explain how she was hearing it. It must have been her imagination. Were all kisses supposed to be like this? Her previous boyfriends had never made her feel like she was on the verge of such sweet madness.

Their kiss finally broke apart, and he pressed his forehead to hers. She closed her eyes, hands gripping his shoulders as she tried to slow her racing heart. His muscles were taut beneath her palms, and she could feel the heat radiating off him. It didn't soothe the aching need her body now had for him. For the first time in her life, she understood what her friends had joked about when they'd talked about wanting a man so much they were ready to beg for it. She was *ready* to beg.

"Club's going to close soon," he said in a low rumble.

"What?" She was distracted by his intimate embrace and how much she didn't want this moment to end. His body was warm, and the leather of his jacket smelled so good. She wanted to bury herself against him, rub her cheek against his chest like a cat in heat. Her lips felt bruised, swollen from his kisses, and she licked them.

"We've been at this for over an hour, little one. I would like to continue, but I must close down the club." A surprisingly rueful smile twisted his lips.

Reality crashed down around her. An hour? She had spent an *hour* making out with a dragon shifter? A dragon she knew was dangerous. The dragon she'd come to capture... God, no wonder her brothers wouldn't let her become a hunter. She'd walked right into the lion's den—er...dragon's lair—and had all but jumped his bones. Mortification heated her face as she tried to shake the lingering flames of desire that his kisses had left burning within her.

"I should go." She released his shoulders and looked away, but his green eyes kept drawing her focus back to them. She raised a hand to her kiss-swollen lips and almost smiled but had to shake herself to remember that this was dangerous. She shouldn't have gone this far.

He cupped her chin and forced her to meet his gaze.

"Will you wait for me? After I close the club we can go to dinner." The earnest desire in his words made her hesitate. Could she stay near him and not lose her head again?

"Please, my little rose, do not make me beg." He winked at her, and the harsh lines of his scarred face seemed to fade into boyish playfulness.

"Eat? It's after midnight!" she said, half laughing.

"An early breakfast then."

She knew the logical thing to do was to thank him for the amazing evening and leave—but she couldn't.

If I can keep control over my hormones, I can learn more about him. That's what a smart hunter would do, right?

She needed to learn his weaknesses if she was going to figure out a safe way to inject him with the serum and call the Brotherhood to come and get him. Rurik was the key to one of their biggest crises at the moment. He feathered another kiss over her lips, and the last of her resistance crumbled.

"An early breakfast it is." She grinned up at him foolishly. Maybe it was okay to play the bad girl and do something wild and reckless. Just once.

"Excellent. Come with me." He led her from the cage to the back of the bar and sat her down on a stool, then waved over the bartender. "Victor, please keep this lovely woman company while I close up."

The bartender spoke to Rurik in Russian, and Rurik responded with a chuckle and nodded. Victor handed Charlotte a fresh glass of wine. Rurik leaned in close and playfully tugged a lock of her hair before he walked through the club's dwindling crowd. He disappeared through the back door she'd spied earlier.

"My boss likes you," the bartender said. His accent was heavy, but his English was decent.

She took a deep sip of her wine. "You think so?"

The bartender chuckled. "He danced in a cage with you. He never does that with other girls."

Charlotte wasn't sure why that mattered, but God, it had been so hot, so *fucking hot*. She was wet just thinking about it. Clamping her thighs together, she tried not to think about what it said about her that a simple make-out session had gotten to her like that. But then, there had been nothing simple about making out with Rurik.

She finished her wine and watched the club close down, the bouncers escorting the last of the partiers out and locking up. The lights dimmed, and the fog cleared from the floors. Only then did Rurik reemerge through the back door. He still wore his black-and-red motorcycle jacket, but he held two black helmets and came over to her.

"Ready?"

"We're not taking a car?" she asked as she took one of the helmets from him.

"I do not take my car to the club. I ride my motorcycle." He held out a hand. She didn't have to go with him—she could see it in his eyes—but there was a longing there, a need that matched her own. She took a deep breath and placed her hand in his.

The bartender handed Charlotte her purse, and she let Rurik lead her out onto the street. A sleek black motorcycle with dark green trim was parked on the curb. He stopped and turned to her.

He helped her put the helmet on, then secured his own. He straddled the bike and started the engine. Rain began to fall around them, misting the streets that were still warm from traffic. Charlotte shivered, glad she'd brought a coat. She pulled it on, slid onto the back seat behind Rurik, and wrapped her arms around his waist.

"Hold on tight, little one. I'll see you are dry and warm as soon as I can." He patted her hands and then gunned the engine. The motorcycle shot forward as they sped into the brightly lit Moscow streets. She watched the world around her blur as Rurik guided his bike into the traffic. Rain made the lights from the cars seem like foggy halos. He was fearless, flawless, and sexy as hell. She never thought she'd have a thing for motorcycles, but tonight she totally did.

There was something magical about the way they had to work together, their bodies leaning in the same direction as he took sweeping curves for every turn. She felt connected to him in a way she hadn't expected. They were one being while they rode together, a single blur on the streets of Moscow. For the first time in her life she felt bonded to another person. A person who was a danger to humans, a person she had every intention of betraying at some point. Charlotte swallowed down the uncomfortable burn in her throat just thinking about what had to be done. But not right now. Not yet. Besides, nobody was going to hurt him; all they needed was information.

Rurik finally stopped in front of an expensive-looking glass building and helped her off.

A young man in a valet's uniform rushed out. Rurik tossed him the keys before he took off his helmet. Charlotte removed her own, and the young man collected both.

She gazed up at the bright lights of the beautiful glass exterior. It looked more like a high-end apartment building. "This doesn't look like a restaurant."

"That's because it isn't. Nothing good is open this time of the morning. This is where I live."

"Here?" She quelled the flutter of nerves at the thought of going up to his apartment and focused instead on the fact that the building was classy, refined, and didn't match the gritty biker vibe Rurik put off. Yet this was exactly the opportunity she needed. He would feel safe at his own home and lower his guard. If she could get invited over tomorrow, after she had the serum with her...

He laughed and took her hand, the moment so natural that she didn't pull away. "Of course. Did you think I would live somewhere else?"

Blushing, she shrugged. "I don't honestly know. This building is beautiful." She marveled at how well their hands fit together and how warm his palm was. They walked through the lobby, and Rurik took her to a set of gold elevator doors. Once inside, he removed a black keycard from his wallet and swiped it through a scanner next to the buttons.

"I thought we were getting breakfast?" she asked.

"We are. In my apartment." He thumbed the button for the tenth floor, and the elevator doors closed.

She started to object. She'd agreed to food, nothing else. "But—"

"Don't tell me you are afraid? You are safe enough with me." A mischievous twinkle in his eyes sent her pulse racing.

"I'm not afraid, but you changed things. You can't do that." She protested a little, but not too much, letting him feel that he was the one who was safe, the one in charge. *So far so good...*

He curled an arm around her waist and tugged her close. "Of course I can. I'm the one in control." She pressed her palms on his chest in an effort to either push him away or touch him. She wasn't really sure.

"Rurik..."

He grinned. "I love it when you say my name." He leaned in and nuzzled her neck. "And you will say my name many times before this night is over."

That should have scared her, but it didn't. From the moment she'd met him, she hadn't been afraid of the dragon side of him—she was more afraid of the man, of how much he affected her. Yet she wasn't able to turn away. The pull between them, at least for her, was so strong that she stared at him, mesmerized, unable to speak. He didn't seem to want to say anything either. He held her close, their bodies touching, their faces inches apart.

Would it be so bad to lean in for a kiss? Just one more? Her resistance wavered, and she was giving in—

The elevator doors slid open with a chime.

"My floor," he announced. The words were simple and direct enough, yet she heard the offer in his voice, the choice of getting off with him or staying inside the safety of the elevator.

"For the record," she began, blushing, "I do not go home with guys...like *ever*." She bit her lip when he smiled at her.

"Then I'm honored to be the first, my little rose." He towered over her and stole a quick, hard kiss. There was only one door in the hallway on the floor, and Rurik led her to it. He turned the knob without using a key or keycard.

"You don't lock it?"

Rurik gave a shrug of one shoulder. "Unnecessary. I own the floor."

As they stepped inside, Charlotte gaped. The rooms had high ceilings and modern furnishings. It was a lot like a five-star hotel. There were glass chandeliers and dark leather couches. It was a mixture of various forms of masculine luxury, right down to the blue diamond fireplace against the interior wall of the living room. The windows were floor to ceiling, giving the impression that she could take a leap out of the building and fly. Which was not a good thing, given that they were ten floors up. About nine floors too many for her liking. They got closer to the windows as he took her to the kitchen, and Charlotte's breathing kicked up.

"What's wrong?" he asked, reading her panic.

"I have a thing about heights." She nodded at the oversized windows.

His dark chuckle distracted her from her fear momentarily. "Afraid of heights? Whatever will I do with you?" He winked and then picked up a slim black remote from the granite countertop of the kitchen, aiming it at the nearest windows. Black screens came down, turning the windows into walls, at least as far as the eyes were concerned. Charlotte's muscles, which had tensed to steel cords, began to relax.

"Better?" Rurik asked.

"Much."

"Have a seat. I'll order some food." He nodded to the table. She sat down, kicking off her heels. She rubbed her sore feet and watched him pull his cell phone out of his back pocket. He dialed a number and spoke rapidly, then hung up and turned to her.

"Food will be here soon. Would you like another drink?"

Why not? She was still feeling a bit buzzed from the club, and she didn't want that relaxed feeling to go away just yet.

"Sure." She pointed and flexed her toes and blushed when she realized he was watching her. "I'm not used to wearing heels." In the lab, she'd always worn sneakers.

"I never understand how you females squeeze into those dresses or stand in those shoes, but I certainly won't complain because the end result is..." He waved a hand at her body, his eyes heating with open appreciation.

She raised a brow, wondering if he'd finish that sentence. He didn't, but the heat in his eyes assured her that he was more than pleased with her appearance. Rather than be embarrassed, she felt emboldened and sexy. Was this how a woman was supposed to feel around a man she liked? He made her feel beautiful and attractive, and she loved it.

"So if you do not go home with men like this, then why me?" Rurik poured a glass of wine for her and a glass of bourbon for himself. He watched her take a sip before he raised his own glass to his lips. Charlotte swallowed, unsure what to say. The truth was more complicated than she cared to admit.

Because you're sexy as hell and I can't think rationally around you? Because I want to know if you make love as dirty and sinfully as you kiss? Because I'm here to capture you and bring you to my brothers because you might be the key to stopping an all-out dragon war?

She had to play it safe—at least enough to keep him from discovering her true purpose, but convincing enough that he didn't try to mesmerize her into revealing the truth.

"I guess there's something about the way you kiss," she finally admitted.

He laughed, the sound dark and forbidden in the best possible way. He took off his leather jacket and tossed it on the counter. He walked over to the table but didn't sit. Instead, he cocked his hip and took another slow drink as he watched her. Charlotte fixated on his throat as he drank and how he licked his lips when he set the glass down. She missed those lips already, wanted them against her own, her skin, her...*everything.*

"What are you doing here in Russia? It's a very long way from home, is it not?"

"It is." She had practiced her story, knowing it was best to stay vague but at the same time keep as much truth as possible. "I'm a biochemist from Michigan. I came here for a vacation." She smiled a little. In a way it was a vacation. A vacation from her controlling brothers.

"A biochemist?" He finished his bourbon and took a seat next to her at the table. "You don't look like a biochemist."

"And what does a biochemist look like?" she countered.

"Not like you."

"Everybody expects me to be wearing a lab coat and glasses all the time or something. Stuck at the lab with no social life whatsoever." And that's exactly what she had been until Meg had consulted her about the shifter-repressing drug. She tried to turn the focus back on him. "So you own a nightclub?"

"I do." He reached across the table and stroked a fingertip

along her arm as he spoke. "My older brother is a respectable businessman. My other brother, well, he's a..." Rurik snorted as though whatever he was thinking was amusing.

"He's a what?" she asked.

His green eyes burned into hers with mischief. "An international jewel thief."

Her heart jolted. "A jewel thief?" Was he kidding? There hadn't been anything in the files on that. All she knew of the brother Mikhail was that he'd lived in England for a few centuries and had recently gotten into a deadly fight with an English dragon. It was part of the reason the serum had come into the Brotherhood's possession. But international jewel thief? Rurik had to be kidding...right? She started to pull away, but he curled his fingers around her arm, possessive but gentle.

"Afraid of me again? I never promised that I was a good man. My family, well, we are quite the opposite, especially me." His words rolled along her skin, giving her goosebumps. They scared her, but not enough to make her run. She couldn't let him know she knew what he really was. She had to pretend that she didn't know what he was talking about.

"Are you in the Mafia, the Russian Bratva or something?" Yeah, *that* sounded like a proper question to ask. No way that could get her in trouble. Sheesh.

The hard smile he flashed her sent a wave of heat through her.

"Bratva? Those fools have nothing on my family."

That was the truth. She'd spent the last few weeks reviewing everything she could about the Barinov family, and they had survived countless numbers of attempts by the Bratva to rub them out or marginalize their power. The smart ones learned to leave the Barinovs alone. The dumb ones didn't last very long.

I really shouldn't be here doing this. But she had to prove that she wasn't a helpless little girl anymore. She just wished she had chosen a less harebrained way to do it.

"So you're a Russian club-owning badass," she said.

His lips twisted into a crooked grin. "Something like that."

"Does that mean you're dangerous?" She was teasing, but she also wanted to see if he would argue he wasn't. He'd already admitted he wasn't a good guy, but she was curious to see how far he'd open up about himself to a "mere mortal" who wasn't supposed to know what he really was.

"I—" The apartment door chimed.

Rurik growled to himself and left her to answer the door. A man in a waitstaff uniform rolled in a cart with covered serving trays. He paid the man, who set the dishes on the table and promptly rolled the cart back out.

"What kind of apartment building has room service?" she asked as he lifted the lid to reveal two steaks with asparagus and mashed potatoes. She'd always loved a good steak.

"I own this building, and I like the convenience, so I had a skilled kitchen built in. My tenants are wealthy and happily pay for room service when they want it. I hope this is all right. I assume it's a more American fare?" He passed her a white napkin rolled over silverware.

"Yes, this is perfect. Thank you," she said. "So if you own the building, I take it the nightclub business pays well?"

"Well enough, but my family has always had money, and my oldest brother is quite good at investing."

Now that made sense. The Brotherhood's files indicated the Barinovs seemed to have a good source of wealth from collecting jewels over the centuries. They were obviously shrewd investors too. She was about to ask another question, but Rurik cut her off gently.

"Enough about me. I'm more curious about *you*." Rurik took a bite of his steak before continuing. "Why visit Russia? Surely Russia in the middle of winter is not a good vacation spot. I could picture you on a tropical island in a teeny red bikini." He winked.

Charlotte blushed. "I'm not really the bikini type." She'd always felt too self-conscious to wear something so revealing on a body so curvy. The tight-fitting dress she wore now was bad enough, but there was no way she would wear a bikini in public.

"Then why Russia?"

Charlotte shared part of the truth. "I've always loved history. I wanted to see the Winter Palace while it snowed, but the forecast for the trip seems to indicate only rain, so I decided not to travel to Saint Petersburg. But still, there's lots to see here." She'd loved learning about the czars and the whole Anastasia mystery when she was younger.

Rurik's rakish grin faded, and his eyes softened with shadows of sorrow.

"The Winter Palace is quite beautiful when it snows. We used to have the most wonderful winter balls there. Outside, the windows would glow with gold light, and you could hear music drifting across the ice and snow. In a world of white and heavy winter silence, the palace was brimming with colorful life."

His gaze grew distant. He seemed to be seeing something past her, many years ago. He probably didn't even realize the slip he'd made by admitting he'd been there when the palace had hosted balls. Charlotte couldn't imagine what it must be like to live as long they did. She wanted to know more. She had so many questions about his life as a dragon, but she couldn't reveal herself. Not yet. It might get her killed.

Rurik focused on her again. "I think I know someone powerful enough to summon snow, if that is what you wish." He reached into his pocket and pulled out a cell phone. He dialed a number and spoke a few seconds later.

"Grigori..." He grinned at her. "Can you make it snow in Saint Petersburg tomorrow, say around noon? I'm taking a lovely young woman to the Winter Palace." He listened to Grigori, the oldest brother, Charlotte remembered from the files. "Thank you." They hung up. "Grigori will make it snow for you."

Charlotte laughed, pretending to assume he was only teasing her. But she couldn't help but wonder if what he was saying was possible. Nordic ice dragons were able to manipulate precipitation. But Grigori, Rurik, and their third brother, Mikhail, were Russian Imperials. Perhaps Grigori would call in a favor?

It occurred to her that while she was here she wanted to gather as much data as she could from Rurik. She would have to collect blood samples from him both before and after the serum was administered. She wanted to see if he could confirm if dragons had anything in common with the latest research coming from studies on Komodo dragons.

Researchers at George Mason University had created a synthetic version of a peptide found in the blood of Komodo dragons. They had dubbed it DRGN-1. DRGN-1 had proved to be tough against microbes. Bacteria stuck together to create biofilms that attached to surfaces and help to protect themselves during an infection. Even infected wounds healed faster with DRGN-1, and the layers of skin were rehabilitated. If Rurik and other shifters had similar peptide structures in their blood, it might explain how their bodies aged so slowly and healed so quickly.

I could change the world, make it a better place. What she really wanted was to find a way to make the human world and the supernatural world have a way to communicate, to build trust. It would solve so many problems, but neither world was ready for that yet, which meant her options were limited. It eased the guilt of what she was planning to do, but only just. She was lucky that Rurik distracted her with his company.

They ate the rest of their dinner, conversation flowing easily between them. She was surprised how much he seemed at ease with her and she with him. He was charming, more so than she ever expected of a nightclub owner who rode a motorcycle, but then, he was more than a thousand years old and had been born into an age of chivalry.

"So, your two brothers..." She pushed her empty plate away and waited to see if he would talk more about them.

"Grigori and Mikhail." A glint of humor made his eyes sparkle. "Both are my elders. Grigori is the head of the family. He only recently married. He and his wife are already expecting a dr—a child, I mean." He corrected himself, but Charlotte suspected he'd almost said *drakeling*, the dragon shifter term for children.

"That's wonderful." She leaned back in her chair, relaxing.

"It is. I cannot wait to see that child run circles around my uptight brother."

"And Mikhail...the international jewel thief and all-around man of mystery?" She tried to sound teasing. Most women wouldn't stay for a midnight snack in a man's apartment when he told her that his brother was a criminal.

His expression was suddenly shadowed with sadness. He played with his empty bourbon glass, rolling it between his palms. "Mikhail was gone for a long time. Our father made a rash decision. He disowned Mikhail and prevented him from returning to Russia, but my father is gone now. Mikhail is finally home. He too has settled down and married. He kidnapped a gemologist when he stole his jewels." That flash of humor was in his eyes again. "It worked out in the end."

She laughed, playing along with his comments as though he were still telling tall tales.

"And you? Any siblings? Any overprotective brothers I should know about?"

Charlotte was caught off guard by the alarmingly accurate query. A nervous giggle escaped her.

"Yeah, actually, I do have two very protective brothers. Neither of them even knows I'm here." Now that was certainly the truth.

"They wouldn't approve of you being here?"

"Not in Russia. Not anywhere, really. I've never even left the United States before, if you can believe it. They would flip out if they knew I'd come here alone."

His brows rose. "You're alone in Moscow? No friends? No one?"

She shook her head very slowly.

A scowl stole over his features. "Your brothers are right. That is very dangerous. Moscow is a dangerous place. You had a taste of it tonight at the club. I love my country, but it has a heart of darkness beneath the glittering surface. You aren't safe here alone." He rose from the table and towered over her again, his eyes darkening to a burnished gold. She backed up even more as he invaded her space.

"Imagine. A man like me could take you, little rose. He could make you his, possess you in every way, and you would have no chance of escape. No way to get home. No recourse. No salvation. Do you understand? A man like me would be very tempted by an innocent young creature like you." His words softened into a deep, threatening purr.

She peered up at him from beneath her lashes, trying to still her shivering. "But you won't...right?"

He curled his fingers under her chin, lifting her face up to his. "Are you quite sure about that?"

3

> DON'T LOOK BACK AND DON'T RUN. YOU MUST NEVER RUN FROM ANYTHING IMMORTAL. IT ATTRACTS THEIR ATTENTION. —PETER S. BEAGLE, THE LAST UNICORN

Charlotte was lost in his gaze all over again. "You... It's like you're making me dizzy... How do you do that?" she murmured dreamily. It was just like at the club when he'd convinced her to dance in the cage for him. She wanted to do anything he asked—*anything*. It had to be the power of hypnosis dragons had. It felt like he was mesmerizing her. Her being turned on by all this, however? *That* had to be the pheromones at play.

He blinked, his eyes no longer golden, and with a low growl he turned his back on her. She watched him pace away from her, and her thoughts soon cleared of that strange fuzziness.

"I should escort you home before I change my mind," he said in a dark tone.

She stood, slipping her heels back on. "Change your mind?" Her body felt a little shaky, as though she'd just had a wild burst of adrenaline and was coming down from the high.

"Yes." He turned back to her, eyes lingering on her face, then sweeping over her body in that peculiar way that felt like a caress. His hands clenched into fists, as though he was suppressing the urge to reach for her. "I'm tempted to carry you over my shoulder into my bedroom. I'd spend the next several hours having my way with you, fucking you into blissful oblivion."

She tensed at his harsh words and the rough fantasies they conjured up in her mind. Rurik was a man who took what he wanted, a dragon in full control. She suppressed the thrill that came with that thought. She'd always dreamt of being with a man like that, who knew exactly what to do next in bed. A man like that was hard to find. It was probably the reason she was still a virgin. She just couldn't picture herself with a man who wasn't like Rurik. She'd probably spend the rest of her life a virgin if she compared every man to someone like him.

"Fuck, you smell sweet." He raked his hands through his chocolate-brown hair, and his eyes seem to turn from green to gold again. "I have no control, not with you smelling like heaven." He braced his hands on the kitchen counter, staring straight ahead, not at her.

"Rurik...I think I should go." She reached for her purse, but he stepped closer and caught her wrist. She looked up at him, and he tugged her to him, pinning her against the counter, hip to hip, as he captured her mouth with his. It was another drugging kiss that set her head spinning. It reminded her of when as a child she'd sat on the swing at the park, twisting her seat around so the chains twisted tighter and tighter. When she let go she was rocketed around in a wild, unstoppable spin that ripped a cry of joy from her before she did it all over again.

"Tell me to stop. *Beg me.*" He cupped her face in his hands and murmured this between slow, deep kisses.

"I..." The words didn't come. He gripped her thighs and lifted her up onto the counter, locking her legs around his slender hips.

"Fuck." The roughness of his palms explored her bare skin. It felt so good, tracing the shapes of her calves up to her outer thighs.

He pushed her flat on the counter by pressing his palm gently on her chest. Then he trailed a fingertip down her throat to her breasts, which were heaving against the neckline. Charlotte threw her head back, panting as her body flushed with wild heat. Every part of her felt electrified by his touch.

"I'm going to rip this dress to shreds."

The words jerked her out of the haze of her body's rising desire.

"No, wait! I *really* like this dress. Give me a sec, and I'll get out of it." She reached behind herself to try to unzip her dress, but he growled impatiently and pulled her down from the counter. She braced herself as he spun her around and bent her over the granite top as he tugged the zipper down to her lower back. She wore a black strapless bra with matching panties, which he bared as he slid the red garment down around her hips. She stepped out of the dress, and he ground his denim-clad hips against her, letting her feel the hard press of his massive erection. She pushed back. God, being with him was like being in heat—

She tensed, turning around so they faced each other, and then placed her palms on his chest and pushed at him. He let her have a bit of space, but he was breathing hard, his eyes a swirling golden green.

"Wait..." She panted and stumbled away from him. She had no doubt at this point that the pheromones she'd been warned about were at work. She was not going to let her first time with a man be under some kind of influence. It needed to be of her own free will.

Rurik was breathing hard, just like she was. Part of her wondered if her special perfume was having a similar effect on him. His hair fell into his eyes, and he watched her in that predatory way that made her shiver. But he didn't try to force her.

"Put your dress back on. I will take you back to your hotel."

He stalked over to grab his jacket from the counter and slung it on. Charlotte bit her lip as she shimmied back into her dress and snatched her purse off the counter.

Charlotte, what have you gotten yourself into? It was supposed to be recon only tonight. Not a half-naked make-out session with your target!

She followed him to the door on shaky legs. Neither of them spoke as they stepped into the elevator. Damn, this night had been a disaster on so many levels. She had gotten too close to him, and he'd manifested some sort of power over her. She hadn't been ready for how things had spun out of control. But he had stopped when she'd asked him to. That was unexpected.

She ducked her head, avoiding looking directly at him. She might have blown any chance of meeting with him again, which would make the rest of her job more difficult. Though she was certain she'd matched the formula they'd found, it still needed to be tested in the field. But if it worked as they'd hoped, they'd have a powerful tool to use in case the dragons ever got it in their heads to take over.

It wasn't as far-fetched as it sounded. Every couple of decades some group of supernatural creatures tried to take over, and the Brotherhood was always there to stop them. Just a few months ago a dragon had been on the road to becoming the next prime minister of England. That man had used this very serum to try to remove some of his rivals.

If she brought Rurik back to the Brotherhood as a prisoner, who knew what further tests they might run to prove the serum worked, with or without his permission? And what if they tried to weaponize the formula? Or find a way to make it permanent? Some members of the Brotherhood were known to be overzealous in their charter, including the woman who'd almost become her sister-in-law. She cringed at the memory of what had happened to Serena, the hunter who'd been engaged to her brother Damien. She'd had a personal vendetta against the vampire "corruptions" of the world for as long as she'd known her. One day she'd crossed the line, taking out a vampire coven without cause. The Brotherhood had known they were a benign group, using blood from a blood bank, but she didn't care. For Serena, the only good vamp was a dead vamp. Given Damien's plans to reform the Brotherhood, it had been a source of constant debate between them.

In the end, Serena's overzealousness had been her undoing. A French vampire assassin had murdered her in cold blood, leaving her for Damien to find as a message to the Brotherhood. Her brother had never been the same since, had never taken another lover. It had broken his heart and made him less certain of his plans to change the Brotherhood's ways.

As Charlotte and Rurik left the building and stepped out onto the street, where the valet had Rurik's motorcycle waiting, she noticed someone lingering by a car, watching them. He continued to watch them while she and Rurik climbed back onto his motorcycle. Something about the man was off. He looked familiar, but she couldn't quite place his face.

※

Dimitri Drakor stood by the black SUV outside Rurik Barinov's apartment building.

"Found yourself a new toy, eh Rurik?" he murmured as he watched the dragon shifter pull a female onto the back of his motorcycle. The woman glanced at him, and for a moment Dimitri had the unnerving feeling that she could see right through him. But he merely inclined his head as she turned from him and gripped Rurik's waist. He was far enough away that she couldn't get a good look at him anyway.

"Far plainer than the last one," he muttered, thinking of the previous woman Rurik had taken under his protection, for all the good that had done her.

Dimitri pulled out a cigarette as he watched the taillights of the motorcycle vanish into the night, trying to keep the memories at bay. But he could never forget the night that had changed everything: the night his son had killed Rurik's possible mate and Rurik had murdered him for it. He had been proud of Ruslan for making a bold move like that, but he hadn't done it in the right way.

Killing a dragon's mate took away a dragon's will to live. None could survive that. But they hadn't yet mated, and instead of glory, Ruslan had forced his own father into battle with the Barinovs—and that had ended far worse than Dimitri could have ever predicted. Now his entire family was dead, slaughtered before his eyes.

But he was still alive, and the need for vengeance burned inside him.

I will not make the same mistake again.

Rurik was the Barinov battle dragon, the fiercest and most dangerous of the family. The other two Barinovs would not go to war, not now that they were mated. If it came down to it, they would flee with their mates to protect them.

But Rurik was still here, the last obstacle that kept Dimitri from taking control of Russia. His family had once controlled the east before the Barinovs had killed all but him. He deserved to rule all of the country. He was stronger and older. A better dragon than the softhearted Barinovs.

He watched and made sure Rurik was long gone before he pulled out his cell phone.

A man with a Brazilian accent answered. "Hello?"

"Luis, he is headed your way. His motorcycle is marked with a GPS. I will send you the coordinates when he stops."

"My men will take him out," was the curt reply.

"Our deal doesn't come into effect until he is dead."

The other dragon hissed. "We *will* kill him. And then the Moscow drug trade is ours alone."

"Of course." It was an easy concession to make. Dimitri had no interest in the drug trade. Luis was a Brazilian Starback shifter, and his little overseas empire was welcome to do what they wanted once the Barinovs were eliminated or neutralized.

His only concern was that the hotheaded Starbacks might draw the attention of the Brotherhood if they weren't careful. He'd faced the Brotherhood before, many centuries ago. He'd witnessed them slay dragons in Europe with cunning traps and deadly weapons. Even though they'd possessed the talents and intelligence of cavemen, the Middle Ages had somehow given these human mortals an unfair advantage. But today the Brotherhood was limited in their ability to fight the preternatural unless it was absolutely necessary. They were more concerned with preventing humankind from knowing that monsters did exist. But times changed, and if the Brotherhood should turn their eye toward his kind again, he wanted to be ready for them.

Dimitri would not let another slaughter of dragons occur, not again. Once he was in control and had a strong alliance with the Starbacks, he would extend his connections to the Chinese serpents next. When the dragons stood united, they could defeat the Brotherhood and truly take over. They would put the humans in their place, beneath the clawed feet of their betters.

But in order for that to happen, Rurik had to die.

4

DON'T BE AFRAID. DON'T BE AFRAID OF ANYTHING. WHATEVER YOU HAVE BEEN, YOU ARE MINE NOW. I CAN HOLD YOU. —PETER S. BEAGLE, THE LAST UNICORN

Tonight was a fucking disaster.

Rurik's dragon growled in agreement inside his head. He revved his engine as he drove through the streets of Moscow, trying not to think about how good it felt to have Charlotte's legs wrapped around his hips. He was supposed to have been busy handling the account books tonight, not getting distracted by a shapely blonde in a killer red dress.

He'd seen her being bothered by those fools, and he knew he had to intervene. But there was more to it than that. There was something about her that he and his dragon couldn't resist. She'd almost seemed to glow when he'd first seen her in his club. And her scent...God, he could have inhaled it for days and never gotten tired of it. If he hadn't known better, he'd have sworn she was a dragoness. But that wasn't possible. She lacked any of the telltale signs of being a shifter.

When she'd been threatened, his dragon had almost lost control. One thing he didn't allow in his club was women being harassed, especially those he was attracted to. His dragon had wanted to rip those bastards limb from limb when he'd caught the scent of the woman's fear in the air. That was one of the reasons he knew she could not be a dragoness. Yet the moment he drew near her, he realized his intervention had been dangerous. Her mouth-watering scent was somehow addictive, like a drug pumping through his veins, and there was something more about her...

A virgin. In his club. A curvy, untouched female of childbearing age. He'd only been around one of those once before, when he'd met his brother Grigori's future mate, Madelyn. The scent then had been unmistakable, almost irresistible. But this woman? It had been impossible to walk away from her. He finally understood what Grigori had told him about the temptations of virgins. Rurik hadn't wanted to believe his brother's warnings, but there was no denying it now.

This new obsession couldn't have come at a worse time. He couldn't afford such distractions, not when his family was so fragile. The Barinovs once had great allies, but over the years the noble dragon families had begun to diminish, until all that were left were the power-hungry lines like the Drakors.

I'm the only one strong enough to protect my family, because I'm not foolish enough to fall in love.

The uneasy peace Grigori had made with Dimitri Drakor after their battle three months ago did not fool Rurik. Nothing would hold Drakor to his word now. He had nothing to lose, and Drakor would do anything to destroy the Barinovs. That made Rurik's dragon pace restlessly inside his head. Danger was always on the horizon. It had already cost him dearly.

Nikita. The Frenchwoman who'd worked in his bar for two years, a possible mate.

Her lifeless eyes flashed across his mind, and he gripped the handlebars of his motorcycle tighter. *Don't think of her. Don't relive that pain.*

Rurik hadn't allowed himself to claim her as his mate, but his heart and his dragon recognized the loss of what could've been. He had no intention of dying young from the loss of a true mate.

And I have no intention of letting Charlotte test my control.

He had to take Charlotte home and walk away from her, no

matter how irresistible she was. There was something *too* tempting about her, and it wasn't just her body that called him. During dinner he'd become addicted to her laughter and her shy smiles, but when she'd danced for him in the cage, he'd almost come undone. She was different from all the other women, even Nikita. He'd come so close to losing control again and again with Charlotte. She made him feel like an untried youth courting his first female. He hadn't been that reckless or desperate with lust in centuries.

It continued to rain as they rode to her hotel near Red Square. Charlotte clung to him from behind, and he could feel the shivers racking her body. She had to be soaked to the bone. He parked near the hotel entrance and waited for a crowd of people on the sidewalk to clear. Then he helped Charlotte off his bike and set the helmet on his seat. A valet appeared and took the bike away.

"You're coming inside?" Charlotte asked. The lower half of her hair was drenched and hung in dark gold strands. For a moment, he was lost imagining curling that liquid gold around his fingers. With a shake, he pulled himself away from the daydream and the dangerous path it could lead.

"I'm taking you right to your door. I told you the city isn't safe, even in a nice hotel like this."

He checked the street, out of habit rather than actual suspicion, and saw a black sedan coming from the same direction they had come. Could be nothing; black sedans were ubiquitous in Russia. It pulled up close to the valet booth. Rurik guided Charlotte away from the street in case it splashed water onto her. The window of the car rolled down, perhaps to hand the key to the valet.

Instead, the lights of the hotel glinted off the barrel of a silencer.

Rurik's instincts, honed by centuries of combat, subterfuge, and betrayal, came roaring back to life. He grabbed Charlotte and threw her to the ground, covering her body with his. The hotel's lobby window exploded behind them. He grunted as a bullet tore into his back, another hit his shoulder, and a third hit his thigh.

All around them, glass tinkled to the ground in diamond-like shards, the light from the chandeliers inside reflected in dazzling sparkles over the broken field of glass. Sounds rushed around him, the jumble too chaotic for him to process. He focused on breathing, his blood pounding in his ears. A dragon, once engaged, focused on sight and movement, not sound.

He gasped at the sharp stab of pain from the bullets, but he stayed down. All around him people were screaming and trying to hide. He looked over his shoulder, squinting as he tried to see the black sedan, but it was too late. Tires squealed as he watched the car speed off into the night. He was in no shape to pursue.

The bullets had to be iron—he could tell from the way they burned inside him. And the fact that the silenced bullets had been subsonic meant they were also lodged in him, instead of passing through. His body fought to seal the wounds, trying to keep his blood from spilling out, but the iron made that difficult, and if they were left inside him too long, it could poison him.

For a long moment, he lay on top of Charlotte, sucking air into his lungs in great gulps as his body tried to adjust to the adrenaline. His dragon was clawing at his insides, wanting to come out and defend itself, but he had to stay calm, keep his other half locked down. If he transformed now, not only would it make the news, but it would draw the Brotherhood down on his family's head. And the iron bullets would only cause more damage to him as he changed from one form to another.

Iron bullets—that was no coincidence. Most bullets were made of lead. This was deliberate. The list of possible suspects dropped to just a few names, and one of them was right at the top.

"Rurik! Are you okay?" Charlotte gasped as she sat up, holding on to him, keeping him up rather than dragging him down.

"I'm fine," he hissed. "Need to get inside... Can't be seen." He tried to stand. She curled an arm around his waist and slung her purse around her free shoulder.

"Come on. I'll take you to my room."

"Hurry." They hobbled into the lobby, which was a scene of chaos. People were shouting on their phones and rushing outside to see if anyone else was injured. Several security guards bellowed into their walkie-talkies and gathered uninjured guests together in small groups. There didn't seem to be any other casualties, for which Rurik was thankful.

He had to get out of sight. If his face showed up on the news, that would risk exposure.

Grigori was the master at changing his hair color every ten years to show signs of aging, before eventually transferring the family's company to a "son" who looked just like him. But Rurik refused to do that. Instead, he sold his club after five or ten years and opened a new one elsewhere, rotating between his favorite locations. Clubs were fickle things, and the routine fit naturally with their natural life cycles.

Charlotte took him to the elevators and punched in her floor. They waited, panting together until an elevator opened up. Thankfully, it was empty. Once inside, she tried to get a better look at his wounds, but he shied away.

"Don't be such a baby," she said. "I need to see how bad they are."

He growled. "I'm not a baby. I was shot—of course they're bad." He finished this last in a childish mutter, but then when he saw her face turn ashen he sighed.

"They can't be that bad, or you'd be bleeding all over the floor."

"My jacket is lined with ballistic nylon" Rurik said, which was true, but that was meant for bike accidents, not bullets. "Still, it hurts like hell, and I don't want you touching them." He also didn't want her to worry or have any reason to doubt his strength.

"We'll still have to get a look at them once we're in my room."

When they stopped at her floor, she offered to help him to her door, but he shrugged off her arm and stumbled there on his own while she found her keycard. The damn bullets were making his skin burn—definitely iron. His dragon wanted out of his skin so he could heal faster, but he couldn't transform in the city. And he couldn't transform with the iron still inside him, because that would only make things worse.

Her room was small and had only one bed. He started toward it, but she caught his arm and steered him to the bathroom.

"Strip," she ordered.

"Didn't know all it took was being shot to make you want me naked." His pained chuckle did not earn him a smile. He peeled off his jacket and then his shirt. He glanced over his shoulder at his reflection in the mirror and winced at the sight of three bullet holes, one in his lower back, one on his left shoulder blade, and a third in the back of his thigh. Blood still trickled down, but very little, all things considered. He was lucky. He would have to get the bullets out before the wounds could heal with them inside. That could be fatal.

"Fuck," he muttered again. He unzipped his jeans and dropped them to the floor.

"What—" Charlotte began until he angled his leg and showed her the wound in the back of his thigh.

"It's... I thought it would be worse. But still, we should get you to a hospital." She held a first-aid kit in her hands, her face pale as alabaster.

"Trust me. I will be fine as long as you can be brave and dig the bullets out."

Charlotte gulped audibly. "Dig them out?"

With a few hobbling steps toward her, he took the first-aid kit from her and tossed it onto the sink counter. From his jacket he pulled out a Leatherman multitool that unfolded into a set of pliers, which also held various knives, screwdrivers, and even a small ratchet. Useful for most bikers, but not exactly meant for surgery. It would have to do.

"The bullets didn't go deep. Here." He handed her the Leatherman and braced himself against the sink, head lowered.

Charlotte shook as she came up behind him. She rubbed alcohol swabs on the wounds on his back, and he uttered a string of Russian curses that would have made his father box his ears had the old dragon been alive to hear it.

"Sorry!" She dabbed at the wound on his lower back. "Okay, here goes." He felt the pliers dig into him as she searched for the bullet. His vision tunneled, and he rested his head on his forearms and closed his eyes.

"You're right, I feel it! Just below the surface. Hang on!" The pressure of the pliers burned as she pulled the first bullet out. She dropped it into the porcelain sink next to him with a little clink. Then she applied more alcohol to the wound. The dragon inside him roared at the sudden flair of fresh pain, but he didn't let a sound escape his lips.

"You want me to bandage it?" she asked.

"No, it will heal fast," he assured her. It was true. With the iron out, the wound was already clotting and knitting back together. A human would have required more serious medical attention. Thankfully, Charlotte was not a doctor; otherwise, she would have had some uncomfortable questions.

She moved on to the bullet lodged in his shoulder. It must have lodged in his bone, because he could feel the pliers scrape as she found it. He bit his lip as she removed that bullet. It joined the first in the sink. Then she knelt behind him and dug into his thigh. That hurt more than his back, because the muscles had more sinew. Hot blood trickled down his leg onto the floor.

"Got it!" She stood and dropped the third bullet next to the other two. Rurik lifted his head and met her gaze in the bathroom mirror. She looked so young and vulnerable, her hair still soaked, her dress damp and makeup smeared. Her trembling hands held the bloody multitool.

God, he was a damned fool. She was human, and she'd been shot at. His little rose was delicate, after all. She wasn't a fierce dragoness used to wounds and bloodshed, yet she was being damned brave right now, and his chest filled with a swell of pride. Her lashes fluttered as she stared up at him.

"Wow... I really thought there'd be more blood. Guess none of them hit any major arteries. Lucky you. Are you going to be okay?" she asked, biting her bottom lip.

He managed a nod. "I'll be fine. It's not the first time I've been...hurt." He reached up instinctively to trace the scar that marred his cheek and forehead, a gift from a battle long ago. It had been a serious wound—it would have to be to leave such a mark—and he had been fortunate to survive it.

"You need to get out of that wet dress."

Her eyes widened. "What?"

"You'll freeze, little rose." He turned her around so that her back was to him and without asking unzipped her dress. She peered over her shoulder at him, so incredibly shy, clearly torn between objecting to and encouraging his behavior. The sexy minx from earlier tonight was gone. Now he was facing a fragile creature who needed his protection, even if she didn't realize it.

"It's all right. I'm going to take care of you." He brushed his hand along her bare shoulder.

"Hey, I'm not the one who got shot." There was a fire in her eyes, but it was dimmed by fear. Her hands were still shaking like hell.

"I've been shot before. You haven't. You are in shock. Go. Get into the shower." He nudged her toward the shower stall, and she got in. He turned on the water, careful to aim the nozzle away until the water heated up.

Charlotte covered her black-clad breasts by crossing her arms over her chest. Her modesty would've been charming under different circumstances.

"The water's hot." He flicked his fingers into the spray before he angled the nozzle toward her. "Remove your underwear." His words were a command, but he kept his tone gentle. She needed him to be firm, but he didn't want to scare her.

"No—"

"Charlotte, I'm not asking." He stared down at her, careful not to influence her too much with his gaze, just providing a nudge in the right direction. He didn't want to make her do anything she didn't want to do, but he had no time to argue with her either.

She stared at the tile floor as she slipped off her panties, then unhooked her bra and tossed it onto the rug outside the shower door. She stepped fully into the spray, rubbing her body vigorously with her hands as her teeth started to chatter, despite the hot water. Her body's temperature had dropped too fast.

He took a deep, controlled breath before he stepped into the shower behind her and covered the back of her body with his.

"You need body heat, sweetheart." He didn't do anything except hold her as the hot water warmed her from the front and he from behind. After a few minutes, her teeth stopped chattering, and she leaned back against him.

"I've never... That was so scary," she whispered. The steam curled up around them, and he pressed a kiss to her shoulder.

"I am sorry you were there." Whoever had fired the shots had meant to kill him. It wasn't the first time he'd faced this type of threat. The Russian Mafia had tried more than once to take control of the city, having put hits out on both him and Grigori, but they had never known to use iron bullets, something their hitmen had not lived to regret. No, this had been no human assassin at work. This was someone who knew all too well what he really was.

"Was someone trying to kill you?" she asked.

"I told you, Moscow isn't a safe place. Not even for me." He nuzzled her neck, and the sweet scent of her mixed with fear made his pulse quicken. Sometimes he hated the predator in him for responding to fear like that. He didn't want her to be afraid.

He wanted to destroy those who had almost killed her tonight. He wanted to release his dragon so it could sniff out those men and tear them apart. But his instinctive need to protect her was stronger than his desire for revenge. Whoever had taken a shot at him tonight would have gotten a good look at Charlotte. They knew what hotel she was staying at, which meant she was still in danger, especially if they believed he had feelings for her. To come after him was understandable, but to target an innocent not once but twice in order to hurt him? Unforgivable.

All because he'd been foolish enough to dance with her, to kiss her...to convince himself for one minute that he could have a normal life with a normal girl. He would leave her now if there was a chance it would help, but the damage had already been done. Leaving wouldn't shift the target he'd inadvertently placed on her back.

"You should wash the blood off your hands." He took her palms and pulled them into the spray, rubbing his fingers along the pads of hers, trying to erase the evidence of tonight's horror.

"What about you?" She turned in his arms, and her full breasts pressed against his chest. He was wearing only his boxers, but it felt like he was damn near naked against her.

"I don't—" he began.

Charlotte shook her head. "You do. Turn around." She was giving him orders. A sweet, innocent virgin ordering around a dragon. His brothers would laugh their asses off if they ever found out. He turned his back to her, and her soft hands ran water over his wounds.

"Your tattoo—it's beautiful," she whispered.

He'd forgotten that she would see it, the large black dragon tattoo on his right shoulder blade. It was a fierce dragon, wings spread wide as it roared and spewed fire when it was in its resting pose. When his emotions were strong, however, it would move, and right now he was battling to stay calm. If she saw a moving tattoo...

Charlotte traced one of the wings, and his dragon buried deep inside him huffed in pleasure. "It's so detailed." It could actually feel her touch on its wings. In his human form, this was the dragon's only outward manifestation. But it could feel everything he felt.

"Your wounds are already healing," she said with a gasp. "How is that possible?"

Rurik turned, curling his arms around her waist and her back, hoping to distract her. He was healing far too fast, and soon she would start asking questions he couldn't answer. He hadn't wanted to use his full powers on her before, but this was about keeping his family safe. Keeping his world safe.

He cupped her chin with one hand and made sure she was paying attention. "Charlotte, I think you're a little confused about tonight..." He let his gaze draw her in and mesmerize her. It was one of the more useful dragon abilities, one that he could use in his human form.

"What?" she asked, her eyes going wide.

"We had a wonderful night together, but you've suffered a bit of a shock. My wounds aren't as bad as you remember. Barely a scratch, see? The ballistic nylon stopped them. All you treated were some minor cuts and bruises. You are unharmed and safe now." He waited until her eyes had a softer look, and he knew that he had buried the fear of the shooting deep in her head.

"We had an amazing time." She grinned bashfully, her eyes returning to normal.

"I am going to spend the night," he added.

"Rurik—I meant what I said. I don't do this." She waved a hand between their bare bodies.

"I know, and that's why I'm going to be good. I promise." He flashed her a wolfish grin, making her laugh. The sound filled his chest with a cottony warmth he'd never felt before.

"I thought you said you were a bad guy?" she asked, raising a brow.

"I am, but tonight I'm *your* bad guy, which means I'll be good to you." He leaned down and kissed her. Not a kiss to seduce or control, simply one to tell her that he would stay with her and protect her through the night.

I'll keep you safe. I won't fail like I did Nikita. He carved the vow in his heart. He would stay with Charlotte until he was sure she was safe, and then he would send her back to America where no one would come after her. The thought of never seeing her again made his chest tighten, but it had to be done.

Charlotte kissed him back, her sweet lips soft as the petals of a rose. Whoever taught her to kiss had been a master. She was a wet dream brought to life, with full curves and a shy side that made him want to tie her down and explore every part of her until she held no more secrets left. Then he wanted to curl his body around hers and ask her to tell him *everything* about herself.

Fuck. What was wrong with him? He would've said it was nearly getting killed, but he'd felt this way long before the shooting. From the moment he'd watched her dance for him in the cage at the club, he'd been sucked in by her. She was a breath of life, a kiss of fire, and completely irresistible.

They kissed until the water started to cool down. He broke the kiss with reluctance and shut the water off. They both reached for the towels at the same time, laughing as their hands met.

"Here." He handed her the first towel and wrapped it around her body, covering those sexy curves. He took the other towel and wound it over his hips before he stepped out of the shower. He glanced at the three bloody bullets still lying in the sink. He would deal with that mess in a few hours, after he got some rest. For now, he hid them before Charlotte could see them and remember what had really happened outside.

"I think I have a T-shirt and some pajama pants that might fit you. They're big enough, I think. I mean, they're not, but they'll stretch." Charlotte was bent over her suitcase that sat on the foldable rack, her towel-clad ass giving him a dozen wicked ideas of what he could do to her.

Behave, he told himself.

She handed him a black T-shirt with an old rock band logo on it.

"Kansas?"

"So what?" she challenged. "My brothers raised me on classic rock."

"Brothers are funny things, aren't they? Mine are both older, but I spent my childhood tussling with them to become stronger and faster." He grinned at her. Then he dropped his towel, stripped out of his soaked boxers, slid the borrowed T-shirt over his head, and pulled the fresh boxers on. They were tight, but he would survive the night.

"My brothers never tussled with me. It was so annoying. My parents died when I was little, and I was treated like a porcelain doll." Charlotte ran her fingers through her wet hair as she talked, and he sat back on the bed, watching her. He'd slept with more than one queen, even an empress, but none of them compared to Charlotte. When he gazed at her, she almost seemed to glow, and her voice with that slightly husky feminine tone was like a choir of angels singing to him. Every time she smiled at him he got a goofy grin on his face. Fuck, she was sexy as hell.

She turned her back to him and slipped on her pajamas, a flannel set of pink-and-black polka-dotted pajama pants and a matching button-up nightshirt. When she faced him again, he caught a hint of her breasts in the low neck of the shirt, and his body responded.

He was supposed to be a good man tonight, not a fierce, possessive, and dominating dragon. Her brothers were right—she was a delicate creature who needed to be handled with care. She reminded him of the hothouse flowers Catherine the Great used to grow in her secret greenhouse. He'd visited her there more than once to steal a kiss and had seen the rare and beautiful blooms thriving in a protected environment. Those flowers would not survive the harsh climate of Russia. But there was a fierceness to Charlotte that rivaled even that of Catherine, which made him wonder if she might not be as delicate as she seemed.

"What?" Charlotte eased down onto the bed and pulled back the sheets to climb in.

"I was just thinking of someone," he admitted. "You remind me of her."

She covered her mouth to yawn, then smiled again. "I hope that's a good thing." That sheepish smile made his heart feel strange and fluttery. It confused his dragon too, which had gone very still inside him. Like it was watching a creature it didn't understand yet was curious about and was afraid that one sudden movement might spook it.

"It is. She was an amazing woman. She was powerful in a time and place where women weren't respected in Russia."

"Was?" Charlotte pulled back the covers on the other side of the king-size bed, and he took the invitation to join her. His wounds had healed enough that they weren't likely to bleed into the sheets.

"She died many years ago." He watched her puff up her pillow and settle into the bed, lying on her side to face him.

"Rurik, you'll really be okay, won't you?" she asked, her beautiful blue eyes cutting through him with genuine concern.

"I'll be fine. It was just a few scratches, remember?" He shifted down to lie beside her, curling an arm around her hips and tucking her against his chest so he could place a soft kiss to her forehead.

Her responding sigh made his dragon shift inside him, restless with curiosity. Normally when he bedded a woman his dragon seemed disinterested. Only Nikita had ever caught the dragon's eye before. His dragon wanted to keep him awake all night to watch her while she slept.

At times like this, sharing his body with another creature was a nuisance. Most of the time he and his dragon were in sync, but sometimes the beast rose to the surface. Right now, still healing in his human form, Rurik was too tired to watch her, and the dragon growled with displeasure.

Soon. Soon I will possess her for us both. Then maybe he could clear his system of this wild, foolish desire for the quiet yet passionate American who'd stumbled into his life.

A battle dragon could not afford to mate. He could not put his family at risk. He had known this the moment he'd learned what he was, when his father had discovered that his strength and skills surpassed those of his brothers.

"A battle dragon is a sacred position, Rurik. You will be the last thing between our family and extinction."

It was a great weight to place on the shoulders of a fifteen-year-old boy, but fate had chosen him over Grigori and Mikhail. And that meant he would *always* be alone. No mate, no falling in love, no spending the next thousand years with a woman like Charlotte.

He kissed her lips, even though she was asleep before he reached over and turned off the light. He wrapped himself around her, guarding her jealously the way a dragon guarded his most precious jewels.

5

MEN HAVE TO HAVE HEROES, BUT NO MAN CAN EVER BE AS BIG AS THE NEED, AND SO A LEGEND GROWS AROUND A GRAIN OF TRUTH, LIKE A PEARL. —PETER S. BEAGLE, THE LAST UNICORN

Damien MacQueen holstered his gun as he reached the old abandoned ruins of the Detroit train station. Many years ago the station had fallen into disrepair, and he had moved the Brotherhood's international headquarters from Boston to Detroit. It was a city that many people had given up on, but for his needs, that made it perfect. A crumbling city with high crime rates tended to draw in supernatural creatures, the sort who would make plays for local power.

Not on my watch...

As he got closer, he touched the barbed-wire fence that surrounded the building. A normal human couldn't see what was really there. Hundreds of cleverly crafted spells projected the illusion of a ruined and abandoned station. Damien placed his hand on the main padlock. The spells around the station recognized him, and the facade of the old crumbling building faded.

Now he could see what the spells had so carefully hidden. The station had been beautifully restored and looked just as it had in its prime—with a few additional features inside, of course. It now housed some of the toughest supernatural hunters and the most magically gifted humans in North America. The best the world had to offer and the last line of defense against the night.

Damien had a laid-back yet vigilant approach to the supernatural. If they kept to themselves and didn't cause trouble, he didn't cause them trouble. But if they crossed that line, his people did what needed to be done. He was proud that his kill rate was low. His predecessors had been tougher, more ruthless, but times had changed, mankind had changed, and Damien knew that sometimes a situation was painted in shades of gray. But some in the Brotherhood still only saw things in terms of black and white.

Serena, the only woman he'd ever loved, had been one such hunter. Beautiful, brilliant, and utterly unforgiving. She'd been killed after murdering a nest of vampires who had been classified as a nonthreat. No such thing in her book. But that action had cost her dearly. They might not have been a threat, but they had friends in high places.

The vampire nobles didn't care how many rogue corruptions the Brotherhood took down. They believed in law and order as much as anyone. But Serena's rogue action had been seen as a threat, and they had responded accordingly, sending their best assassin to send a message.

Damien still remembered the sight of Serena's body laid bare and bloodless for him to find. It had taken every ounce of his self-control not to seek his own vengeance. But Serena had been in the wrong, acted against orders, and Damien wasn't going to continue the chain of bloodshed and take more innocent lives. No matter how heartbroken Serena's death had left him, his job was to make the world a better and safer place.

The gates parted as he pushed them open, heading toward the station's main entrance. He was going to need a shower and a beer after tonight's fun. Damien had spent the last three hours in peace talks between the Snowfall Shifters and the Black Forest Wolf pack.

The names these guys give themselves...

He'd had his gun loaded with silver, ready for things to go pear-shaped, but fortunately nothing had happened. Still, he felt safe enough to holster his gun only now that he was back at headquarters. Werewolves and other corruptions had tempers and serious aggression issues.

One would think the word *corruption* was a derogatory term the Brotherhood had come up with, but in fact it came from the shifters themselves. For some reason no one was really sure of anymore, shifters like werewolves and vampires were referred to as corruptions, but not others like dragons or the thunderbirds of old. The Brotherhood's official stance was that it had to do with the means of their creation. Magic was at the heart of every shifter, but corruptions could pass on their condition through a bite, like an infection, and this seemed to be something that the dragons and other preternatural creatures felt was not normal.

But corruptions were also the ones the Brotherhood had more personal contact with. He was even considering allowing a few of the more levelheaded ones out there into their ranks to help act as liaisons as well as enforcers. Dragons, though, refused to have anything to do with the Brotherhood. And that was a problem, especially now.

As he walked into the lobby, he saw his brother, Jason, leaning against the front desk, flirting with the receptionist. Once he saw Damien, however, he straightened and dropped the receptionist cold, much to her chagrin. "Everything go all right tonight?"

"Fine. Kept me on my toes, though. Archer Falls is one scary bastard." Damien chuckled.

"The panther shifter from New York?"

"That's the one. How about here? Quiet night?" He and his brother walked shoulder to shoulder through the halls.

"Yeah, nothing major. The weres and vamps are all nice and quiet. Nothing at the usual hot spots, bars and run-down motels. I thought for sure we'd have a vamp nest or two to bust into, you know?"

Damien sighed. "You know when it's nice and quiet that means something big is probably in the works, right?"

Jason shrugged. "Well, we can't worry about it until we know what's going on."

Damien punched his brother in the shoulder. "And that's *exactly* why you aren't running the show."

Jason gave him a mocking sneer. "Ha ha."

"Come up to my office, and we'll have a beer. I'm wound tighter than hell after tonight."

They waited at the elevator bay. "You hear from Charlotte yet? She's supposed to be in New York by now."

"No. She hasn't called you?" There was a ding as the elevator doors opened. Damien got in, and Jason followed.

"No. That's what I'm saying. She hasn't checked in. That's not like her. You know how lonely she gets when she goes to those out-of-town conferences. She *always* calls." Jason shoved his hands in his pockets, frowning.

Damien's stomach began to knot. The week before Charlotte left she'd been distant and quiet. Neither he nor Jason had been able to get her to cheer up. He'd been an idiot and ignored his baby sister all night to talk to Jason about dragons, and she'd been upset. He'd thought her feelings had only been bruised a bit, but maybe the damage was deeper than that. She hated being left out of the loop, especially being denied the chance to work at the Brotherhood. But that was something he would never change his mind on, even if she grew to hate him for it. As long as she was safe, he kept his promise to his parents intact.

The elevator stopped at the top floor. The office at the end of the hall was Damien's. It was elegantly decorated, sleek and modern, with a view of the Detroit River. It was winter now, and thick chunks of ice were floating south. During the coldest months, it was one of Detroit's nicer natural wonders. It was always incredibly blue.

"Why don't you call her?" Damien said.

Jason pulled out his phone and dialed. He placed the phone on speaker, and they listened to it ring. It went to voicemail.

Jason ended the call and pocketed his phone. "Trace it."

Damien took a seat at his desk and logged into the Brotherhood's secure mainframe. He accessed their tracking systems. Everyone in the organization plus their family members had special locator chips in their phones for emergencies. It wasn't unusual for a family member of a hunter to be kidnapped by those looking for either leverage or revenge.

The trace gave GPS coordinates that matched Charlotte's apartment in Detroit.

"She's not in New York," Jason growled. "Where is she?"

"Hang on." Damien pulled up a new menu and typed in a code he'd memorized.

His brother leaned over Damien's chair, peering at the screen. "What's that?"

"My backup. Remember that Coach suitcase we bought her for Christmas? I put another transmitter in the lining." He tapped his finger on the desk anxiously as a blue sphere rotated on the screen, indicating it was searching.

"You bugged Charlotte's luggage?" Jason grinned.

"Better safe than sorry." Damien almost smiled, but when the screen changed and the coordinates popped up, his heart stopped.

"Looks like your bug's got a bug in it." Jason's usually good humor was subdued.

"No, it's working fine."

"Then what the hell is she doing in *Moscow*? She's never been out of the country."

Damien knew. She'd gone to Moscow because of what he and Jason had been talking about last week. They had been discussing their concerns about an imminent dragon war in Russia. Jason had been in charge of trying to lure Rurik somewhere he could be contained safely and questioned about the situation. But Rurik continued to slip out of the Brotherhood's grasp. Had Charlotte gotten the idea into her head that she could bring in a dragon? Surely she wasn't that foolish. But the second the memory of her hurt gaze flashed in his mind, he knew the truth. She wasn't thinking straight. She'd rushed off to Moscow to catch a dragon to prove him and Jason wrong.

Shit.

"She's gone after the dragons. I don't know what her plan is, but that's the only thing I can think of."

"You mean...the Barinovs? Is she nuts? She's not a hunter."

"I know." Damien rubbed his eyes with his thumb and forefinger. "Call Meg in, along with whoever else is in the building. I want a task force assembled in ten minutes."

"Consider it done." Jason sprinted from the room.

Damien stared hard at the screen.

"What the fuck are you doing, Charlotte?" The weight of his past and his burdens settled even more heavily upon his shoulders. When their parents had been killed, Damien had taken over the Brotherhood and had vowed to protect his sister at any cost, even if it meant protecting her from herself. He'd already lost Serena to this life. He wouldn't lose his baby sister too.

But dragons? How could he protect her if she was already in their territory?

Ten minutes later, he faced a team of the best hunters in North America. Meg Stratford stood close to his desk, her red hair pulled back in a ponytail. She was alert, even though it was getting late. Next to her were Nicholas Rubin, Tamara Gilbert, Jason, and Kathryn Rubin.

"We have an extraction situation, and time is of the essence. We're going to Moscow."

Meg's eyes widened. "Why us? Why not let Saint Petersburg handle it?"

"I would, but I don't trust anyone else to handle this."

"Who's the target?" Nicholas, one of the trackers, asked.

Damien frowned, unable to hide the truth from them. "Charlotte MacQueen."

Meg's face paled. "Charlotte?" She and Charlotte were close friends.

"I'm afraid it gets worse. We're going to be facing dragons, the royal Barinov house."

"Russian Imperials. Aren't they the ones Saint Petersburg were trying to extract information from?" Tamara said. She shared a look with Nicholas, the magical tracker she partnered with.

"Right, but the Drakors, the other Russian dragon line, also operate in Moscow—or used to. A few months ago, the Barinovs all but wiped out the Drakor line. As of right now we're still sketchy on how that happened or if it's going to stop. Historically, the Barinovs haven't been troublemakers, but we can't take the chance that that hasn't changed. With the Drakors all but extinct, a new dragon clan might sense the power vacuum in Moscow and make a play or form an alliance against the Barinovs. The situation is tense and incredibly volatile, and it's why Saint Petersburg were keen on interviewing one of the Barinovs. I'll send you all reports on the two dragon families tonight, as well as any other potential players. We leave at dawn."

The hunters and trackers left, but Jason and Meg stayed behind. She was biting her lip, something she rarely did. Damien had known her since she was a child, and it was obvious something was bothering her.

"What is it?" Damien stood, facing her. Meg rarely showed any nerves, but she looked ready to bolt.

"You're going to kill me for this, but I think it's my fault that Charlotte is in Russia."

"What? Why?" Jason demanded.

"When I was in London tracking the Belishaw dragons, I came across something." She turned on her cell and pulled up a picture of a needle in an evidence bag. "I found this at the scene. It was in that Sinclair dragon's other house, a residence he kept a secret from the public."

Damien nodded. He remembered all too well Meg's report on the British member of Parliament who'd managed to hide his identity as a dragon for centuries. Sinclair had designs to take out or subdue the Belishaw family in a power struggle. He had been killed by one of the Barinov dragons, Mikhail.

"You found that where you said Sinclair tortured Randolph Belishaw," Damien clarified.

"Yes. Whatever was in this needle weakened Randolph Belishaw and cancelled out his ability to heal. I've never heard of such a thing before. When he looked at me, he looked human. His eyes didn't have that otherworldly glow. Whatever was in this, it made him vulnerable."

For a long second Damien didn't speak. If Meg was right, this drug was a game changer. And in the wrong hands it could be incredibly dangerous.

"How does Charlotte fit into this?" Jason asked, crossing his arms.

"When I got back stateside, I didn't submit the evidence to our lab. I'm sorry, Damien, but this drug could be a potential dragon killer. I didn't want just anyone to have access to that. You talk a good game when it comes to peace, and you keep your promises, but if someone else took over tomorrow, it could be a different story. We could be ordered to kill our enemies on sight, like they did back in the fifties. I didn't want to hand that kind of power over until I knew we could use it wisely." She looked down, her face flushed. "So I called in Charlotte. I wanted her to examine the formula on the sly. She was going to see if she could reverse-engineer the drug based on the notes we found at the crime scene."

"So you recruited our sister," Jason growled. "You know we kept her out of this life on purpose—so shit like this doesn't happen!"

"Jason," Damien warned him. His little brother had more of a temper, but Damien had learned patience. He had lost too much as a young man.

Meg's defiance grew. "Listen, I didn't tell her to go to Russia. She was supposed to stay here. I don't know how she got it in her head to..." She paused a moment, and her eyes began to water. "This can't be my fault. It can't..."

"Not looking like that from where I sit," Jason huffed.

"It's all right, Meg." Damien's chest tightened with guilt at upsetting her. She was one of his best hunters. He never should have let her get so close to Charlotte over the years. "Right now what matters is figuring out our next step. So knowing Charlotte, she succeeded in developing this drug. Now what, she's run off to test it out? Why didn't she go after one in America?"

"You guys have been obsessing over the Barinovs for weeks, given the powder keg that area is right now. She's probably trying to prove herself to you by getting what you can't—an interview with a Barinov."

Damien sighed, looking back and seeing the pieces laid bare before him and how they fit together. She had seen the file he had left at their house a week ago. It had pictures of the three brothers. And they'd been talking shop at home far more than usual. But still, this wasn't like her. Charlotte was always so calm, so well behaved.

Shit.

Meg chuckled. "Besides, the Barinovs are freaking gorgeous, so that's a perk. I can respect that."

Jason struggled for words. "But Charlotte isn't..."

Meg snorted. "Isn't what? A hot-blooded woman? You do realize you two have made her dating life *impossible*."

"Now hold on," said Damien.

"Oh, spare me, Damien. You had me tail her on half a dozen dates and run background checks on three boyfriends while I was in training. And I know for a fact you scared one of them off with a friendly 'talk,' Jason. I'm sure in your little macho brotherly heads you're just looking out for her best interests and don't even realize that you were smothering her. Hell, she's probably still a virgin. If I'd been in her position, I would have run at those dragon hotties myself."

Both Damien and Jason froze at this.

A virgin? He went over the list of her boyfriends. She'd never seemed to be that close to any of those men. Was it possible...?

"Fuck," Jason muttered. "She's like candy-coated ecstasy. They won't be able to stay away from her. Did you tell her about that? How virgins are like catnip to dragons?"

Meg shook her head. "Look, I was trying to help her prove her worth to you meatheads, but strictly in a research capacity. I'd never encourage her to go into the field. We just talked about the serum…" Her eyes widened as a new revelation dawned on her. "And I might have let her analyze the synthetic dragon pheromone we've been working on."

"So let's just recap for a moment," Jason added sarcastically. "Charlotte has created a dragon-suppression serum, she's headed into a preternatural war zone, she's a virgin, and oh yeah, she's got her hands on a dragon love potion? Great—just fucking great."

Damien raked a hand through his hair. "She's going to be fine. She's only been there a day at most. She might not have even made contact yet. We can extract her before she gets too close. She's not a trained agent. She won't be able to get into too much trouble before we arrive."

"Right," Meg echoed, but he sensed her disbelief.

"She'll be fine. She's probably asleep in her hotel right now." He hoped. Or else he would rain fire down on those damned Russian dragons.

"Meg, I want you to swing by the lab Charlotte was working in and grab any of the serum she might have left behind. We could use any help we can get." Taking on the Barinovs would be dangerous if it came down to that, and they'd need every advantage they could get to bring their baby sister home.

6

MARVELING AT HIS OWN BOLDNESS, HE SAID SOFTLY, "I WOULD ENTER YOUR SLEEP IF I COULD, AND GUARD YOU THERE, AND SLAY THE THING THAT HOUNDS YOU, AS I WOULD IF IT HAD THE COURAGE TO FACE ME IN FAIR DAYLIGHT. BUT I CANNOT COME IN UNLESS YOU DREAM OF ME." —PETER S. BEAGLE, THE LAST UNICORN

Charlotte was having the most exquisite dream. It was snowing outside, and she was in a warm bed, the curtains half-closed, and a man was kissing her neck. His hot body was flush against hers from behind. She let out a soft moan of pleasure and tilted her head to give him better access to the sensitive spot just behind her ear, which sent powerful shivers down the rest of her body.

"Yes," she whispered in encouragement. Her dream lover murmured something she couldn't understand, and his dark, warm chuckle against her ear made her feel like she was doing something wicked in the best possible way.

She pushed back the covers and searched for his hand. When her fingers curled around his wrist, she guided his hand to the waistband of her panties and pajama bottoms.

"There? You're sure?" he asked.

"Yes." She rubbed her bottom against his groin, teasing the hard shaft by rubbing it against the cleft of her ass. "Touch me."

She closed her eyes, allowing her body's senses to take over. The rustle of the sheets, the mix of his sighs and hers, and his smell, darkly masculine with a hint of pine and winter, wrapped around her. It was the most erotic dream she'd ever had. She'd never had a dream that felt this good—or this *real*. She wasn't about to waste a single minute.

"Be patient, little one." Her lover's rough laugh sent shivers of longing through her. She wanted him to take her, to shove her flat on the bed beneath him and take her so completely that she felt *owned*.

She tried to move his hand again. "Please...I need..." Her clit was throbbing, and her channel was wet and ready.

"Oh, little rose, how you torture me," he rasped as he sank his teeth into the sensitive area between her neck and shoulder. The possessive hold made her whimper, but not from pain. The bite rooted her in place, and her body went limp with pleasure at how safe she felt while being so incredibly aroused.

He slipped his hand beneath her panties and cupped her mound, then explored her folds with his fingertips. She wiggled, encouraging him to plunge his fingers inside her, but he resisted, and she was held still by his gentle but firm bite. When he finally slid one finger into her, the ripples of building pleasure began in earnest. He toyed with her, thrusting, withdrawing, and then his fingertip brushed over a spot that made her jolt and her belly quiver.

He let go of her shoulder to speak. "This, right here?"

"Yes, right there!" she gasped, and he began to rub on that spot deep inside. He pushed a second finger in, and the tightness gave way when he kept rubbing on that spot. His hips pushed hard against her ass as he rocked against her from behind. He continued to torture her with his fingers while nibbling on her neck.

"Bite me again, please!" she begged. There was something about the way he did that. She needed more of it.

He sank his teeth into her shoulder, and she screamed as pleasure ripped through, robbing her of thought and breath. She lay there, feeling the heat of him behind her, wishing she didn't have to ever leave this bed. Charlotte sighed, the tension in her body seeping out of her, and a small smile curled her lips.

"How do you feel?" The deep rumbling voice snapped her out of her trance. Her body went rigid as she tried to process everything that had just happened. It hadn't been a dream at all.

Oh my God, what have I done?

She'd crossed the line and done the one thing she shouldn't have. She was lying in a hotel bed with a dragon shifter who had just made her climax using only his hand. Overwhelmed by a wave of embarrassment, she rolled away from him and buried her face in her pillow.

Rurik didn't let her escape that easily. He slid up behind her, bending a muscled arm around her waist. The delicious heat of his body made her relax, but she still couldn't meet his gaze.

"Still so shy," he teased, nuzzling the back of her neck. It felt tender and raw. She lifted her head and brushed her hand over her skin.

"Ouch!" she yelped when she reached a tender spot.

Rurik gave a gentle rumbling laugh. "My apologies. I got carried away when you begged me to do it. You will be sore for a few days."

A few days? It would be at least a *week* before she stopped feeling sore.

"Look at me." He pulled her onto her back and leaned over her. She finally met his gaze. The green of his eyes was now strangely golden, as if the color had been put through a filter.

She reached up to touch his cheek, and a lock of his dark hair fell across his eyes. "Your eyes..."

"What about them?"

"They're golden-green. I swear, yesterday they were pure green, like jade."

He shrugged and rolled off her. "It's a trick of the light," he answered casually, but Charlotte knew that wasn't the case. Eye color changes were a magical trait in dragons, along with rapid healing. The wounds from last night were almost healed. The once bleeding raw holes had healed over and looked like pink knotted scars from old injuries.

But then she remembered, he'd just been scratched, hadn't he? But hadn't she removed the bullets herself? Her mind fought with what she had seen versus what her gut told her was true. Had he planted the idea in her head?

"How are you feeling?" How could she pretend not to notice that he had healed far too fast from something that would have killed a mortal man? "Have the wounds reopened?"

"Fine," he answered carefully. "Just a scratch, remember?"

There was something about the way he said "remember." He *had* planted the idea in her head. He looked over her head toward the window and grinned. "I see your wish has been granted. Look, snow." He pointed at the landscape outside, which was full of fluffy flakes.

"You'll have to thank your brother for me," Charlotte joked. "But I won't be able to get to Saint Petersburg to see the Winter Palace. It's a five-hour train ride." It had been on her bucket list, but she'd come here for a particular mission, one that she was failing at spectacularly. She shot a guilty glance at the mini-fridge where she'd stored the vials of suppressant and their injector needles.

I was too busy freaking out over nearly getting killed and almost having sex with a dragon shifter in the shower. Get it together, MacQueen. You just need an opportunity to take him down, and then you can call the Saint Petersburg team to secure him.

"Why don't you shower, and I'll call my jet? We can be in Saint Petersburg in under three hours." Rurik came over, his shirtless chest level with her eyes. His skin was slightly tan, like he'd spent time in the sun even in the midst of a Russian winter. She tilted her head back, and he traced his fingertips along her throat, making her tremble with delight.

"Your jet?" she asked, trying to contain her excitement. If he took her to Saint Petersburg, they would be that much closer to the Brotherhood offices. A twinge of renewed guilt dug like a small but sharp knife between her ribs. She smiled up at him.

"It's one of the perks of my family. The jet is always on call." He leaned down with a crooked grin and pressed an open-mouthed kiss on her that sent sparks of arousal through her exhausted body.

"Okay. I'm in," she said with a sigh.

"Good. You should shower first. I'll make the call." He stole one more quick kiss that made her head go fuzzy. She forced herself to climb off the bed and go into the bathroom.

As she stripped out of her clothes, she heard him speak in Russian to someone on the phone. She heard him chuckle, the warm sound making her smile too. She gave herself a little shake.

What am I doing? I can't fall for him. He's the target. I have to get close to bring him down. That's it. Then it occurred to her that perhaps his affections toward her weren't genuine, but were brought on by the experimental pheromone she'd put on. Still, it didn't make her feel that much better about what she was planning to do.

Was this how her brothers always felt? Did they have to get close to preternatural creatures to betray them? For the first time in her life, she had to face the fact that maybe her brothers were right about her. She might not be cut out for their line of work.

Charlotte took a quick shower and dressed. Rurik was already in his clothes from last night, examining his motorcycle jacket with a dark scowl. He slid a finger through one of the bullet holes and let out a stream of curse words. When he saw that she was watching him, he swung his jacket on. It was funny, she knew she should be freaked out over him being shot, but whenever she thought about it, she calmed and focused on one thought—she was safe and she was with him.

"We will need to stop at my apartment again before we leave."

"Okay." She collected her purse, her coat, and her camera. Then she walked over to the mini-fridge and opened the door, careful to angle herself so she blocked his view.

"I'm grabbing some snacks for the plane. You want

anything?" She tucked a small black carrying case between two candy bars and crammed them into her purse, burying them deep.

"No, my plane will have the necessary amenities." Rurik laughed. "Caviar from the Black Sea, if you wish."

"Not much of a caviar fan," she said as she shut the mini-fridge door. She had jeans and a nice sweater on, along with a thick blue peacoat. She hoped it would be warm enough for where they were going.

"Nor am I," Rurik said with a chuckle. "But it is expected."

She waved a hand over herself. "Do I need different clothes, or are these okay?"

Rurik smiled. "I much prefer you *without* clothes, but it is cold outside and I wouldn't want you to freeze."

"Ha ha." She laughed sarcastically at his teasing, even though she liked it. A hot blush flooded her face.

"There it is." His low rumbling chuckle made her burn with desire.

"There what is?"

"Your blush. It's quite a fun challenge to see what makes you turn red, my little rose." He slid a hand beneath her coat to stroke her lower back, giving her ass a playful squeeze.

She smacked his chest. "Are we leaving now?" If they stayed here much longer, she was afraid they would end up back in bed and doing what they'd almost done last night and this morning. It was exactly what she wanted. And that's what made this game they were playing so dangerous.

❈

"You *failed*," Dimitri snapped at Luis Silva. Luis, the battle dragon of the Silva family who controlled most of Brazil, curled his lips in a challenge. He slammed his hands down on Dimitri's desk. Dimitri looked at those hands, unimpressed by the cracks they'd made in the wood finish.

"Last night wasn't my fault," Luis said. "Those bullets you provided me? Completely underpowered."

"That is the nature of a *subsonic* silenced pistol," Dimitri countered. He'd overestimated this man's intelligence. "You didn't want to attract attention to yourself, now did you?"

"Yes, but to do it right, I'd have to go right up to him and shoot him point-blank. You think I'm going to do that in front of security cameras?"

"And what the fuck were you doing shooting up one of the nicer hotels in Moscow in the first place? You were supposed to take care of it from the shadows, not in the limelight. Don't make me regret this alliance, Silva."

Luis's black eyes were as dark as obsidian, but Dimitri didn't back down.

"He was with a woman. A human. I was curious to see if she would be given his protection."

Dimitri calmed a little. "I know the woman. I saw her too." If Rurik was protecting a woman, they might be able to use her.

"He took at least three bullets when he shielded her from the attack. That was instinct. She means something to him." Silva pulled out a slender switchblade and flicked it open. He tossed it into the air, catching it by the handle as it came back down. A pointless display of agility, Dimitri thought, common among those compensating for actual talent.

"You plan on kidnapping her to lure him in?"

Luis nodded with a sly grin. "To the shadows, as you put it. The Ramirez family, do you remember them? They controlled most of Brazil a hundred years ago."

"I remember." Dimitri hadn't liked Pablo Ramirez. He reminded Dimitri too much of Grigori Barinov and his brothers, no doubt part of the reason the two houses had once had an alliance. Pablo had believed dragons were supposed to be guardians to humans rather than their rulers. In other words, he'd been a fool.

"Pablo mated a mortal woman. We took her, and after we had

our fun, we used her to lure Pablo's family into a trap." Luis snapped his fingers. "And that was the end of the Ramirez line. It cost me ten of my men, but men can be replaced."

Dimitri didn't smile like Luis did. "Pablo was too trusting. Rurik is no fool. You won't catch him off guard. Not enough to kill him. And he won't take a mate. He's resisted the lure before."

Luis was still grinning like a jackal. "Perhaps. But I believe I know something you do not."

Dimitri steepled his fingers and leaned back in his chair. "Oh?"

Luis flipped his knife again, and this time the blade landed point down on the pad of his finger, yet no blood was drawn.

"That woman he was with? She is human, but that isn't *all* she is." Luis continued to draw out the suspense a little longer.

"What is she?"

"She's Damien MacQueen's sister."

The announcement hit Dimitri like a sledgehammer. The sister of a Brotherhood hunter? And not just any hunter. The *head* of the entire organization.

"Are you sure?" he asked.

"Positive. We keep track of MacQueen's family closely."

"Is she a hunter or tracker?"

"Neither," Luis said. "She's a civilian, as they say. She has some degree, I forget the word, but she does not work for the Brotherhood. She has no real training, no protection."

Dimitri scoffed. "No protection? I doubt that. MacQueen wouldn't let his sister go unwatched."

"Yet she is here with a dragon. Do you think if MacQueen was watching her closely he would have allowed that? You know how the Brotherhood feels about our kind," Luis spat and closed his switchblade as he got to his feet. "If you want Rurik dead, you let me do this *my* way."

Dimitri got to his feet as well. "What's your plan?"

"We tip MacQueen off, let him know who his sister is shacking up with. Odds are he will lose his shit and come in guns blazing.

And"—Luis grinned—"we'll tell Rurik's brothers. They can't know who he's with, but once they do, they'll close ranks, ready to fight."

"You would give the Barinovs a heads-up? I don't think—" Dimitri began.

"No, we tell them that she's a spy, a hunter sent by her brother. You have to admit playing both sides against each other is the best way to handle this."

Dimitri considered it. Perhaps Luis wasn't an idiot after all. It wasn't perfect, however. Grigori didn't trust him, and he would trust Luis even less. However, one thing all dragons agreed upon was that they had to be careful around the Brotherhood. It was one of the few unifying forces between the dragon families of the world.

"Fine. But let me tip off MacQueen and Grigori."

"Excellent." Luis reached into his leather jacket and pulled out a pair of Cuban cigars, handing one to Dimitri. Luis snapped his finger at the end of his, and a small flame ignited the cigar's tip. Dimitri did the same and took a slow drag of his exquisite Cuban.

"If anyone is still standing after this is over, we'll snuff them out." Luis puffed out a circular ring of smoke, which transformed into the shape of a dragon and then a shapeless cloud.

Dimitri watched the ghostly image of the dragon made of smoke fade. "Agreed."

The Barinovs would finally be eliminated, and Ruslan and the rest of his family would be avenged. Dimitri began to laugh, hard enough that tears even came to his eyes.

7

I THINK LOVE IS STRONGER THAN HABITS OR CIRCUMSTANCES. I THINK IT IS POSSIBLE TO KEEP YOURSELF FOR SOMEONE FOR A LONG TIME AND STILL REMEMBER WHY YOU WERE WAITING WHEN SHE COMES AT LAST. —PETER S. BEAGLE, THE LAST UNICORN

Charlotte stared at the interior of the luxury jet. "Holy cow, you weren't kidding!"

Rurik leaned against the plush leather seat closest to him as he watched her. A smile crossed his lips, one he couldn't seem to stop, nor did he want to. She made him want to hoot and holler like a child, her innocence was so infectious.

"I'm glad you're pleased." He found he wanted to be more formal around her now, to play the gentleman the way he had with the queens and princesses of old. Charlotte brought that out in him; it was amusing and a little disturbing. He'd always been good at adapting to the changing times, yet with Charlotte he felt his past self coming back, the old-fashioned side of his dragon that would cherish and guard her.

"Rurik!" A voice from the plane's open door made him jerk in surprise. Grigori and his mate, Madelyn, were coming up the steps.

He blocked his brother's path to the plane's cabin. "Grigori, what are you doing here?"

Grigori arched his brow when they came face to face. Neither dragon flinched. "You tell me you want the plane to show Saint

Petersburg to a girl? I'm guessing this is the same girl who asked for snow? So I am curious. I want to meet the woman who's enchanted my baby brother." From behind Grigori, Madelyn gave a stifled giggle.

Rurik curled his lip in the face of this age-old brotherly challenge.

"You can meet her later."

"I've already told the pilot that he's taking four of us." Grigori punched Rurik playfully in the arm, and Rurik, still sore from the bullet wound, winced. Grigori didn't miss his reaction, and his eyes narrowed.

"What's wrong?"

"Not here. I'll fill you in later," Rurik whispered. Charlotte was approaching. He didn't want to explain things to his brother with her around. "Charlotte," he said, changing his tone, "this is my brother Grigori. He and his wife, Madelyn, have decided to join us."

"Hi." Charlotte beamed, shaking hands with Grigori and Madelyn. "It's so nice to meet you. I take it you helped arrange the plane? Thank you so much." Charlotte's cheeks pinkened, and Rurik's body grew hard. Would it be such a bad thing if he shoved his brother out of the plane en route? He could fly, after all. He wanted Charlotte alone so he could introduce her to the mile-high club. A meddling older brother would only get in the way.

"It's a pleasure." Grigori shook Charlotte's hand, and Madelyn did the same.

"Come on, let's sit down. I have so many questions." Madelyn tugged Charlotte to the back of plane, and they seated themselves in two chairs side by side. It gave the brothers a few minutes to talk alone. Rurik had no interest in being lectured by his brother, but it seemed it was inevitable.

"What happened?" Grigori asked, studying his brother. "Who hurt you?"

"I was taking Charlotte home from the club last night. A sedan pulled up and opened fire on us. I took a few bullets. They were made of *pure* iron."

Grigori's eyes widened, and he leaned in closer, touching Rurik's shoulder.

"Are you all right?"

"Yes. Charlotte is good in a crisis, it turns out. Fortunately, they hadn't gone deep. She dug the bullets out of me. I've almost healed."

Grigori jerked his head toward the back of the plane. "Then she knows what we are?"

"No." Rurik grimaced. "I altered her memories so she remembers my jacket as stopping most of the damage."

Grigori relaxed, his features losing the harsh tension. "Good. But this news concerns me. We will have to talk more of it later, when we are assured of more privacy." He sighed and smiled. "Let's sit so the plane can take off."

Rurik followed his brother to where Charlotte and Madelyn sat, their heads bent together. Madelyn said something, and Charlotte blushed and laughed. Rurik sat spellbound by the sight of Charlotte laughing and smiling so easily. Grigori joined them, choosing a seat across from her. She smiled again, her expression open and free. In that moment, when Rurik watched her with his family, how open she was and how easily she fit right in with them, as though she had always been there, his heart jolted.

She could be my true mate.

Charlotte was slipping past the barriers he'd erected around his heart. But he could not let her in, could not let her become a part of him.

If I let her, she could destroy everything. She would live another seventy years at the most, and I would die with her. Then who would protect my family?

With a ruthless heartbreaker smile, he joined them at the back of the plane. He sat next to Grigori, facing Charlotte.

"So, Grigori, tell me—what was Rurik like as a child?" Charlotte asked as she grinned at Rurik. He couldn't resist chuckling before he turned to his brother.

"Choose your words carefully, Grigori, or I'll start sharing your secrets with Madelyn."

When his brother laughed, the sound was infectious. How long had it been since he'd heard Grigori laugh? Too long. Being mated had been good for him, just as it had been with Mikhail and his mate. Both of his brothers had relaxed ever since they'd found the women fate had chosen for them. Madelyn was a thunderbird, an immortal in her own right, though she hadn't known it until recently. Piper, Mikhail's mate, had triggered an ancient dragon stone and became a dragon shifter herself. But the odds of such luck happening with Charlotte to make her immortal? Impossible.

"Rurik as a boy... Where do I begin?" Grigori tapped his fingers on his chin in mock contemplation. "He was an absolute rascal. Always scrambling off to places he shouldn't go or doing things he knew he shouldn't. And he was tough. He had a knack for wrestling, far more than Mikhail or me." Grigori shared a glance with Rurik, a twinkle in his blue eyes. There was a compliment there, one rarely given between the brothers, and it made Rurik want to puff out his chest with pride.

"Of course, he's also stubborn and reckless, but I'm sure you're figuring that out just by being around him." Grigori laughed again, and Charlotte nodded.

"I am." She laughed, but it wasn't at him. "He certainly keeps me on my toes."

They continued to talk as the plane rose into the sky. After the flight attendant brought them refreshments, they relaxed for a while, enjoying their newfound companionship.

Madelyn suddenly paled, holding one hand to her stomach. "Grigori?"

"What is it?" Grigori was out of his seat in an instant, taking her hands in his.

"I'm feeling nauseous. Can you help me to the bathroom?"

Grigori unbuckled Madelyn and walked her to the bathroom.

"Is she okay?" Charlotte asked. Her concern warmed his heart.

"I suspect it's morning sickness."

"That's right, you mentioned she was pregnant." Charlotte's eyes softened, and Rurik wondered if Charlotte ever dreamed of having children. He couldn't imagine her not wanting them. She was warm, sincere, loving, and brave, everything that made a good mother. But if they mated, he could never give her children. Only a dragoness or another of the immortal kin could have drakelings. Or would it be a thunderling? He honestly had no idea how this would work out, and it caused him some concern.

"Yes, only a couple of months."

"Wow, that's wonderful. She and Grigori must be thrilled."

"They are." Rurik changed seats, settling in beside her. He buckled up and reached over to take Charlotte's hand, stroking the back of it and studying the delicate veins just hinted at beneath her skin. *So fragile and so beautiful. She's incredible.*

"I like your family," she said softly, ducking her head. He cupped her chin and raised her head so that she peered up at him beneath those dark lashes. His body flared to life at her seductive yet shy gaze. The woman knew how to turn him on without even trying.

"Seems like they like you too." He leaned over and traced his fingers down her cheek. He gazed at her lips, neither too plump nor too thin—the perfect shape for both kisses and smiles. His hunger to taste her in every way he could was almost overpowering, and her intoxicating virginal scent was damned hard to ignore. He'd teased Grigori mercilessly about how he hadn't resisted Madelyn, but now he understood his brother's loss of control. A true mate was difficult to resist, a virgin true mate all but impossible.

"Are you going to kiss me?" she asked.

His lips quirked into a wicked smirk that earned a giggle from her. "Maybe."

She made a soft little noise of excitement as she gripped the collar of his jacket with one hand and tugged him toward her.

Their lips met in a mix of searing heat and sweetness. Joy ran through his veins, like the old lullabies his mother had once sung when he was a drakeling. There was tenderness, fire, sorrow, and delight all mixed in their kiss that rocked him to his core. He held a hand at the nape of her neck as he kissed her more urgently, demanding she open herself, give him everything she had. The burning desire to connect with her went beyond physical need. Behind his closed eyes he saw his home, the Fire Hills of Russia, the rippling shades of fiery leaves in the fall, the joy of flying low over the valley. His body surged with adrenaline and excitement as he shot up through the clouds and into the bright light of the morning sun.

Then the images changed. He saw a little girl chasing two blond-headed boys across a sandy shore, laughing as she tried to catch up to them. They stopped, each holding out a hand to her. Their palms, much bigger, much stronger, curled around her small fingers as they led her to the lapping waves. She screeched in delight as the cold water kissed her toes, then rushed forward to clean her feet of sand before the water pulled back out. The eldest boy smiled down at her. *"Don't worry, Charlotte, we'll protect you."*

"Yeah, always," the other boy agreed. Their sunny smiles and dark-blond hair seemed familiar, and the heartache that poured through him was strong enough to drown him. Something about this made Charlotte's heart heavy, and he was feeling that through her as they kissed.

The vision faded as he and Charlotte broke apart. His arms were locked around her, and she was clutching his jacket as though her life depended on it. Ghosts of tears clung to her lashes. Her lips were parted, and he could sense the questions on the tip of her tongue. It was as though his mind and hers had been on the verge of becoming one.

"What was that?" she panted, a little frightened.

"I..." He couldn't tell her the truth, or that he'd made a dangerous mistake. Shared memories and emotions were a sign of a mating in progress. He could not ignore it or dismiss his fascination with her. This was infinitely *more*. He'd never let things get this far with Nikita—he'd been far more careful around her.

A true mate... But to claim her would be to defy my father. He could already hear his father's voice in a commanding tone.

"One to lead, one to gather jewels, one to protect. That is how it must be. We have no other children, so you must each bear a burden."

And Rurik's burden was living the rest of his long immortal life alone.

"Rurik, what's the matter?" Charlotte asked, her brows knitting together.

"I..." Again, he was at a loss for words. Thankfully, Grigori and Madelyn returned at that moment.

"Sorry. Sometimes I get a little sick," Madelyn said, her face still pale, but she was smiling. "I'm pregnant." She touched her belly gently, and Grigori sat down beside her, lacing his palm over hers.

"*We're* pregnant," he corrected with a warm smile, and his mate leaned in to nuzzle him.

"Oh yeah? You can carry the baby for a few months then," Madelyn retorted, but she returned his nuzzling embrace with a soft smile.

Rurik watched them enviously. He could never have that. Charlotte was watching them too, and the longing and loneliness in her eyes broke through the cool distance he'd tried to put between them. She may not be a mate he could claim, but he could still provide her with comfort. He slid an arm around her shoulders and lifted the armrest between them so she could slide closer to him. She was stiff only a few seconds before she settled against him with a sigh.

"Congratulations to you both," Charlotte said, smiling. "You must be so happy."

"Thank you," Grigori replied. "We are indeed happy." He murmured something in Madelyn's ear, and she blushed.

Rurik bit his lip to keep from laughing. Big, scary Grigori—a warrior in corporate boardrooms and a fierce dragon in his own right—was grinning like a young boy and whispering sweet words of love in his wife's ear. Grigori noticed Rurik grinning and frowned before he leaned over and socked Rurik in the arm.

"Ow!" Rurik snapped.

"Whatever you're smirking about, brother, I will repay it in bruises," Grigori warned.

Madelyn laughed and glanced toward Charlotte. "That has to be a brother thing. I'm an only child. I don't know how brothers do it, always tussling, punching, growling."

"It is definitely a brother thing. I've got two myself. They shove each other all the time. Sometimes they do it to me, but not intentionally."

Another pang of jealousy hit Rurik as he listened to Charlotte speak of her brothers. Two men who would have the rest of their lives to spend with her, while he would have to walk away, leaving only these fleeting moments with her and a lasting emptiness inside.

"Would you ladies like another drink?" Grigori asked.

"Water would be great," Madelyn said.

"Yes, water, please," Charlotte echoed.

"Come on, Rurik." Grigori pulled him away from Charlotte, and they walked up to where the flight attendant stood ready to serve them.

"Two bottles of water, please," Grigori said. He and Rurik then stepped away to a careful distance.

"You're playing with fire, Rurik."

"How so?"

Grigori stared hard at him. "Charlotte is a virgin. You know that. But there's something else—there's something about her that is intoxicating even to me, which it shouldn't be, since I'm mated."

"If you get any ideas..." Rurik raised his shoulders slightly in defense.

"Don't be stupid. My point is, something doesn't feel right. You must take care. I see the way you two are together. It's only less than a day, and you are already fixated on her. I want you to be careful."

"It's a temporary fascination," he lied. "It's not as though she is my mate."

Grigori slid a finger under his collar and then loosened his blue silk tie.

"I've never seen you like this before. Not even with Nikita. Are you sure she's not?"

"She's not," he lied again, the words stinging his lips.

"How do you know? I see a different side of you. The burden you bear as a family battle dragon takes a heavy toll on you. But around her it seems to fade."

"And that's *my* burden to deal with," Rurik growled. "Not yours, not Mikhail's."

Grigori's gaze turned soft in a way that reminded Rurik of their beloved mother.

"You're going to let Father's old nursery rhymes of our duties define your life forever? He should never have told you that you could not have a mate. With our dwindling numbers, he was wrong. What's more, you deserve happiness. If that means taking a mate, Mikhail and I will both support you."

"I can't," Rurik whispered.

"Why?"

Because Nikita's death wrecked me, and if I had a real mate, it would someday kill me. And if I die, you won't stand a chance if Drakor rebuilds somehow and strikes again.

"I am..." He hesitated, searching for the words that would hide his fears. "I'm not like you and Mikhail. I'm not cut out to have a mate."

"I didn't think I was either. I was obsessed with work and forgot how to live. Having a mate changes everything. You can't imagine going back to your old life once you find her."

Grigori took the bottled waters back to Madelyn and Charlotte, leaving Rurik feeling torn and alone in a way he never had before. He couldn't ignore his father's instructions. It had kept the family safe for thousands of years. His father had been the eldest of three brothers, the established leader. His two younger brothers, Rurik's uncles, had died centuries ago during a battle with Nordic ice dragons on a quest for special gemstones, ancient and mysterious in nature. One had watched his mate die and had vanished, most likely perishing in the icy mountains. Since then, Rurik's father had trained his sons to fill their roles as leaders, guardians, and battle dragons. If Rurik turned his back on his father's wishes now, everyone he loved could die.

My family must come before my happiness.

But as he looked at Charlotte, tiny fractures in his resolve seemed to splinter wider and wider. He had to face the rising truth. He didn't want to lose her.

8

IT IS NOT IN THE STARS TO HOLD OUR DESTINY BUT IN OURSELVES. —WILLIAM SHAKESPEARE

Charlotte could still feel the ghostly press of Rurik's kiss on her lips. Something had happened between them. She hadn't just seen stars. She'd seen herself through his eyes, running on the beach with Damien and Jason. Before that she'd been flying high above the clouds, without fear or panic. Just an amazing, thrilling sense of joy. She'd experienced his memories, and he'd experienced hers through a single kiss.

There had been nothing in the Brotherhood files about that. At this rate she was going to have to write an entirely new set of rules about dragons, starting with mind-blowing kisses that make you share memories. But that was a problem. What if the next time they kissed the memories she shared exposed her for who she was?

Rurik's voice interrupted her thoughts. "Are you okay?"

"Sorry, just thinking," she admitted.

Rurik tapped her temple with a finger and winked. "I'd love to know what's running through that head of yours."

She smiled shyly. "Wouldn't you?"

Rurik bit his lip, trying to contain his smile, and for a moment she forgot they weren't alone. Then Grigori coughed politely.

"You two going to disembark or stand here and ogle each other? I'm sure the pilot would like to refuel, and the flight attendant is cold because she can't shut the door until we leave the plane."

Embarrassed, Charlotte slipped her coat on and descended the airstairs ahead of Rurik, ignoring the chill of the wintry breeze. Her head and heart were still in the clouds, and there was no coming down, at least not yet. She and Rurik bid goodbye to Madelyn and Grigori and caught a cab to the center of Saint Petersburg, where they had a chance to explore the city.

"Hungry?" Rurik asked as they passed by a row of buildings close to the Winter Palace.

She nodded eagerly. "Starving." Charlotte was dying to try one of the local restaurants and actually take the vacation she'd told Rurik she was here to experience.

Rurik led her to a cozy Serbian restaurant on the palace embankment of Saint Petersburg. The Gosti was famous for its Serbian specialty dishes, like pies with sweet and savory fillings, of which he ordered two and quickly found them a table.

Charlotte took a bite of her beef-filled pie as she studied the little eatery. It was painted in a deep emerald along the bottom of the walls, with a butter-yellow wallpaper with a delicate, somewhat faded floral pattern along the top half. A floor-to-ceiling bookshelf against one wall contained dozens of books—not that she could read any of them. The intimate setting reminded her more of summer cottages by Lake Michigan than what she expected to see in Saint Petersburg. Outside, the snow was falling thick and heavy, just how she'd always imagined it would.

"I can't believe I'm really here." Charlotte beamed at Rurik, unable to contain the excitement and rush of actually being in Russia, living an adventure she'd thought she'd never have. She reached out to take his hand. "Thank you for this. *Truly.*"

"Anything for you, my little rose." He brushed her fingers with his other hand, and they sat there quietly until they noticed an old woman staring at them. She wore a thick shawl around her head and shoulders, and the deep wrinkles in her face seemed as ancient as her brown eyes.

"*U vas yest 'sil' naya sud'ba.*" The woman spoke in a rusty old voice, pointing at them, then to her own chest.

"What did she say?" Charlotte whispered.

Rurik seemed to consider the woman's words. "She believes we have a strong destiny, and she wants to tell our fortunes."

"Oh, can we? I've always wanted to do that!" Charlotte exclaimed. "Please?" Ever since she'd learned that magic was real as a child, she'd always believed in seers or people who could see glimpses of the future. Sure, most of them were just con artists, but some of them had to be real, right?

Rurik chuckled. "If you wish." He spoke to the older woman and offered her the chair between him and Charlotte. "I will translate for her as she reads the cards."

The woman hobbled over and eased down into the chair with a sigh, then removed a set of very old and worn tarot cards. The edges were rough and slightly crinkled. The illustrations, while faded, were still stunning in their design. She began to lay out the cards on the table. She made a horseshoe shape from left to right using seven cards. Her withered hands trembled slightly as she turned over the first. Then she began to speak in Russian, and Rurik translated.

"The Magician is the past, the cunning master of all he surveys." The card showed a magician in a warrior's pose, a sword in his hand, with roses and lilies all around his feet. His tunic was white with red robes, and he wore a belt that was made of an ouroboros, a snake eating its own tail. The old woman's brown eyes flashed on the serpent ring that Rurik wore. It had a green jewel in its single eye, and its mouth was consuming its own tail. The ring was stunning, and Charlotte wondered how she hadn't noticed it before. Of course, she'd been distracted by the rest of Rurik most of the time. The woman reached out and touched the serpent ring, then pressed her gnarled fingers gently against Rurik's chest, speaking softly.

He translated for Charlotte. "Skill and confidence are yours but if misused can be your downfall. Beware of pride and arrogance." Then she turned over the next card above it in the horseshoe formation and spoke again. "The High Priestess, guardian of secrets. She knows the secrets of life but shares them only with the wise."

The card bore a woman with an enigmatic smile. She stood between two columns with a curtain suspended between the pillars. A crescent moon rested like a crown in her hair.

The old woman looked at Charlotte, speaking softly. Rurik did his best to match her tone. "You bear a great secret, hiding it from those who would betray it. You must trust your heart, or you will make a grave error."

Rurik reached over and took Charlotte's hand. She glanced at him, guilt making her feel hollow inside. How could this woman know the secret she harbored about the formula?

The old woman turned over the third card. It depicted a woman holding the head of a lion and facing its open jaws, controlling the beast, keeping it from eating her.

"The future. Strength," Rurik translated. "Together you can control your destiny, but stand apart and all will burn to ash around you." The woman touched both their hands, her eyes soft and serious.

Then she turned over the next card. A naked couple entwined together. Charlotte knew very little about tarot, but she recognized that card.

"The Lovers," Charlotte said.

The old woman nodded, and Rurik translated again. "Opposition and attraction. You must both choose between your desires. Family or each other. You cannot split apart."

She turned over the next card with a frown. With a little mutter, she slid another from her deck, putting it next to the card that had displeased her.

"The Emperor and the Sun. You have two forces in your life. The authoritative leader who brings order out of chaos." She stared at Rurik. "He speaks to you." She touched Rurik's chest again. "He tries to guide you—listen to him or you will fail."

Then she pointed to the Sun and spoke to Charlotte. It took a moment for Rurik to catch up. "He's your guiding Sun. He is the center of all, the source of your love and trust—he illuminates you. He is a man of action but does not understand you are guided by the moon. Yours is a different path. The Emperor and the Sun will try to destroy each other, and they may succeed."

Rurik's green eyes met hers, and she swallowed hard. They were destined to be on two different sides if a war between dragons and humans broke out.

She turned over the second-to-last card, revealing a man hanging by a noose. It was upside down. She traced the line of the rope and addressed Rurik. His words came out soft and low as he translated.

"You sacrifice comfort and passion, even your heart, believing things will be better as a result, but you are destroying yourself and hurting her." The old woman curled her fingers over Charlotte's, and a ghostly smile hovered about her lips, one born of sadness rather than joy.

She reached for the final card and turned it over, revealing a beautiful woman pouring water into a lake. Behind her a star shone brightly against the night sky. The old woman brought Rurik and Charlotte's hands together and then spoke one last time.

"She is your star, your guiding light. If you forsake her, you will fall into darkness. Every shadow does pass, but if you go on without her, your light will die and so will the fate of your people."

The hairs on Charlotte's neck and arms rose, and sharp tingling raced like an electric spark along her skin. She sucked in a breath, almost afraid she wouldn't be able to breathe. The fair-haired man on the Sun card looked like Damien as a boy, and the Emperor looked like Grigori. The Magician looked like Rurik. The High Priestess even resembled herself. How was this possible? Was she just seeing what her subconscious wanted her to see? An invisible energy seemed to vibrate from the table and the cards. The old woman moved, touching each card as though counting them in a soft murmur of Russian, but Charlotte wasn't listening.

It felt as if she were facing a thin veil made of gossamer threads. The curtain in her mind rippled, whispers coming from the other side. But they weren't loud enough to hear. She wanted to push the curtain aside and cry out to the voices, demand they speak in a way she could understand. The answers seemed so close, yet she had no way to move the curtain.

How long can you last? a quiet voice asked. *How long before you fall?* But she didn't comprehend. Fall into what? Or where?

She came back to herself in a violent rush.

"Charlotte, are you all right?"

She looked for the woman, but she was gone and the cards had vanished with her. "Huh? Oh, yes, fine."

"Lost in your thoughts?" He gave her hand a gentle squeeze. She managed another nod. She felt open, raw, and vulnerable—from a tarot card reading, of all things.

"Yeah, I guess I was." Charlotte wiped at her eyes, shocked to find tears coming away on her fingertips.

Rurik's mouth softened into a smile. "You were shaken by the reading?" he mused. He ran his fingertips along the back of her hand.

"Weren't you?" Her eyes burned with fresh tears. *I am the guiding light for the man I plan to betray? Our brothers stand in opposition to each other, and we are the lovers who must overcome our opposite natures.* It was all so close to making sense.

Her secrets weighed heavily upon her heart. The older woman had somehow known about the serum. The secret that, if shared unwisely, could upset the balance of the world. Who knew what the consequences of that might be?

Rurik smiled, but there was a bittersweetness to it. "Why don't we go see the palace? It's still snowing, and the view will take your mind off your worries."

He's trying to pull away. He's afraid of whatever it is we could be together. So am I. But she could not imagine a world where she was apart from him, either. The old woman's words trembled in her head like dew collecting on the delicate lines of a spiderweb.

Everything was connected, but she still couldn't see how—she could only feel it.

"Come." Rurik stood and held up her coat. She sighed and let him help her slide it on. Maybe he was right. She needed a distraction from the heavy weight she was carrying inside her.

As they left the restaurant, a light breeze rustled along the row of buildings facing the river. The wind played with her hair, tugging strands of it about her shoulders. Rurik stopped and watched her with a gleam in his eyes. Reaching up, he caught one of her loose locks, staring at the intricate snowflakes that clung to the dark-blonde strands without melting.

"You're breathtaking." He cupped her face, and his hands were warm even without gloves. "Just when I think I've gotten used to looking at you, it's like the sun opens up and it shines on you all over again."

Rurik, her beautiful scarred battle dragon, was murmuring sweet words that were breaking her heart. The serum in her purse seemed to weigh a thousand pounds. His green eyes glowed with an inner fire that mesmerized her. She leaned into his body, pressing herself against him. She didn't care if anyone was watching. She was flooded with a hunger for this man, but it went beyond physical. It went to the farthest depths of her very soul. The truth was on the tip of her tongue. Could she tell him everything?

"Rurik..." she began, her voice breaking. Could she confess future sins to this man? Because she couldn't deny it any longer—she was falling for him. Like a shooting star, she was burning up in his atmosphere, and there was no going back to the safety of the lies she'd spun.

"What is it? Are you cold? You're shivering." He curled his arms around her. The leather of his jacket was warm; his body heat defied the snow and icy wind. She rubbed her cheek against his chest, breathing in the scents of leather and man.

"I know." The words shot out of her mouth.

He raised her chin so she had to look up at him. "Know what?"

"I *know*. I know what you are."

His concern sharpened in an instant to a cold, almost feral gaze.

"What I am?" he said slowly.

"Yes. I know about you...and your brothers." She drew a soft deep breath, her body shaking from fear. "You're a dragon shifter." There. It was done. Nothing could take the words back.

Rurik's arms tightened around her. "How?" His eyes left her face as he searched the crowds on the palace embankment. He then jerked her away from the people. She almost tripped trying to keep up with him. When they reached the gilded gates of the Winter Palace, he stopped her hard enough that she fell into him.

"*How?*" he repeated.

This had been a mistake—she shouldn't have told him. The rage in his eyes was chilling.

"A friend of mine saw your brother back in London. She knew he was a dragon. She—"

"Who is your friend?" Rurik snarled. His gaze turned from green to gold, and a fuzzy dizziness swamped her. She couldn't look away, even though she wanted to. A compulsion to speak overcame her.

"Meg Stratford."

"And how did she know what I am?"

"She's a hunter." She hadn't meant to tell him that, but she bit her tongue before her brother's name could slip out too.

"The Brotherhood?" Rurik's face was pale, the dark scar turning pink on his cheek and forehead. The dizziness in her head faded slightly.

"Yes."

He gripped her by the arm and started to drag her away from the snowy grounds of the Romanov palace. "You're coming with me, right now."

"Where are we going?" She tried to break free of his hand. Her heart beat hard against her ribs, and she swallowed the lump of panic lodged in her throat.

"We are going somewhere safe so I can get some answers. Do not scream for help. No one will come to your aid." He glanced back at her, a fierce look that gave her chills. "You know what I am, so you know what I can do. If you cooperate, you won't be harmed, but I *will* get my answers out of you—one way or another."

Charlotte knew she was in serious trouble. The sweet, sexy man who'd caressed her this morning was gone. In his place was the dragon shifter she'd feared before she'd stepped into the nightclub. The intimidating enforcer from the Brotherhood files.

Telling him the truth had seemed so important. But now she feared it might cost her everything—perhaps even her life.

9

HEROES KNOW THAT THINGS MUST HAPPEN WHEN IT IS TIME FOR THEM TO HAPPEN. A QUEST MAY NOT SIMPLY BE ABANDONED; UNICORNS MAY GO UNRESCUED FOR A LONG TIME, BUT NOT FOREVER; A HAPPY ENDING CANNOT COME IN THE MIDDLE OF THE STORY. —PETER S. BEAGLE, THE LAST UNICORN

Damien stepped off the Boeing C-17 Globe Master military transport, tactical gear backpack slung over one shoulder. His team followed behind him.

"Welcome to Russia," Damien called out to the rest of the hunters and trackers.

They'd touched down on a private airbase run by the Russian military. After the end of the Cold War, the Brotherhood had created secret agreements with local military bases in every major country to have safe passage in and out of any region. The local military assumed that they were some kind of special forces, though the use of an American transport no doubt raised some eyebrows. The Brotherhood's true identity was only shared with top government officials, and sometimes not even then, depending on the country's stability. The last thing anyone wanted was for word of the supernatural to reach the general population.

"So do we get to try the local vodka?" Jason asked as they walked toward the four Mercedes SUVs waiting for them.

"Sure, between fighting dragons and saving your sister, vodka tastings are top priority," Nicholas joked. Everybody laughed except Damien; his mind was firmly on the mission. Humor was good for morale, and Jason could always be counted on to make wisecracks. They all knew the danger of what they would be facing —it was part of the job.

Except this time his sister was involved.

Damien vowed that once he got her safely back to Detroit, he was locking her in her apartment for a month until she understood just how foolish she'd been.

Yeah, that will prove Meg wrong, his inner voice said sarcastically. She'd mostly kept quiet during the trip, but the way she'd looked at him... He couldn't help but worry she was angry with him over what had happened with Charlotte.

They loaded their gear into the vehicles. Just as Damien opened the driver's-side door, his cell phone vibrated. He pulled it out and glanced at the screen. The number was blocked. He was used to getting unknown calls in his line of work. "Hello?"

"MacQueen." A Russian man spoke his name with a familiarity that put Damien on guard. It wasn't a voice he recognized, and he knew every hunter on the Saint Petersburg team.

"Who is this?"

"A concerned citizen. I thought you should know that your sister is being held hostage by Rurik Barinov. I trust you understand how dangerous that is?"

Hostage? Charlotte was a prisoner of the Barinovs already? He clutched the phone tight and tried to remain calm. She'd only received minimal self-defense training, nothing compared to what Brotherhood hunters went through.

"How do you know this?" Damien demanded. Jason and the rest of the team were watching him closely. If someone had figured out how to contact him on his secure cell line, it couldn't be a good thing. If they had his number, they could know a number of other top secret things that could put his hunters in jeopardy.

"How I know doesn't matter. I thought *you* needed to know.

The Barinovs go too far and must be stopped. Check your phone if you don't believe me. I'll send you a picture. Make them pay for what they've done to your sister." The call disconnected. His phone suddenly buzzed with a text message. A picture downloaded, and his heart leapt into his throat.

It was a photo of Charlotte being dragged to the ground by Rurik Barinov. Glass from a window behind them was shattered, and a look of terror was splashed over his little sister's face.

"Who was that?" Jason asked.

Damien stared at his phone for several long seconds before he spoke. There was no way he was showing them the photo, especially not Jason. His brother's temper was legendary. Jason was the shoot-first-ask-questions-later-maybe type, and the last thing Damien needed was to give him a reason to be trigger-happy.

"The Barinov family has taken Charlotte as a hostage. I assume they will use her to get information about us and then eventually contact us for some kind of exchange."

Damien forced himself not to let panic take over. This was not the first hostage situation he'd handled, but this was different. This was his baby sister. The promises he had made his parents burned deep inside his chest, reminding him that he could not afford to fail. He'd already lost one woman he loved to this job; he wouldn't lose his little sister as well.

"Damien?" Nicholas's voice broke through the rush of his panicked thoughts. "What are our orders?"

Orders—right. Get your head in the game, MacQueen.

He pocketed the cell phone. "We continue as planned. Converge on Charlotte's last known location and secure the area. If she isn't there, gain access to every camera and video recording in the surrounding area to track her down."

Damien took his seat in the SUV. The rest of his team spread out across three vehicles and left the base. The distant lights of Moscow acted as a beacon, calling him to Charlotte.

I will find you, little sis. Just hang on.

Madelyn sat on the couch in her and Grigori's Saint Petersburg apartment. "I think he really likes her."

Grigori poured himself a glass of wine and his wife a glass of water. "I think so too." He joined her on the couch, giving her a kiss before he handed her the glass of water.

Madelyn stared at the glass with contempt. "I miss wine."

Grigori chuckled. He adored his stubborn little wife, but she had to be careful during her pregnancy. He was nervous, as was she. They were treading unknown waters, not knowing if a dragon shifter and a thunderbird could have children, or how it would develop. So far, the baby seemed healthy, but would it possess a dragon's spirit or that of a thunderbird? Was it possible to have some kind of chimera, possessing qualities of both? No one knew. He'd hired the best doctors money could buy, those who knew shifter biology and could be trusted to keep the nature of Madelyn's child and any unnatural test results secret. Even within their world, this was dangerous information.

"Is Rurik afraid of taking a mate?" Madelyn asked.

Grigori stared into the burgundy depths of his wine. "Our father was rigid in his ways, though he was a good man—*mostly*." He amended the last bit quickly. Grigori's father had killed Madelyn's parents out of fear and the need for revenge. Thunderbirds had killed Grigori's grandfather, because he had killed a number of thunderbirds in retaliation for the death of *his* grandfather...and so the cycle had gone for uncounted centuries. Now the thunderbirds had become all but extinct. It was a sobering thought, that Madelyn might be the last of her kind, and he prayed deep down that it wasn't true.

"He gave us roles—one to lead the family, one to collect jewels, and one to defend us. Battle dragons are formidable at what they do, so most houses would kill them by killing their mates. Even the strongest dragon can't survive a broken heart. My father convinced Rurik that he couldn't take a mate. You remember

Nikita, the human woman Ruslan Drakor killed a few months ago?"

Madelyn nodded.

"She was a potential true mate for him. It hurt him deeply to lose her, even though he never claimed her."

Madelyn cuddled closer to him, her gray eyes filled with sorrow. "So if he gets too close to Charlotte, he could mate her by accident? I still don't fully understand how dragons do that."

Grigori chuckled. "Do you need a reminder of exactly how we mated?" He leaned in, kissing her and relishing her sweet taste. Madelyn finally put a hand on his chest and gave him a little push back.

"You know what I mean. How do you choose to mate someone at that *exact* moment?"

Grigori set his wine down on the coffee table and took her hands in his, lacing their fingers together as he tried to find the words to describe it.

"For me, mating was like...catching the wind with your wings and harnessing its strength. When I kissed you, it was as though I was spinning an invisible cord around us and binding us together. I opened up my mind and heart to you in a way I never have to another soul. I didn't have to think about it, but I also couldn't stop it. One's true mate is a gift. I honestly don't know how Rurik managed to resist Nikita." Grigori squeezed her hands gently. "With Charlotte he's already falling hard. I've never seen him like this. If he continues to spend time with her, he will cave and claim her."

"Is that bad?" she asked.

"I believe he will fight falling in love and hurt them both."

Madelyn frowned. "That would be horrible."

"He's stubborn enough to hold out longer than me or Mikhail."

His cell phone resting on the coffee table suddenly vibrated. The name showed that the ID was blocked. Nothing unusual there, given his family's ties.

"Do you have to answer that?" Madelyn asked.

"It might be important. If it's business, I promise to hang up immediately." He reached for it and answered.

"Barinov here."

"Grigori." Dimitri Drakor's voice was instantly recognizable.

Grigori growled. "What do you want? I thought we finished our business when we saw each other last time." If Drakor made any threats, Grigori would kill him.

"I thought that given our peace treaty has been restored, you deserved a warning."

"Warning about what?"

Madelyn sat up, eyes wide with worry.

"Your brother is romantically involved with a Brotherhood hunter. Did you know that?"

"What?" Grigori got up from the couch and started pacing.

"Your brother is entangled with a MacQueen, Grigori. Charlotte MacQueen. She's a *hunter*. What's more, she's the sister of their leader, Damien."

Grigori went still, his heart racing. The Brotherhood had never been on good terms with his people. In recent decades they'd left shifters and their kin alone unless they threatened human affairs, but that hadn't always been true. Some were notoriously proactive, and it wasn't that long ago, during the Cold War, that they had been especially unforgiving.

And Rurik was interested in MacQueen's sister? Another truth hit him like lightning. She was Rurik's true mate. How was that possible? It wasn't. There was something else at play.

He remembered his meeting with her, the attraction he'd felt because of her scent, despite his true mate being right there with him. It wasn't natural.

Of course. It *wasn't natural*. The Brotherhood must have found a way to manipulate a shifter's senses. It could be she wasn't a true mate at all but somehow was made to seem like one. Pheromones, perhaps? And she had been sent to bond with Rurik, tie his life with hers. He could already see how this would put them in a position of power over the Barinovs.

This could destroy them all.

"How do you know this, Drakor? Are you spying on us?" he asked, his voice deadly calm.

"I stay in Moscow on occasion, as per our treaty. And I see things. I keep track of the Brotherhood, which it seems you do not." Normally, this chastisement would have enraged Grigori, but he was right, and the fear for his own mate and unborn child was too strong.

"You must stop her, Barinov. You know that as well as I do. If there's only one thing we could ever agree upon, it's that the Brotherhood of the Blood Moon is our enemy."

That much was true, Grigori had to admit.

"I assume you're leaving Moscow?"

"Of course. I'm going home, back to my lands. If I am to die, I wish to be on my own soil when it happens. Take care, Barinov." Drakor hung up.

"What did he say?" Madelyn demanded, her voice breathless.

"Charlotte is not what she seems to be. She lied to us."

"Lied?"

"She is a hunter for the Brotherhood." He stared deep into her eyes, his every nightmare reflected in them.

"Are you sure? Can you trust Drakor? He tried to kill me."

Grigori looked away. "That I will never forget, but..." How could he explain it to her? That some things were deeper than hate? Shifters lived long lives and did not easily forget past transgressions. The Brotherhood could not be trusted.

"But what?"

"Our families have stood against the Brotherhood for centuries. He wouldn't make this up."

Madelyn's gaze was serious. "So then we assume for now that he's telling the truth," she replied slowly. "What's next? Do we need to confront Charlotte?"

"Talk?" Grigori scoffed. "She plans to ensnare Rurik in her web, and he doesn't even have a clue."

"To what end?"

"I don't know," Grigori admitted. "If he were to bond with her, then she would effectively hold his life in her hands. Our entire family might be held to ransom or be forced to fight for their causes. And we would dare not retaliate. There are many possibilities, and none of them are good."

"Oh God, Grigori, we have to stop her!"

"*I* will stop her. You must stay here." He touched her belly, his heart breaking.

"But—"

"Madelyn, I won't let you go anywhere near the Brotherhood. I need you to stay here and call Mikhail. Tell him everything. If something happens to me, you must immediately go with Mikhail and Piper."

"If you die, then I die anyway," Madelyn countered.

"Perhaps not. We do not know if the bond will work the same way between us. And it's possible that your love for our unborn child could keep you alive. Regardless, there are fates other than death that might await me. I won't have you put yourself at the same risk."

Grigori dialed Rurik's number, but it went straight to voicemail.

"Rurik, pick up your damn phone! Where are you?" He hung up and came back to Madelyn, catching her in his arms.

"My heart," he whispered against her lips. "I love you with all that I am. Please don't forget that."

He knew she was feeling his fears. They had known the joy of love so short a time. It was unfair that they had only been together a few months. Grigori didn't let himself finish the thought of what would happen if he couldn't come home. It was too dark, too awful.

"Stay safe. Let Mikhail and Piper protect you and the baby."

Before he could stop himself, he left her, his heart still aching. He had to find Rurik and save his family. He only prayed he wasn't too late.

10

I HAVE BEEN MORTAL, AND SOME PART OF ME IS MORTAL YET. I AM FULL OF TEARS AND HUNGER AND THE FEAR OF DEATH, ALTHOUGH I CANNOT WEEP, AND I WANT NOTHING, AND I CANNOT DIE. —PETER S. BEAGLE, THE LAST UNICORN

Charlotte didn't protest as Rurik took her into the lobby of the Grand Hotel Europe. She had to trust that he wouldn't hurt her after everything they'd been through.

He wouldn't, would he?

He took her straight to the front desk and spoke to the hotel steward in rapid Russian, then slid the man a black credit card. The steward's eyes widened as he took the card, then hastily prepared a set of keycards, handing them to Rurik.

"Come," Rurik growled, his grip on her wrist still tight as they headed to the elevators.

"Rurik, please..." she begged as the elevator doors closed, sealing them in. "If you would just listen—"

"*Not now.*"

How different this was from the other night. Then she had been safe, the secret she kept still a secret. Now he was taking her up to a hotel room to interrogate her.

They stopped on the third floor. He led her down the hall, where he used his keycard to open the door. He shoved her through and closed the door behind him, then raised a hand to point at the bed.

"Take off your coat and sit down. *Now*."

Something about the way Rurik spoke to her in that dominating and dark way made her rush to obey. She was afraid. The Rurik she was falling in love with wouldn't hurt her, but this Rurik, the one who feared the Brotherhood? He might be capable of killing her to protect his brothers and their mates.

Breathe, Charlotte, just breathe. You have to stay calm so you can think this through.

She turned away from him, taking in the splendor of the room as she shrugged out of her coat. Her hands shook as she set it down over the back of a chair. The dark green brocade walls made the room feel warm, like she was stepping into a summer forest. The table and bed were carved from antique cherrywood. Everything about the suite murmured of money in the best way. The large sitting room had two wide windows with white curtains that allowed sunlight to softly filter into the room. A gilded chandelier hung above the table, where an old ivory chess set sat. There was even a bar with a trio of full decanters and glasses. It was a beautiful room to face an angry dragon in, and it had to cost a fortune to stay in. A massive king-size bed with a green satin coverlet embroidered with gold thread was in the adjoining room.

A pang of regret hit her. This could have been a wonderful room to lose herself in Rurik's arms, to give herself to him entirely, but now that would never happen.

Charlotte set her purse down on a table, her legs trembling. Rurik flipped the lock on the door, set the keycard down, and walked over to the curtains, tugging them closed. He removed his jacket and laid it over the back of the nearest chair. Charlotte watched his muscles flex beneath the black sweater he wore as he faced her, his arms crossed.

"What am I going to do with you?" he growled. There was a strange mixture of cool distrust and a simmering heat behind his words.

"Please don't hurt me," Charlotte begged as she retreated into the adjoining bedroom. They'd been so connected before. Every time they'd kissed she'd seen a part of his soul through his memories. The man she'd seen didn't seem like someone who would kill a woman, but she was the enemy. What reason did he have to trust her? She didn't want to die here, so far away from the only family she had left.

Rurik walked up to her. She tensed as he cupped her chin, forcing her head back as he stared down at her.

"Hurt you? I would *never* hurt you," he growled. "But I do not trust you either. How do you know what I am?"

"I've studied you," she admitted. "We have files..."

"So you *are* a hunter!" His tone deepened, and his eyes began to swirl that beautiful shade of gold.

"No! I'm a biochemist!" Her temper flared, temporarily dispelling her fear.

"Hmmm." He made a noise of disgruntled disbelief. For some reason that pissed her off. She hadn't lied, not about that. She smacked his hand away from her chin and pushed him hard in the chest. He didn't budge, the damn muscled bastard, but his nostrils flared.

"If I was a hunter, do you think I would have ended up in this position?" She waved a hand between them.

Rurik arched a brow, coolly meeting her glare. "What do you mean?"

She blushed as she realized what she'd said. "Nothing." She turned away from him and stalked away.

"Oh, you mean how you can't resist me?" He stepped up close behind her, his hands settling on her waist. Charlotte jerked free of his hold.

"I can resist you just fine," she muttered, but the words were a lie.

"You are not the first woman the Brotherhood has sent to try to seduce me, you know," Rurik said. "They *all* wanted to end up alone with me. But I could smell their intentions a mile off."

"What I *mean* is that I wouldn't have admitted my connection with them to your face. And I certainly wouldn't have ended up here, defenseless in a hotel room with you. If I was a hunter, I would have probably had a backup plan to incapacitate you so I could escape."

Rurik crossed his arms over his chest, a smile curving his lips. "Finally, you're telling the truth."

"What?"

"That you're not a hunter—I didn't believe it until just now." He was still grinning, but there was a flash of surprise in his eyes.

She stilled, studying him. "Why do you believe me now? What did I do?" She'd been snapping at him, and now he was claiming he believed her?

"It's not what you did—it's what you *said*."

She tilted her head slightly. "What I said?" What had she said? She'd been rambling and frustrated.

"You'd incapacitate me and *escape*. A hunter would never escape. A hunter would have tried to take me down, capture me. A hunter would probably even kill me if they thought it necessary. But escape? That is something a hunter wouldn't think about. They're fighters. You're not fighting me. You came quietly."

"Oh…" She whispered the word, realizing he was right. And it seemed her brothers were right after all. She wasn't cut out to be a hunter. She'd already failed by being discovered. Hell, she'd confessed who she really was without him even interrogating her.

She placed a palm over her belly. Knots of worry built inside her, making her sick. "I need to sit down." She fell back onto the bed and tried to still her heart, which was beating hard enough to bruise her chest. Rurik approached her, towering over her as he reached her at the foot of the bed, and she lifted her gaze to his face. He reached up, hesitant this time as he cupped her chin.

"You aren't a hunter, and you haven't attacked me. You know the truth about me, and it is a *dangerous* truth." He brushed the pad of his thumb over her lips. "Tell me, little rose, what do you really know of dragons?"

She shivered at his intimate caress, feeling an ache deep inside because he wasn't touching her out of desire, but to invoke fear.

"You are immortal, but you can be killed. You're susceptible to iron, but only if it is pure. You hoard gemstones and precious metals, and you can transform almost instantly. You can use pheromones and other means to hypnotize and influence people, especially those of the opposite sex."

"Pheromones?" He suddenly laughed at this. "Oh really? So if I were to kiss you, you would spill all of your secrets? Even the darkest ones?" His green eyes grew warm, and she was lost in their color for a long moment.

"I guess. I don't know..." She trailed off. The Brotherhood's reports on that particular factor had been vague, at least in the reports she'd had access to. Information was a weapon, and the Brotherhood kept it under tight lock and key to all but those who needed it.

"Let us test this little theory..." He leaned down and captured her mouth with his. He cupped the back of her neck, holding her captive for his ravaging lips. It wasn't a tender kiss—it was a conquering one, yet it wasn't violent. She whimpered, swept away by how conflicted he made her feel. Every cell in her body was humming with a languid and slowly building fervor that would explode if he continued.

"You're sure you aren't a hunter?" he asked between kisses.

"No, I'm a biochemist. They would never let me join the Brotherhood." She sighed as he kissed her again and then gasped as he lifted her up and placed her farther back on the bed. Then he lay on top of her, kissing her again, and all shock faded beneath the pleasure of what his lips could do.

"Do you wish to hurt me or my family?" he asked. His hands lifted her sweater. The heat of his body burned her, not letting her feel the cold kiss of air on her bare skin.

"Hurt you?" she echoed dreamily as he kissed her collarbone, working his way down to the slopes of her breasts, which were covered by her black bra.

"Yes, do you want to hurt us?" he repeated. His words, dark and soft, with that Russian accent, made her tremble. She'd come here planning to drug him, but she couldn't anymore. Not after everything they'd been through together. Not after how she felt about him now.

"No," she answered honestly. The two vials of the serum lay in her purse, but she wouldn't reach for them.

"Then why did you come after me at the club?" he asked.

"I..." She tensed, fear still fluttering inside her despite her building arousal. "We know about the dragon war, the power vacuum it left behind and how things might escalate into something worse. I wanted to get you alone so the Brotherhood could talk to you. We want to do what we can to help avert a full-scale war, but your people and mine have never really been on talking terms."

Rurik's gaze burned into hers. "Dragon war? That's what this is about? You think my family can't handle one Drakor dragon?" He chuckled. "You can tell the hunters there is nothing to fear."

"But without the Drakors, there are others who will try to take their place...from China, maybe, or other continents. People could get hurt."

"We would take the war to the countryside as we did a few months ago. There will be no casualties."

"You're assuming that they will play by the same rules as Drakor."

This seemed to give Rurik pause, like she'd touched on something he hadn't considered and that she might in fact have a point. That relaxed her enough to enjoy what he was doing even more, and it cut a little into the edge of fear she teetered on.

He kissed her stomach, flicked his tongue into her navel, and she dug her hands into his hair as he unzipped her jeans.

"I have more...questions," he warned her. "Will you give me answers, or must I continue your interrogation with kisses?"

She could have sworn she heard playfulness in his tone, but it didn't make sense. He should want to kill her for her deception.

He had no reason to trust her, and she was a danger to him. So why was he kissing her when he should have been wanting to kill her? Weren't dragons supposed to be ruthless? Maybe the synthetic pheromones she'd taken from the Brotherhood lab were keeping his temper down and his arousal up.

"I will answer," she insisted and then gasped as he tugged her boots off her feet, then began to pull her pants down. God, *his* pheromones really were affecting her. She'd tell him just about anything to make him continue what he was doing.

"I don't know if I trust you. You've lied before. Why not now?" He dropped her jeans onto the floor and then removed his shirt, tossing it down as well. He crawled back up her body, and she wrapped her arms around his back. Her cold fingers warmed instantly as they touched his hot skin.

"I swear, I'm telling the truth." She panted as he traced one fingertip down her inner thigh, outlining her underwear before he hooked that finger under the fabric of her panties and began to tug them down.

"I want to be *completely* sure." His silken tone sent ripples of erotic delight through her. Her panties and bra fell onto the floor, and she was lying completely bare beneath him.

"Are you still afraid of me?" Rurik brushed the backs of his knuckles over one taut nipple. Her breasts were heavy, the nipples ready for his mouth, but she couldn't ask him, couldn't tell him what she needed. Saw a playful tenderness in his eyes, mixed with an inferno of desire. Then she understood. He was playing some game with her. His idea of interrogation wasn't painful—it was intensely pleasurable. The more she resisted, the farther he would go. And that was what she wanted most.

"Kiss me," she urged in a desperate whisper, digging her nails into his shoulders. His green eyes changed, the pure color swirling with a honey gold. A dragon's desire. It was so strong it changed the color of his eyes. She had a thousand questions, but when he dipped his head and nibbled her bottom lip, she decided they could be asked later.

His gaze raked down her naked form. "I will have all of your secrets, just as I will have *you*."

She'd never dreamed she would meet a man like Rurik, all firepower, and have him want her back like this. But he did. She could see the hunger in his eyes. This wicked foreplay was more than just a game. The stakes were climbing higher and higher, because she was falling in love with him.

Rurik leaned over, kissing her ruthlessly, branding her as his, and she embraced it. She wanted to be his in every way. He slid one hand down, cupping her breast, kneading it gently. Then he moved that hand lower, cupping her ass, giving it a hard squeeze that sent jolts of pleasure through her. Then his hand slipped between her thighs, and one finger pushed into her wet, aching sex.

"Tight little thing, aren't you?" he growled. "It is going to hurt to take you." He bit her earlobe and tugged on it. She hissed and arched her back, pressing her breasts against his chest.

"Please, take me," she moaned, and he growled low at the back of his throat. He shifted above her, unzipping his jeans. She lowered her head, watching him as he shucked off his jeans and boxers. The man was gorgeous. Fucking perfect, scars and all.

"Take a deep breath," he warned her, his tone impossibly gentle.

She gasped as he started to enter her. When she tightened, he murmured sweet words she didn't understand into her ear. But when he kissed her, images exploded in front of her eyes. Mountains wreathed in fiery-colored leaves, halls of empty palaces, the beating of his lonely heart—it was all there, just within reach. Charlotte plunged deep into him, bathing in his memories and sensations.

"Your mind…" Rurik whispered as he thrust into her over and over again. "It's beautiful. I can see everything—I can see *you*." He stared down at her, the edges of his lips curved in a boyish grin. Wonder filled his eyes. She felt the same way. They were tied together now, the bonds unbreakable.

"Rurik, *faster*." Her body ached for a hint of roughness, a bit of that ferocity he seemed to promise.

He clasped her hands in his, lacing her fingers as he pinned her hands down on either side of her head. He rotated his hips, driving into her in entirely new angles. It made white dots dance in front of her eyes. She'd always fantasized about how she would lose her virginity, but she'd never believed any of those fantasies would come true.

"You're perfect." Rurik's heavy accent showed just how close he was to losing control. He spoke again in Russian, leaned down to kiss her neck, and she moaned.

"Bite me." She needed to feel his teeth in her neck. "Now!"

Sharp pain hit her as he bit down. She screamed as her body went up in flames. It was as though she stood in the center of a blinding snowstorm, watching the glittering flakes envelop her, but there was an inferno at the heart of the storm. Rurik's heart. She reached through the ice to touch the fire.

11

AS FOR YOU AND YOUR HEART AND THE
THINGS YOU SAID AND DIDN'T SAY, SHE WILL
REMEMBER THEM ALL WHEN MEN ARE FAIRY
TALES IN BOOKS WRITTEN BY RABBITS.
—PETER S. BEAGLE, THE LAST UNICORN

Charlotte blinked as the visions faded. It was the strangest thing in the world to see through another person's eyes, to feel what he felt, to taste and smell everything he had. And she had shared those same experiences with Rurik, being a part of him in a way she didn't know was possible. But it was. Now she was back in bed with him, that bond still in place even though she could no longer see his memories. Her body shook from the pleasure and the shock of what she'd just experienced with him.

"What...was that?" She lifted her head and tensed when she felt him move inside her. Her body was raw and sore down there, but it still felt good.

"I..." Rurik paused and then closed his eyes, a shaky breath escaping him before his dark lashes flew up again.

"What happened? That wasn't dragon pheromone–related, was it?" she asked, unable to resist her natural scientific curiosity.

A ghost of a smile passed his lips. "It wasn't. I don't know where you heard that. The pheromones we give off don't have any effect on humans or even our own mates."

"Really?" She shifted beneath him and winced again. "But I was told that dragons are irresistible, that women throw themselves at you..."

His soft laugh made her face flame with embarrassment.

"If that was true, women would have been flocking to me while were walking around the city. But that didn't happen."

"Then why do I get all fuzzy-headed whenever you kiss me?" She felt really stupid now. If that was true, the synthetic pheromones they'd engineered in the lab wouldn't have had any effect. What was happening to her?

"That is because you and I have a connection."

"A connection," she muttered, then winced when she shifted. Soreness twinged at her inner thighs.

He noticed, his eyes narrowing. "I was too rough." A dark frown marred his face as though he didn't like admitting that.

"No, you weren't. I was a virgin, remember? I knew I would end up sore. Now explain what you meant by a connection." She should have felt shy admitting that, but things had changed between them. Something had clicked like two gears in an antique clock, and for the first time in her life, she felt whole.

"It is complicated."

She bit her lip. "Why not try me? I'm a biochemist, remember?"

He pulled out of her, and the sudden feeling of emptiness was unwelcome. She wanted that connection again. Rurik picked her up, making her squeak in surprise, and carried her into the adjoining bathroom with its massive tub. He set her down on the edge and turned on the taps, testing the temperature with his fingers. Once it was hot enough, he climbed into the tub and waited for her to join him. She'd never shared a bathtub with anyone before, but Rurik was fast becoming a first for just about everything.

"Lie back against me," he urged, and she did so.

"I'm not too heavy?" She hated to ask it, but she was so aware of herself and didn't want to remind him that she had a full figure.

"You're perfect." He kissed her cheek and wrapped his arms around her waist.

It felt good to be held by him. The hot water rising at her legs felt good too.

"Now will you tell me about how you can affect human women, or at the least me?"

His raspy chuckle made her laugh too.

"We attract women because of our confidence, power, and wealth. We're like catnip just by being who we are."

"Catnip?" She snorted. "But like you said, women weren't flocking around you, so..."

Rurik drew the pad of his index finger around one of her nipples, making it harden as he chuckled. "We're irresistible, but there is intent required on our part. Desire. Would you like me to remind you just how much you want me?" He gently pinched her nipple, and a bolt of pleasure made her moan and arch her back.

She giggled when he lowered his head to her breast and sucked on the tender peak. "Stop distracting me."

His laughter was warm and sinful, and she squirmed as he continued to lick and suck on her nipple. When he started to move toward her other breast, she caught his cheek in her hands and forced him to look at her.

"But you do have *some* abilities. You said you could manipulate the humans by the palace to walk away."

He stiffened slightly at the mention. "We can mesmerize others, yes, but that is not the same thing. We can erase memories or bury them. We can convince people to do things or not to."

"Including sex? You didn't..."

"No. The only time I ever used that power was to alter how you remembered the shooting, to rationalize why I healed so fast. I didn't want you to panic. You reacted well enough, but I expected you to be in shock. I feared the reality of almost dying would set in." He stroked a hand along her waist, finding a sensitive spot that made her wriggle and almost laugh.

"I remember the shooting. And I remember being worried at

first about your wounds." She stared at him, trying to remember everything. Flashes of it came back. "Wait, I did pull out some bullets, didn't I? They weren't just scratches."

"No, they weren't. Now you remember everything." He used one hand to brush soothing fingers along her collarbone. Drops of hot water trickled down her breasts.

She couldn't believe that he had influenced what she had thought. "Only you didn't take my memories away?"

"I try never to remove memories. I change them as little as possible. A dragon could get carried away with exerting that sort of power."

She couldn't argue with that. If she'd been in his position, it would have been tempting to make someone believe a different version of events in order to hide a more difficult truth.

"But I admit, I did convince you to dance for me in the cage in my club," he added with a chuckle. He couldn't seem to resist.

"The cage—" She blushed deeply, burying her face against his shoulder as she remembered. "Oh my God, the *cage*." He massaged her shoulders. The water sloshed around them, and she moved forward so she could twist the knob and turn off the water before leaning back against him.

"So what we just did, that was something, wasn't it?" She knew what had transpired between them had changed everything. There was something between them now; she felt it whisper at the back of her mind. She needed to know what it was.

Rurik was silent for a long while before he spoke. "What do you know of dragon mating?"

She ran over the Brotherhood file in her mind. "Um...not a lot. They say you mate for life, but I assumed that was a cultural thing, old habits dying hard, or to keep the dragon lines going."

"Well, dragons do mate for life, but there is more to it than that. When we mate another being, the bond is..." He murmured a few words in Russian, as though unsure how to describe it. "Unbreakable. That is the closest I can get to describing it."

A prickling sensation skittered along her skin, lifting the fine hairs on her neck.

"Okay." She held her breath as she waited for him to continue.

"We cannot mate just anyone. It has to be destiny. A *true* mate. I once had a possible mate, but I never claimed her."

"What happened?" She shifted to lie on her side against him in the massive tub. She was bothered by the idea that he might have loved another woman, yet had chosen not to. What made her situation different?

"I never succumbed to the temptation to claim her as mine. The dangers were too great. And then she died a few months ago..." Rurik's voice trailed off.

Charlotte was torn. She wanted to comfort him, but she feared he would not accept that.

"I'm sorry," she finally said.

He gave the barest hint of a nod. "It is dangerous for dragons to mate." He lifted one hand and settled it on her hip beneath the hot water, holding her close.

"Dangerous?" She couldn't see how something like mating would be. Maybe he meant the consequences of being in their world?

"Yes. When dragons mate, it's for life."

"But you're immortal," she added. "How can that be dangerous?"

"We bond so deeply to each other that when the mate dies, we die. And if we mate a mortal..."

Charlotte realized just how short her life was compared to his. For a dragon, getting involved with a human was cutting your own life tragically short. Her stomach fluttered as she sensed there was something he still wasn't saying.

"Rurik, please just tell me." She turned to face him, the water splashing as she straddled him. Despite the way their bodies intimately rubbed, she was determined not to get distracted. This was too important.

"As I said, I had one possible true mate before, and she died.

The grief I felt was great, because I realized all that I had missed in life. I feared there would never be another chance. Then I met you...and discovered you were a possible mate as well."

She couldn't process what he was saying. *A true mate? How was that even...*

"I mated you, Charlotte." He cupped her face, his thumbs brushing over her cheeks in soothing strokes. "I didn't want to, and I tried to stop...but you are *irresistible* to me."

Mated. She was mated to Rurik. Charlotte still had no idea what that meant.

"But, wait, you didn't want to?" She hung on that fact first, probably because it hurt the most.

His eyes, those pure jade pools, softened to a dark emerald that made her hungry for him. "Want? I've wanted you from the moment I saw you. But my position means I must protect the family first and foremost. If something happens to you, I will die. And my family will be left vulnerable." He sighed, closing his eyes, and then inhaled deeply. "But I couldn't stay away from you, even knowing all that. And then, when you begged me to bite you..."

"How does it happen?" she whispered, her heart thudding against her ribs.

"Mating is like two pieces of a puzzle sliding into place. We've gotten closer and closer since we danced at my club, and just now in bed, we stood no chance of resisting you."

She tilted her head. "*We?*"

He threaded a hand through her hair. "My dragon. He and I knew we had to have you."

She cuddled closer, spellbound by the look in his eyes. "What does it mean that we're mated now?" Part of Charlotte still couldn't believe she was having this discussion, but she had to know everything about being mated to him.

"We share memories. We see into each other's hearts in a way that no other species can, because we share actual vivid experiences, even thoughts. It's as though our beating hearts become one, and when one part dies, the other cannot survive."

The weight of his words finally sank in, and Charlotte's eyes filled with tears.

"So...what does this mean? For us?" she asked, the words escaping from her trembling lips.

"We are bound together, you and I. We stand as one, fight as one, live and die as one." She could feel his gaze burn into her. Part of her wanted to open herself completely to him, but she was afraid. Mating him might mean leaving her brothers and the life she'd known behind forever.

"Am I...allowed to go home?" She swallowed hard, fear shooting through her as she waited for his response.

"You will go wherever you wish, but I will go with you. I *must* protect you."

That stung like a sharp slap. He had to protect her to protect himself.

"No, stop," he growled. "I can see you misunderstand me. I protect you because you are mine. I go with you because my heart craves closeness to yours. I would miss you if you left me."

Was he saying he loved her? Or that he could he come to love her? Just as she now realized she was in danger of falling in love with him?

"Rurik, we're practically strangers. How can this make sense? What about my family...?" Oh God, when her brothers found out, they would kill him...unless of course that would kill her.

"If you die...will I die, as a human?"

"I'm not sure," he admitted. "Few of my kind have mated humans, and as far as I know, none have died before their human mates."

He nuzzled her cheek and closed his eyes briefly with a heavy sigh. "We will make it work. Both of my brothers mated Americans. I'm sure you and I will manage, just as they have." He smiled at her, but she didn't miss the shadow of sorrow in his eyes.

"You never wanted this, did you?" He hadn't, and neither had she, but now they were tied together.

"I have always longed to mate, but my duties were clear from the moment my father saw my strength. He told me a battle dragon could never mate—it was too risky for the rest of the family. But now that I have you, I won't ever let you go."

Charlotte didn't know what to say to that. She wanted him to want her, but...

"Rurik, I can't put your family at risk."

"What's done is done. We are mated, and I *do* want you." He brushed away a tear that trailed down her cheek. "I never want to see you cry. A mate is a sacred gift, and you are sacred to me, Charlotte." He kissed her as though it could last for days. As much as she had loved his rough, frantic, dominating kisses, she loved this kind even more. It was sweet, a dozen emotions welling up inside her that filled her with warmth. She could lose herself in that strange and beautiful world of snow where he kept his heart. The flames of his soul were there, so close, if only she dared to reach for him.

"Why don't we continue this on the bed? I'll order room service. We'll stay here today and fly back to Moscow this evening with Grigori and Madelyn."

Rurik slid Charlotte off his lap and climbed out of the tub. Rurik grabbed a towel from a rack and wrapped it around his waist. She sank deeper into the tub, soaking in the hot water as she watched him leave the bathroom.

I just had sex with a man who turns into a dragon, and it was amazing! What a way to lose her virginity. She'd bet even a hunter like her friend Meg hadn't done something this crazy.

Part of her was still in shock over everything that had just happened. She was mated to a dragon, and she didn't know what that would mean for her in the long run. A flurry of thoughts stormed her mind. Where would they live? What about her job? What about if he died before her? She had a thousand questions. Could they have children? She didn't know where to start.

She bit her bottom lip, holding back the sudden grin on her face. *And I'm mated.* Damien and Jason were going to be furious, but in a way she'd done what she had promised herself she would do. She'd captured a dragon—she just hadn't needed the serum to do it.

She stretched languidly in the tub as she listened to the sound of Rurik's voice as he ordered room service. Then he appeared in the bathroom doorway, leaned against the doorjamb.

"Out of the tub, my little rose. I have many wicked things I wish to do to you."

Even though she was sore, she scrambled out of the tub, laughing as she grabbed a towel to dry herself.

He watched her with a crooked grin. "I'll only get you wet again." His green eyes promised wicked things, and now that she'd had a taste of him she wanted *more*. She walked up to him and stood on her tiptoes, her towel wrapped snugly around her, and kissed him. His lips curved against hers. There was something magical about a kiss built upon a world of shared secret smiles. When they broke apart, she was still grinning.

"Wow," she said, still shy at her brazen behavior. Her face was hot, and she knew he'd seen her blush.

He caressed her cheek with the backs of his knuckles. "Fuck, you are so beautiful."

"So are you. I mean—" She shut her mouth, blushing harder.

His green eyes swirled with gold. "Go lie down on the bed, on your stomach."

When she reached the bed, she had the sudden urge to be impish. Charlotte dropped the towel and glanced over her shoulder at him. Then she shook her hips at him and started to climb onto the bed. A second later, he was behind her, his hands on her hips.

"I was going to give you a massage until you shook that fine ass at me." Rurik's growl was almost like a purr.

"A massage sounds nice." She started to crawl forward on the bed on her hands and knees, but he tugged her hips back, and she felt his pelvis bump against her backside.

"Oh no, you little tease. I demand more." His words came out rough and sexy.

She jerked when he pressed his cock in at that angle. It felt different from before, and it stretched her in a new way. She dropped her head on her arms against the bedding and moaned, absorbing the soreness of her channel and a whisper of pain mixed with the building pleasure of this new way of lovemaking. She'd fantasized about this, a man taking her from behind, someone who was completely in control, but she'd never imagined the reality would be so much more intense. Rurik thrust his hips, pushing deeper into her. They both shared a moan.

"More," she begged, shifting her ass, encouraging him to move faster.

Rurik gave her a little spank. "I'm trying to be gentle. You are still sore," he reprimanded her.

"I don't want gentle," she replied as he withdrew until he was almost fully out. "I want you to let go of your control. Take me hard. Hard as you want." She lifted her head and met his burning gaze over her shoulder.

"You don't know what you're asking." His voice was gravelly, and his eyes swirled with that honey color. She now knew this meant his dragon was fighting to get to the surface.

"I *know* what I'm asking," she promised. "We're in this together, remember?" She pushed back, driving him a little deeper into her.

"Fuck," he muttered. "Tell me if I'm too rough." He drove into her, his hands digging into her hips as he penetrated her over and over. The feel of him so deep inside her was heaven. She hissed out a breath as he moved faster, harder, but she didn't want him to stop. It felt *amazing*.

He reached around her hips and teased her clit with the pad of his finger, causing her to explode. He kept fucking her, his hips pumping even as she sagged on the bed, her body limp.

Rurik thrust a few more times and gave a guttural cry as he pulled out of her, and something hot splashed down her thighs. He retrieved her towel from the floor and set about cleaning both of them, with surprising gentleness given the way he'd just claimed her. She collapsed on the bed, stretching out on her stomach.

"Wow," she gasped.

Rurik chuckled as he ran a hand from her shoulders down to her bottom in a soothing caress.

"Scoot up on the bed," he ordered, but his tone was gentle.

Charlotte clawed her way up the bed and collapsed when she reached the pillows. The bed dipped behind her, and large warm hands settled on her shoulders while Rurik's knees settled on either side of her hips. He began to massage her, just as he'd said he would, rubbing deeply into her muscles. It felt so wonderful that she couldn't...keep...her...eyes...

***

RURIK KNEW THE MOMENT SHE FELL ASLEEP. HE CAREFULLY picked her up and pulled back the covers before tucking her in. He wasn't sure how long he stood there, watching her, feeling like the most blessed man alive. He had a mate. The one thing he'd believed he would never have. He could have had this with Nikita, but he'd enjoyed a gentle contentment watching her work alongside him at the nightclub, and he'd convinced himself that was enough. And it had been, until she'd died. Losing Nikita had changed him in a way he hadn't expected and had driven him to throw caution to the wind. His heart ached at the thought of what might have been with Nikita, but he couldn't regret that he'd found Charlotte either. The complexity of the situation left him feeling lost until he looked down at his mate and the turmoil inside him eased.

He'd risked his family's future, but he'd spent the last thousand years thinking of others. Wasn't he due some measure of happiness? She was perfect. He hadn't lied when he told her that. She was perfect in every way. Rurik brushed a lock of her hair back from her face and drank in the sight of her.

My mate...

He collected his jeans and sweater, putting them on before he searched for his cell phone. He'd shut it off to better enjoy the day with Charlotte, but now he need to call his brothers. There was much to discuss.

He saw he had missed several calls from both Grigori and Mikhail. He also had half a dozen messages.

Rather than listen to them, he called Grigori back. He answered on the first ring.

"Where the hell are you?"

His brother's panicked tone scared him. "What's wrong?"

"Is Charlotte with you? Just say yes or no."

Rurik answered carefully. "Yes." He knew the drill. When there was a risk of being compromised, everyone answered questions in a way so no one could overhear and understand the subject of their conversation.

"Can she overhear you?" Grigori asked in Russian.

Rurik replied in kind. "No. She is asleep. What's wrong?"

"She's a hunter for the Brotherhood."

The words were a punch to Rurik's gut. "How do you know this? I know of her ties to the Brotherhood, but I swear on my life she isn't a hunter," Rurik said quietly. She couldn't have lied to him, not after the way he'd questioned her. She was chemist, not a hunter.

"You can't trust your instincts. Your dragon is blinded by desire. Remember what happened to Mikhail five hundred years ago? He got too close to the queen of England and ended up in an English prison for forty years."

Rurik didn't care for the reminder of their brother's suffering. He wasn't Mikhail, and this wasn't the sixteenth century. He trusted Charlotte. If she said she wasn't a hunter, she wasn't.

"I know you don't want to believe Charlotte could lie to you, but it's true. Drakor called. He has been monitoring the Brotherhood, something he reminded me I've been failing to do. We have to take care of this. We need to—"

"First of all," Rurik interrupted, "since when do we listen to

Drakor? I've never trusted that bastard. And second, we can't do anything." Rurik closed his eyes and prepared to confess his mistake to his older brother.

"I understand, but I trust Drakor on this. This is the Brotherhood we're talking about. That issue transcends all our rivalries. And what do you mean, we can't do anything?" Grigori snapped. "We can restrain her and get the truth out of her."

"We can't because I *mated* her. She is *mine*. She's part of our family now, hunter or not."

There was a long silence, so long that Rurik started to wonder if Grigori had hung up on him.

"Then it is too late. They have what they came for."

"What?" Rurik didn't understand what his brother was talking about.

"If you're mated to one of them, they can control you through her," Grigori said with a growl. "Think about it. They'll have a leashed dragon as a weapon now. If you don't comply, they can use your own mate against you."

"She's not what you think, brother. I'll just have to convince her to leave that life behind." There was no way Charlotte would be used against him, not like that.

"It won't be that easy, Rurik. She's a MacQueen."

The name was one that sent witches fleeing to their covens, vampires deep into their nests, and werewolves running off to their packs. In the past, the name MacQueen meant death to the creatures in the supernatural realm. It was a name that brought fear and panic, even to dragons, even today. Damien's grandfather had been ruthless in the 1950s.

"How could she be a MacQueen?" he asked. From what little he knew of Damien MacQueen, he couldn't imagine Charlotte being anything like him. She was sweet, sensitive, and open to trusting someone like him.

"She's Damien and Jason's younger sister. Even if you convince her to leave them, they will come looking for her. And we have no idea of her true purpose in finding you in the first place. They may have trained her as a secret weapon. This bond is exactly what they wanted."

"What do you suggest we do?"

"Until we know more, I want Charlotte secured. Act normal and convince her to come back with us tonight on the plane. I'll slip a knockout drug into her bottle of water. Then we'll figure out what to do with her. We can't take any chances. Do you understand?"

Grigori was right, and Rurik hated that more than anything. He'd surrendered his heart and soul to a woman who was most likely there to betray him. But the thought of drugging her made him sick nonetheless.

"We will see you at the airport in a few hours. Text me the flight time."

"Be careful, brother." Grigori hung up.

Rurik set his phone down on the table. He was halfway back to his bed when the door chimed. He met the hotel staff member at the door and took the cart from him, slipping him a handful of bills that would tide the man over for at least two weeks.

Rurik took the tray with the two plates and carried it over to the bed. Charlotte was still sleeping. She started when he set down the tray and lifted the metal lids, sitting up without thinking, and her bare breasts were exposed as the blankets fell away. Rurik had to remind himself that even though she was his mate, he could no longer trust her, couldn't just take her back to bed, not when he needed to find out if she really was a hunter after all. If she really did plan to betray him.

"Eat," he encouraged, sitting beside her. Only when she was finished did he speak. He cupped her chin, controlling her enough that she had to look at him. "Were you ever going to tell me the truth?"

Her eyes widened, and she opened her mouth but didn't speak.

"You are a hunter, and you're MacQueen's little sister—two very important facts you left out of your confessions." He wanted to see if she would deny it. There were flashes of fear in her eyes, but they were tempered by an unexpected resolve.

"Damien is my brother, but I am *not* a hunter. I've never been a part of the Brotherhood or its mission." She reached out and touched his chest. He barely resisted the urge to pull away and had to remind himself she was his mate—he shouldn't want to pull away from her.

"I'm *not* a hunter," she insisted. "Mesmerize me. Make me tell you the truth. Let me prove it to you."

Rurik considered it. He could use his power on her, but he didn't want to. He still wanted to trust her. He also worried that she might have a way to resist him. It was possible hunters had trained themselves against this power. Yet he didn't think she could be so cold, so heartless to lie to him this entire time. She'd made him feel so happy, so full of hope, and his brother had crushed that joy with a single phone call. How could he ever trust her now?

He rose from the bed and collected her clothes. "Get dressed. We fly back to Moscow in a few hours." He couldn't look at her—it made his stomach coil into knots.

"Rurik, stop!" she shouted. "You want the truth? All of it?"

"Yes," he snarled as he spun to face her. "Tell me every damned detail. Leave *nothing* out." He clenched his hands into fists as he glared at her.

Charlotte, to her credit, didn't cower. But he would never hurt Charlotte, not even if she betrayed him to his worst enemy.

"I am just what I said. A biochemist. A lonely woman whose brothers left her out of everything. They refused to let me join the Brotherhood because it cost my parents their lives. But a few weeks ago, my friend Meg, who is a hunter, told me about a serum that someone had created that suppresses the dragon shifting ability. She asked me to try to re-create it. But I wanted more..." She paused, her face falling. "I wanted to show my brothers I have value, that I could be a part of their world. I thought I could help prevent a dragon war from spiraling out of control. So I took the serum I made and left for Moscow. My plan was to catch you, but the moment I met you...I couldn't use it on you or take you to my brothers." She pointed to her purse. "You will find two syringes inside. You can pour the contents down the drain and throw the syringes in the trash. There's a third one in my hotel room in Moscow. I don't care anymore. You matter too much to me. I couldn't hurt someone I—" She halted abruptly, wiping a stream of tears from her face.

"Someone you...what?" he asked. His dragon had been ready to fight, just as he was, but now he and his dragon were both confused and panicky.

Tears rolled down her cheeks as she met his gaze and said the only words that could change the way he felt.

"I couldn't betray someone I was falling in love with." The pain in her eyes was unmistakable. No one could affect that level of fear unless they were telling the truth.

Rurik held his breath, trying to process what she'd just said. She was falling in love with him.

Charlotte stumbled away from the bed, wrapping a sheet around herself. She looked so vulnerable and small as she approached him and the table where her purse sat. She held the small bag up to him.

"Please. Take the syringes and destroy them." His dragon paced inside his head, still puzzled. His enemy...his mate...what was she really?

12

I HAD FORGOTTEN HOW MUCH LIGHT THERE IS IN THE WORLD, TILL YOU GAVE IT BACK TO ME. —URSULA K. LE GUIN

Rurik dug through Charlotte's purse, his dragon tense inside him, as though afraid of what he might find. His animal side wasn't used to fearing anything, but the idea of a drug that could suppress that part of him, even temporarily, was terrifying.

There were no weapons, no magical tokens or talismans to help her inside. Just...there it was...

He pulled out a black case out and unzipped it. Two small syringes with gleaming green liquid were tucked in elastic straps. He removed them from the pouch. Without a word, he walked over to the bathroom sink. He depressed the plungers on the syringes and drained their contents. The third one in Moscow would be handled soon. There was bound to be more of this back at the Brotherhood labs, but he felt a small bit of relief destroying the immediate threat.

Rurik flipped the taps on, splashing water to wash down the remnants of the drug. Charlotte stayed where she was, sheet wrapped around her body like a loose toga. Her blonde hair was in a wild tumble around her shoulders, and the light from the lamps illuminated the drying tears on her cheeks. It was a shock to his heart, strong enough that for a moment he couldn't move, couldn't speak. He recovered at last and approached her, stopping just inches away.

The apprehension in her eyes cut his heart. She had no reason to be afraid, but she had no reason to believe that. The mistrust between their worlds ran deep.

"If you are being truthful to me, if it is your intention to stand by my side, then from this moment on, we are in this together. No more secrets, no more lies, from either of us. Do you understand?" He needed to hear her say yes. If she couldn't, it was going to rip him apart.

She nodded. "Yes. No more lies or secrets," she vowed, and he knew she was telling the truth. The defenses around his heart crumbled. He wrapped her in his arms, holding her against him, her feet dangling off the ground. She curled her arms around his neck and choked on a sob as she nuzzled him. Their emotions, so close to each other in their bond, were only magnifying.

"I'm so sorry, little one. So very sorry," he murmured over and over again as he carried her back to the bedroom.

He felt her heart, like a faint gold glimmer through a thick silver curtain. She was falling for him, and she wasn't going to keep any more secrets from him. In that moment, knowing she was in love with him was all that mattered. He would face the problem of her family and his tomorrow. Right now, he needed to hold her and reassure himself and his dragon that she was all right.

"How did you find out?" she asked. "About my brothers, I mean." Charlotte cuddled on his lap as they settled back on the bed. He pulled the comforter up around her, wanting to keep her warm. They had a few hours yet before they had to leave.

"Grigori received a call from another dragon. An enemy to our family. His name is Dimitri Drakor. I don't trust that bastard, but Grigori had his reasons for believing him."

"Drakor? I know that name. His house is in control of eastern Russia, right? Or was, anyway. Didn't you kill most of them recently?"

Rurik gazed at her in surprise. "Yes, how did you—"

"That's what got me involved in finding you. The power vacuum the Drakors left is what's got the Brotherhood worried. The idea that whoever is left might ally themselves with other houses, or others might try to move in. Russia's a powder keg right now," she said. "I had to know everything I could about dragons before I came over."

Rurik was torn between smiling and frowning. He liked that his mate was resourceful, but he didn't like that she had access to files on him and his family. They worked hard to stay undocumented and off human radar.

"How much information do they have on us?" he asked.

She shrugged and told him as much as she knew from the files. "You have to believe me—the Brotherhood is more worried about you fighting each other and causing harm to civilians than fighting you themselves. Those agents they sent after you before were just going to bring you in for questioning. They never planned to kill you. They hoped you had answers about the war with the Drakors, and they needed to know how serious the situation was from your perspective."

As she talked, she ran her fingers up and down his chest, seemingly unaware that she was stroking him in a soothing way. It felt good, *really* good. It would have felt even better if she'd wrapped her fingers around his cock, but now was not the time for that, much to his body's disappointment.

"The problem is, your people close ranks and vanish whenever we try to get close," she added.

"It is hard to blame us. It wasn't that long ago that we were hunted down by your people for the mere crime of existing," Rurik countered. "And it wasn't that long ago that the name MacQueen meant death for shifters."

Charlotte's head dropped. "I know. But things have changed in the last fifty years. My parents and my brothers have made sure of it. My grandfather's way was half a century ago, born out of the same fear as McCarthyism at the time. The rules have changed.

They don't kill anymore. Not without cause. They observe. Hell, my brother has even helped negotiate peace treaties."

"Still," Rurik said slowly. "It makes trust for dragons difficult. Half a century for you is half your life, but it's merely an instant of mine. We have long memories. And who's to say your brother's successor won't fall back on old habits."

Charlotte was silent a long moment. "I don't know, but we have to start somewhere. Will your brothers help us figure out what to do?"

"Yes." He nuzzled her cheek before pressing his forehead to hers and closing his eyes. "But they won't be happy about it. Do you think you can make your brothers see reason?"

"I hope so," she said with a sigh. "We're a little like Romeo and Juliet, aren't we?" The smile that stole across her lips was tinged with sorrow. He hated knowing that mating her had caused that pain.

He tried to tease her. "Yes, if the Capulets carried flamethrowers while the Montagues were trained Special Forces. And I, for one, would prefer to avoid their fate if at all possible."

Charlotte sighed and kissed his lips. Her sweet taste was the only reassuring thing about this mess of a situation.

"Promise me you will help protect my brothers and their mates." He would never have asked that of anyone else. But if there was a chance she could help protect them from the Brotherhood, he had to ask.

"I'll do everything I can, but you have to promise me that my brothers and the other hunters won't get hurt. They're my family."

"We are your family now as well," he corrected as he lifted her chin with his fingers. Their gazes locked, and he dove into the warm hazel pools of her eyes. "You're not just a MacQueen now. You are Barinov too."

"And that makes you a MacQueen," she added.

He winced. "That will set my brothers in an uproar."

Charlotte's face reddened. "So...me being a Barinov, does that mean... Er... Do dragons get married like humans? You know, with a fancy ceremony and everything?" Her voice was slightly husky, and it made him wish he had hours to listen to her moan his name in bed with that low, breathless tone.

He nodded, keeping his eyes on her. "We do. The mating was enough in the old days, but we marry now in the human world in order to secure property and protect our loved ones. We adapt to local and regional customs as they change over time."

She traced the seam of his T-shirt collar around his neck, her lashes fanning up so he could see those lovely eyes of hers.

"So...does that mean *we'll* get married?" He sensed her unease and the lack of trust that came with the idea of marrying a stranger. He couldn't blame her. They'd only known each other for two days. And while the mate bond was in place, they didn't truly know each other or completely love each other. Not yet. But love would come, he knew it. A dragon could sense such things within its mate. The bond wouldn't have occurred otherwise. He measured his response carefully before he replied.

"We will, when the time is right. I want us to have a chance to bond, to develop the feelings that we share for each other. I want to earn your love fully and give you mine."

When she sighed in relief, he knew he'd said the right thing, so he couldn't resist teasing her.

"We also have to make sure the wedding party doesn't try to kill each other. A great wall built down the aisle, perhaps?"

She giggled, wrapped her arms around his neck, and buried her face in his neck again.

"Can you hold me, just for a little while?" she asked.

He could sense her emotions beneath the surface, like listening to a muffled conversation. She was a strong woman, but she'd been through much in the last two days.

"As long as you need," he whispered, kissing her temple. Then he rested his cheek against her hair, and they both breathed together. His dragon stirred, cautious, but also hopeful.

She raised her head, and her eyes flashed with a new light. "How long before the plane leaves?"

"About two hours. Why?"

"Could we see a palace or two before we go? I really wanted to take some tours—"

He smirked playfully. "You don't need tours. You have me."

Her eyes widened. "Because you lived through all this... *Holy cow*. I keep forgetting. You seem so modern most of the time."

"Most of the time?" He quirked a brow.

"Yeah, mostly. Sometimes you slip and say something adorably old-fashioned."

"I'm not old fashioned." He shook his head, and she grinned at him.

"Yeah you are, like when you call me 'delicate flower' or 'little rose.'"

"I call you 'flower' and 'rose' because of your scent." He nuzzled her neck, chuckling before he took a playful nip of her shoulder.

"My scent?" She wrinkled her nose, and then she lifted her forearm to her nose and inhaled. "I don't have a scent, except for my body wash from the shower." She sniffed again, and he couldn't help but laugh. She had no idea what he could smell. And then she tensed.

"What?" he asked, his eyes serious.

"The lab...I stole a dragon pheromone the Brotherhood had been synthesizing. I wore it whenever we were together, but it's washed off now."

"Synthesized pheromones?" Rurik rolled his eyes and sighed in exasperation. "Why would you want to create that?"

"I figured it would get you to relax around me. None of the hunters who tried to contact you got very far because you sensed something was off around them. I thought it might help get you to trust me."

Rurik rubbed her back, thoughtful. "That first night you did smell...wonderful." He tilted his head. "That could explain why Grigori told me he found your scent irresistible. Interesting, but also concerning." He leaned in and brushed the tip of his nose along her throat, inhaling deeply. "But I don't smell it now. And you still smell wonderful, but it's more...natural. Before, the scent was overpowering. It made me a little crazy. Now when I breathe in your aroma, it makes my dragon purr rather than pace."

"That's a good thing, right?" She loved the way he spoke to her now, gentle and low.

"Oh yes. Your natural scent is layered beneath those you use from day to day, perfume, shampoo, and so on. It stands out to me. In time I will be able to track you across great distances," he explained. "Our dragon abilities give us some advantages, even while we are mortal."

She eyed him in a critical and assessing manner, the look of someone who liked puzzles and challenges. "What kind of advantages?" It was the way he expected a scientist with a thirst for knowledge and natural curiosity would look at him.

"Well, we have an excellent sense of smell, eyes like an eagle, the ability to create and manipulate fire, and mesmerizing, of course."

"Wait, fire? I know you guys can breathe fire like in the movies, but what do you mean create and manipulate? How does that work? Do you have gas stores somewhere?" Her intense scrutiny and flurry of questions made him laugh.

"Fire for us isn't about storing gases, but the manipulation of energy. You would call it magic, but it's the most basic kind. After all, fire is just very excited molecules." Rurik snapped his fingers. A small red flame burst from his fingertips. He opened his hand, and the flame hovered an inch above his palm, flickering slightly.

Charlotte started to reach out, but before her fingers could touch it, he curled his fingers into a fist, extinguishing the flame.

"That's amazing."

"It has its uses," he replied, but he remembered all too well that those uses could be for dark and bloody ends. Just then he realized the long-standing mistrust between his kind and the Brotherhood wasn't one-sided. The power they wielded was unlike anything normal humans could comprehend. Of course they feared it. They always would, unless they understood it.

They were silent a moment, simply holding on to each other before Charlotte spoke again.

"Rurik, how did you get that scar?" She reached up to trace the line from his brow down to his cheek.

"That is a very long story," he said. "But if you want to hear it, I suggest we go to the Catherine Palace. I can show you."

"The Catherine Palace? Not the Winter Palace?"

"I have more of a personal history there than with the Winter Palace. My brother Grigori spent much time with the Romanovs in the early twentieth century. I was more involved with Russian royalty in the eighteenth. Much of court life was centered around the Catherine Palace then."

She sat up on the bed as she looked around for her socks and boots. "So you spent time around the czars?"

He watched her, wondering how his next words would affect her.

"You could say that. I was once Catherine the Great's secret lover."

Charlotte whirled to face him. "What?" She gaped at him. "Seriously?"

"The Russian court joked that none but a stallion could satisfy Catherine in bed, but the truth was, she needed a dragon. Her husband was a child who played only with toys and never came to her bed. She was lonely and in a marriage without love, and I saw her for what she was: a woman ahead of her time. I adore intelligent women." He flashed a little wicked smile.

She shook her head with a mixture of shock and amazement. "No—really? You were her lover?"

"Would you like me to show you a few of my special moves?" He pounced on her, and she fell back onto the bed laughing.

"As amazing as that sounds," she said, "I'm dying to see your former lover's palace." She stole a soft kiss that made his dragon stir inside, and Rurik felt damn good.

"All right, let's go. We don't have much time before we need to get back." He stroked a fingertip down her nose playfully.

She bounced up out of his arms, grabbing her purse and coat. "Let's go then!" He missed holding her almost right away, which shocked him. It had only been two days, and she was already someone he couldn't live without. How could it happen so fast? Was it just the allure of finding and mating her, or was there something more about Charlotte? She was worming her way into his heart, and he couldn't stop her.

※

LUIS AND DIMITRI STOOD IN THE ALLEY ACROSS FROM THE HOTEL the MacQueen sister was using in Moscow. Luis took a slow drag off a cigarette. They didn't speak; they only watched the three black SUVs that were parked at the front of the hotel. Two blond-haired men climbed out of the first, and their familial resemblance to the woman they'd seen with Rurik was obvious.

Drakor smiled. "Damien MacQueen and his brother Jason are here."

"They'll be waiting awhile," said Luis. "My men tracked Rurik and the woman to an airport today. They flew out to Saint Petersburg. Not sure when they're coming back." Luis flicked the tip of his cigarette, spraying ashes on the ground.

"MacQueen will have plenty of time to set his trap then," Dimitri said with a grim smile. "Patience."

"Patience," Luis agreed. "Once we have her and take care of the battle dragon, my men will take out his brothers."

They watched the hunters remove large duffel bags from their trunks and carry them into the hotel. Dimitri wondered what weapons, magical or otherwise, might be inside them. With the Barinovs gone, he would make the other dragon families of Asia fall in line, then the world. Once they were united, they could finally take out the Brotherhood. Then the world would know their true masters. Dimitri held no illusions about their alliance.

Once the Barinovs were out of the way, Luis would no doubt seek to remove him as well. But Dimitri was old, older than most realized, and with that came cunning and knowing how to play the long game.

Patience. If you had enough of it, an opportunity would always show itself, a weakness to exploit or a means to control others. It wouldn't be long before Luis was the one being removed, and then Dimitri would have a new family to rule over.

But that was the future. For now there was the alliance.

"We should go before we're seen," Luis growled, sinking into the shadows of the alley. Dimitri followed him, allowing the darkness to swallow him whole.

13

SOMETIMES BEING A BROTHER IS EVEN
BETTER THAN BEING A SUPERHERO.
—MARC BROWN

Damien stood in the small office of the hotel manager, watching the shooting that had occurred the previous night. The office was cramped with Jason standing behind the manager's desk as the manager pulled up the security footage.

The picture the unknown caller had texted him had shown Charlotte being dragged to the ground with glass everywhere, but it hadn't been clear what had happened. When they'd found the hotel where her bags had been left behind, they'd seen the shattered windows of the lobby, still in the process of being replaced.

"This is all we have on the cameras," the manager said. His thick accent was punctuated with a nervous glance between the brothers. He tapped a few buttons on the keyboard of his computer, and the video began to play again.

Charlotte and Rurik Barinov stood near the valet booth when the glass suddenly shattered behind them. Chaos descended on the scene. The dragon shifter flinched as he was hit, but Damien couldn't tell how many times or where he was wounded. Rurik took Charlotte down to the ground, covering her body with his. A few seconds later, Rurik stood up and lifted Charlotte up with him.

Damien leaned in close, placing a hand on the desk as he peered intensely at the security footage on the monitor. Charlotte seemed to be okay. It was not what he'd expected. "Do you have footage of them in the lobby?"

"No, I'm sorry." The manager's face was pale, but that wasn't a surprise. Damien and his team had walked into his office like they owned the place. At the first sign of objection, Damien had called his contact in the Russian government and handed the phone to the manager. After that, the manager had agreed to anything Damien requested.

"What room is she staying in?"

The manager exhaled with relief. "That I do know. You will need keys, yes?"

"Yes." He watched the manager collect a couple of blank keys and program them.

"These should work."

"Thank you." Damien pocketed the keys and wrote down his cell number. "If you see that man from the video, call me immediately."

"Of course."

The team took the elevator up to Charlotte's floor. Damien motioned for everyone to draw their weapons and take ready positions outside her door. There was a chance Rurik and Charlotte were still inside. A few silent hand gestures let everyone know what was expected of them.

Damien inserted the room key. The green light flashed on the reader, and he flung the door open, pistol raised. The room was dark, the lights off, and no sounds came from within. Charlotte's suitcase stood on a wooden luggage rack, lid open. The rest of the team flowed in behind him and fanned out, each checking the room and bathroom.

"All clear."

"Clear."

"Clear here."

Charlotte was nowhere to be found.

"Search everything," Damien ordered. For the next ten minutes, he and his team scoured the hotel room.

"Damien. Over here." Nicholas was kneeling by the mini-fridge, pointing at a glass vial filled with green liquid inside.

"Meg, take a look at this," Damien said.

Meg took the vial from Nicholas, holding it up to the light. "That's the serum. Charlotte showed it to me when she made her big breakthrough."

Damien stared at the bright liquid. The spare vials they'd taken from Charlotte's lab didn't have the same tint to them but rather looked blue-green, which made him wonder if there was a reason she'd left those versions behind.

So this was the magical dragon repressor his sister had reverse-engineered. It was a game changer to be sure, but Meg was right—if this fell into the wrong hands, it could lead to genocide. He didn't want his name connected to such an event. The Brotherhood had enough blood on its hands, and he was committed to finding a better way. Nevertheless, he slipped the vial into a pocket in his coat, just in case.

"Listen up," he said, addressing his team. "I want you to start prepping in the rooms on either side. Jason, get the manager to give us those rooms. Relocate anyone in them. Nicholas, review the security footage again, look for anything we might have missed, then put some wards around us. I want silencing spells, anti-fire spells, anything you can think of in case Barinov decides to put up a fight. Triple redundancies. Remember, this one's a battle dragon."

"I'll set up a post outside the hotel," Tamara said. "Meg might be recognized. Red hair sticks out here in Moscow."

Meg sighed. "And me without my wig collection."

Kathryn held her hands out, magic sparking from her palms. "I'll get the spells started." She began to twine her fingers and whisper ancient incantations. Shimmering blue waves passed through the room, tinting her skin and her brown eyes, so much like her older brother, Nicholas.

"Okay, people, let's do this." Damien watched his team get to work. He stared at Charlotte's open suitcase and tried to ignore the uneasy feeling he had about this situation. Flashes of the video kept replaying in his mind. There was something about the way Charlotte and Barinov had fallen, the guarded posture the dragon had while on the floor, and the way he'd pushed her through the lobby, shielding her—*shielding her*. Something about all this didn't ring true.

But the danger was there, even if the dragon had protected her, and Damien had to prepare for the worst.

I know I promised to slay your dragons, baby sis, but this battle could set the world on fire.

༺༻

CHARLOTTE STOOD IN THE SHADOW OF THE BEAUTIFUL IMPERIAL palace of Catherine the Great, her mind torn between the baroque architectural detail of the building and the legendary history of its onetime owner. Catherine had been an ambitious German lady who married into a Russian royal family that had been less effectual than its predecessors, and she soon became a better ruler than her own husband, much to the annoyance of most of her male contemporaries. History had not been kind to Catherine, even if it had allowed the beauty of her home to continue to flourish through the centuries.

There was a healthy amount of snow on the ground, despite the weather reports from the previous day, and still more snow danced about the robin's-egg-blue palace. Charlotte felt as though she stood in the middle of a vast snow globe that had just been shaken. Rurik stood quietly beside her, his emerald eyes tinged with melancholy. Was he thinking of his former lover? Or simply burdened by memories of the past?

"It's so strange coming back here," he said. "A part of my life, part of everything I once knew is crystalized here like a world trapped in a snow globe, yet it's closed off from me forever."

Charlotte tucked her arm in his and squeezed his arm.

"We don't have to go inside."

Rurik shook his head. "No, I want to. It's just that my brothers and I have lived so long, dozens of lifetimes, yet we rarely talk about the past. It holds too much pain for us. I'm just not used to it."

"My brothers are the same way. They never talk about our parents. The Brotherhood has taken so much from us, especially Damien. First our parents, then the woman he loved." She paused, drawing a slow breath. "I understand why he doesn't want me involved in his world, but shutting me out hurts just as much. He doesn't even let me talk about them. It's like I'm stuck in a half-life with my own family." Sometimes she wanted to talk about her parents, because not talking about them only made their memories fade faster. She wasn't even sure she remembered their voices sometimes.

They started walking toward the palace, the snow crunching softly beneath their boots. "How did your parents die?" Rurik asked.

"A vampire. My father was the head of the Brotherhood, trying to undo his father's unforgiving policies, and my mother was a tracker. They were paired together, and worrying about each other is what got them killed. At least, that's what I heard. It's against policy now for teammates to become romantically involved." She knew little of the details. Damien wouldn't let her see the files or the crime scene photos. They wanted to spare her that pain, and she was okay with that.

"I'm sorry," Rurik murmured. "I lost my parents as well, but it was my father's fault. He was obsessed with hunting down the last of the thunderbirds."

Charlotte frowned. She knew the name but hadn't read up on them. The Brotherhood had them listed as extinct, so she'd seen no need to learn about them. "Are they also shifters?"

"Yes. They change into large golden birds, similar to phoenixes.

One flap of their wings and they can kill a dragon with a sonic boom."

"And your father killed the last of them?"

"Not exactly. Grigori's mate, Madelyn, is a thunderbird. Our father killed her parents, but he died during the battle. Before she passed from grief, our mother took the baby and convinced a couple to adopt her."

"How did she end up marrying Grigori?"

"It is a long story," Rurik said. "With the most unlikely of coincidences. You might argue that fate brought them together. For Grigori to mate her, our natural enemy, it is..." He trailed off, and Charlotte suddenly smiled.

"He's like us—mated to someone who's supposed to be his enemy. Maybe this will work out okay after all." For the first time in a few hours Charlotte was filled with hope, but Rurik's dark chuckle snuffed out that small flame.

"Madelyn is the last of her kind. You have a secret international organization, trained to hunt my kind."

Her smile faded. He was right. This was different. How would her brothers react when they learned she'd mated a dragon? Would they feel betrayed? Would she be disowned? Would Rurik face the same fate from his family?

"Enough of this. Let me show you the palace." Rurik helped her up the front steps and knocked on the doors. A man in a security uniform opened the door and stared at them. He spoke in Russian, clearly telling them to leave, but Rurik looked deep into the man's eyes and replied in Russian. The guard stepped back, allowing them to enter. Charlotte didn't miss the vacant expression on his face.

"What did he say?" Charlotte whispered as they came into the hall.

"It's closed to visitors. I convinced him we can have a quick tour."

"You mesmerized him," Charlotte said.

Rurik's only answer was a sly grin. "A private tour is better than sharing it with tourists, trust me."

They walked down the main hall, and Charlotte marveled at the way the light reflected off the white walls and gilded lintel panels. It was the closest thing she could imagine on earth to what heaven must be like.

"An Italian sculptor, Count Rastrelli, created all this. He used more than a hundred kilograms of pure gold on the interior. Stand here." Rurik guided her in front of one of the doorways.

Charlotte gasped as she let him position her just right. At least seven more doorways extended down the hall ahead of her, the gilded paneling around the frames making the lengthy hall look like it went on forever.

"It's like holding two mirrors against each other."

Rurik led Charlotte through a number of ornate rooms, until they came into a massive one with beautiful pale wood floors and tall windows on either side. Between the windows were panels of mirrors with gilded edges and hundreds of candles in front of each.

"What is this room?"

"The Great Hall." Rurik took her by the hand and spun her around. "We used to dance for hours here." He twirled, and she danced back into his arms, where he held her close.

"The Russian court in those days was magnificent—the candles, the grounds, the click of heeled shoes on the floors, and the flutter of silk fans. It was..." Rurik seemed to struggle for words. "Quite a memorable time for me."

"How old are you?" she suddenly asked, almost afraid of the answer. She hadn't wanted to think about their age difference, but this had brought it all home to her, and she had to know.

"I'm over thirteen hundred years old."

Charlotte gasped. "Thirteen hundred?"

Rurik's smile wilted. "What's the matter? You're pale."

"It's... I just... I hadn't thought about your age. What happens when I get old and you don't—"

He cupped her face and silenced her with a kiss. "Don't think about that. We have time yet to worry." He kissed her again, harder, and a rush of images filled her head. Rurik's memories...

Colorful silk gowns swirled in candlelight, and the empress sat on her throne with a secretive smile on her lips. Dancing and laughter and joy were all around her. Time seemed to blur, and she felt a growing gloom, a press of evil drawing closer and closer. Men rushed through moonlit halls. She saw them through Rurik's eyes. He wore a leather bomber jacket and was calling for men to help him. Then there was a room full of amber panels and mirrors...

"They must not take the amber!" Rurik shouted to his men. Charlotte, in his memories, could understand the Russian being spoken. A mighty roar shook the palace as bombs exploded in the distance, making the walls creak and groan.

"The beast is coming!" a man shouted, and then he fled the room. Others followed him. Rurik stood alone at the entrance to the room as Dimitri Drakor came into view. His hands held balls of flame, and his eyes were bright yellow.

"Stand back, Barinov. This does not concern you."

Rurik snarled, his hands creating his own fire. He could let his dragon loose, but it would put the priceless amber room and the rest of the palace at risk. Drakor dove at him, snarling violently, and the flames consumed the air around them...

The vision of the bloody battle slowly faded.

Rurik panted against Charlotte's lips, his forehead touching hers. Her heart still pounded from experiencing his memories and the pain and terror of those final horrifying moments when the two dragons had lunged at each other.

"What was that place?" she asked in a shaky whisper.

He brushed his thumbs over her cheeks, and she reached up to stroke his scar.

"That was the Amber Room. It was once considered the eighth wonder of the world. During the Second World War, I fought with the Soviet Air Forces. I didn't agree with their politics, but the German Luftwaffe was annihilating my countrymen, so I chose to fight. We had so few experienced flyers, and I knew the humans needed my help, but I couldn't help as a dragon. Being a pilot was the next best thing. Germans were bombing the palace and the cities, and I had made a promise to Empress Elizabeth when the Amber Room was installed that I would always protect it. I failed in that promise when the Germans bombed Russia."

Rurik's green eyes darkened. Charlotte hugged him close. "What happened?"

"Dimitri Drakor happened. He betrayed the czars in 1918, then betrayed his own country in the Second World War. He came into the palace as the Nazis broke into the Amber Room to loot it. I couldn't shift. If I had, it would have wrecked the palace and its priceless treasures. Drakor didn't have the same concerns, so he transformed and clawed my face. He wounded me in other places as well, but those wounds healed better than my face." He touched the scar, gaze dropping to the floor. "Does it bother you? That I'm...marked?" The vulnerability in his voice surprised her. The man who had lived so many lifetimes and fought in countless wars was afraid she would find his scar offensive?

She stood on tiptoes and kissed the base of his scar, then his forehead.

"It is a badge of courage, the very outward mark of the kind of man you are. *A good man.* I love...the scar." Rurik pressed his lips to hers in a slow kiss. It burned inside and out, making her dizzy. "Are you *sure* you don't have pheromones? Because every time you kiss me, I go a little crazy—in a good way."

Her dragon shifter grinned wickedly at her. "It's a mate thing, my delicate rose. It will only grow stronger the more time we spend together."

"You know about a lot about mates for not having one," she noted.

Her mate sobered. "I've wanted one for so long, even as a boy. I knew I couldn't have my own, but I could at least dream about it and help my brothers recognize theirs. Keep them off the path that was mine alone."

Charlotte gazed at him, her heart tight in her chest. To think of this beautiful, brave man longing for a life he would never have and yet fantasizing about it was, she had to admit, a bit of a turn on.

"So let me get this straight—you, the sexiest man I've ever met, who could have *any* woman you want, your dream was to have one mate for the rest of your life?"

He nodded, his lips pursed as though he had been afraid to admit it.

She pulled his mouth down to hers, kissing him hungrily. "That is the most romantic, the *sexiest* thing I've ever heard." Each time their lips met, something seemed to tighten between them, like threads being woven closer and closer together on an elaborate tapestry.

I will love this man, this dragon. It's already happening. It's been happening since I met him. But she was seeing things from Rurik's point of view as well now. A human lifetime was nothing to him, so even if the drug was in the right hands now didn't mean it would be a century from now. The only way she could picture the Brotherhood changing for good would be if they established real ties with families like the Barinovs. She thought of the old woman with her tarot cards and the message she felt they had sent her.

"Rurik," she whispered, "I think we have to find a way to bring your family and mine together. Make them understand they don't have to be enemies."

He shook his head, a rueful smile upon his lips. "Bring the Capulets and Montagues together? I know how this story ends. 'Thus, with a kiss, I die.'"

She rolled her eyes. "You're really melodramatic, you know?"

He shrugged. "I've been around a long time. I've seen the Brotherhood at its worst. Dark times where they hunted my kind, killed mates and drakelings who were only protecting themselves. They *murdered* children. It's hard to forget that." He still held her close, but she felt the distance between them span like a vast abyss.

"Hey." She tugged his coat, catching his attention. "Don't shut me out like that. I believe you about the past, but my father spent his life changing how the Brotherhood works, and Damien's carried on that legacy. This isn't the Brotherhood you know. Damien has..." She puzzled over the right word. "He has a soft heart. He's all exterior roughness, but there's gold inside him, like you. Jason..." She paused again, finally realizing the dichotomy of her brothers for the first time. "Jason acts like a sarcastic teddy bear. But deep down, he's all steel." It wasn't that he was a stone-cold killer, but he wouldn't hesitate in a situation where Damien would. Jason would go with his gut instead of stopping to think through all the options.

"You really aren't convincing me that meeting your brothers is a good idea."

"It will be fine. I know it. I just have to explain everything before they meet you. If I call them with an entire ocean between us, they can't do anything rash. I'll call them after we get back to Moscow."

"Aren't they wondering where you are?" Rurik asked. They started to walk through the rest of the palace, their heads close together and their fingers laced.

"They think I'm in New York at some boring conference. I've gone to a lot of those. It was my only real way to travel. They never let me vacation alone or go anywhere exciting outside of the United States. It's been really..."

"Controlling," he finished for her.

She laughed. "I was going to say *lonely*, but you're right. They are controlling. I don't think they've ever understood me. They had their fellow hunters, the ones who understood the organization, but me? I was never allowed to be a part of that life. To them, I was a civilian, yet they didn't let me have any freedom, either. Worst of both worlds."

Rurik murmured in assent. "It is smart, to keep you close and protected. You can't fault them for that."

"Can't I?" she challenged. "They're so focused on keeping me alive that I've never had the chance to *live*. I would have risked anything to feel like a normal girl for just five minutes. I couldn't even go on a date without a background check and someone tailing me. Believe it or not, I met my best friend Meg that way. Damien had her tailing me when she was a trainee. She felt bad for me and told me about it, and we became friends."

"Seriously?" Rurik burst out laughing. The sound was rich and warm, and it dispelled some of the anger that had been building inside her. She thought of the crazy things Damien and Jason had done to keep her life safe but unfulfilling, and she laughed.

"Let's just say my senior prom date doesn't remember most of our date. Damien and Jason found out he had a few misdemeanors and interrogated him for the better part of an hour. With truth serum. I had to practically hold him up during our photos after the dance."

Rurik was still laughing as they reached the glittering hallway. He stopped at the top of the stairs and brushed her hair away from her face, staring deeply into her eyes in a way that made her knees buckle.

"I don't want you to ever be lonely again." He leaned in and pressed his lips to hers in a deep, soft kiss that filled her with dreams of warm sunny mornings in a shared bed, whispering sweet nothings and kissing for hours. She melted into Rurik, unable to hold anything of herself back. When they finally stepped apart, his gaze had become serious.

"Charlotte, I have a home in the Fire Hills. It's a few hours from here. I would love to take you there."

She bit her lip, considering it. She knew for sure that she didn't want to leave, but to stay... Were they rushing this whole thing? Going too fast?

"I'd love to..."

He picked up on her hesitation. "But?"

"Are we rushing this? I mean...I know so little about you other than that we're mated." When Rurik's eyes grew shadowed, she reached out to touch him. "But I *want* to. So talk to me. Tell me something."

Rurik relaxed as they ascended the stairs, and the erratic pulse of her heart calmed a little. She didn't want to upset him, but she meant what she said. The fact was he was a stranger to her. He knew more about her than she did about him.

He chuckled, pausing. "Where to start?"

"What about the nightclub? Why did you choose to go into that business?"

He stroked his chin, considering his answer. "The clubs aren't just about dancing. They are about letting go of control, about living a fantasy, even if only one night. I'm addicted to that feeling. As a battle dragon, I have to stay in control all the time."

"Except with your mate?" she asked, a blush heating her face as she remembered how they'd made love the last time, with her on her hands and knees and him behind her. There hadn't been *anything* controlled about that.

"Yes. That's the one time I can be me, in bed and out. But the club helps me feel close to that. It was why I had you dance in that cage."

"I still can't believe you did that." She was half teasing, half admonishing.

Rurik moved to the side of the stairs, cornering her against the wall, grinning.

"I gave you a mental nudge, nothing more. I could see how much you wanted to try it, but you were holding yourself back." He trailed a fingertip down the column of her throat. What was it about him that made her feel so reckless and wild? He carried an edge of danger that made her forget her worries and want to live only in the moment.

She saw the grin on his lips and slapped his shoulder. "Stop playing games."

"Ah, but there are so *many* games we can play," he whispered darkly. "Games that will leave you wet and breathless, perhaps even hoarse from screaming my name." His lips twisted in a seductive smile that weakened her knees and made her womb clench. "I've had thirteen hundred years to perfect my lovemaking skills." He closed the distance between them, kissing her hungrily, as though she were the cure to a fever that was burning him up.

His chin was covered in light stubble, and it burned her skin in a wonderfully erotic way. He bit her bottom lip, tugging on it, and she moaned helplessly, always wanting more. Her body needed to be connected to him. Now.

"What kind of games?" she asked as he released her lower lip. Her breath quickened as he pressed a thigh between her legs, rubbing her sensitive clit. She clutched at his shoulders.

He licked the shell of her ear. "Any kind you want. I admit I like the idea of you being bound. I'd love to tie you down and torture you with my hands and mouth. Any fantasy you have, I can make it come true." He pressed his thigh against her core again, whispering all the things he wanted to do to her and how it would make her feel. The need to come was so strong she couldn't stand another—

Smack!

He'd given her ass a little slap at just the right moment, and she exploded. He covered her mouth with his, silencing her cry of pleasure. Her eyes flew open for a few seconds as she tried to breathe through the violent riptide of her climax. Above her, the gold lights of the electric candles bounced off the mirrored walls of the hall and the tapestries lining the stairs. She'd always wanted to live a princess fantasy, but this was close enough: having an orgasm on the stairs of the Catherine Palace with her dark Russian prince.

It was a perfect dream, and she was so afraid it was going to stay just that, a dream that would never be a reality within her reach.

14

"I LOVE WHOM I LOVE," PRINCE LIR REPEATED FIRMLY. "YOU HAVE NO POWER OVER ANYTHING THAT MATTERS." —PETER S. BEAGLE, THE LAST UNICORN

Rurik held Charlotte's hand as they stood in his apartment in Moscow, facing down his brothers. Charlotte had been brave when they'd flown back with Grigori and Madelyn, but she'd said little. But now she had to officially tell his brothers the truth and explain everything.

The more difficult task would be having them believe her.

She trembled hard enough that he could feel it through her hand. The gold lighting from the modern chandeliers cast shadows between them, accentuating the distance between him and his brothers. He had put his body slightly in front of hers, just in case his brothers didn't believe her and decided to treat Charlotte like a possible threat.

Madelyn and Piper were also studying Charlotte, Piper openly curious, Madelyn a little wary. Mikhail's eyes glinted with mischief, though, which boded well, at least for Charlotte. Rurik knew his brother would most likely tease him for the next hundred years over this. He tugged Charlotte closer, lending her his strength and warmth. Her shaking softened.

"So this is your mate?" Mikhail asked, smirking.

He let go of Charlotte's hand so he could put his arm around her shoulder. "She is."

"Of all the women in the world to mate, you mate a MacQueen," Mikhail mused with a wicked grin. "Perhaps we should have her secured? Handcuffed to a chair? Fair is fair, given your family history."

Charlotte tensed, leaning into Rurik.

"He's teasing you, little rose," Rurik murmured in her ear, then added louder, "And if he's not, I'll remind him who the stronger dragon is."

Mikhail chuckled. "Fair enough. You can save the handcuffs for bed." He winced when his mate, Piper, jabbed him in the ribs.

Grigori tugged at his tie, still frowning. "Rurik, we have to discuss this. Your mate has reverse-engineered the drug that was used on Mikhail in London. Can you imagine if Drakor got his hands on it? He would use it against any dragon who dared oppose him, make them swear fealty to him out of fear. What if the Brotherhood decided to use it to eliminate us? We can't have anything out there that can give our enemies the advantage. It must be destroyed."

"I know," Rurik growled. "But the genie is out of the bottle. The Brotherhood will have her notes. We cannot live in a world of what-ifs. It exists. We must deal with that fact."

Grigori considered this. "Charlotte, could you make an antidote?"

"It's certainly possible. I had planned on working on that next when I got back. My hope was that the Brotherhood would only use the serum for their own safety during interviews and interrogations, and then the antidote could be given upon release."

"Good. We'll need it in case Drakor learns of Charlotte's formula. And if he does, we'll have to alert the other houses as well."

"You have to relax, brother," said Rurik. "You're helping no one by acting like we're on the verge of war."

Grigori sighed, accepting but reluctant at the same time. "Very well. Are we still having dinner?" His tone was calmer, but Rurik knew that was only for Charlotte's sake. The tension was rolling off his brothers in waves. But tonight was supposed to be a "meet the family dinner," not an interrogation. His brothers and their mates walked ahead of them into the dining room, and Rurik held Charlotte back.

"Don't worry, they will like you. It's just...this news has everyone on edge."

"I know. I hate that I replicated that stupid drug." A tear rolled down her cheek, breaking his heart. He didn't want her to ever be afraid, but reality had to be faced.

He cupped her chin. "I promise we will sort all this out. Besides, if you hadn't made the drug, you might never have come to Russia, and I never would've found you." He kissed her, trying to tell her with that kiss what words could not. He needed her in his life, and now that he had met her, had known the bliss of having a mate, he would never wish to change the past.

"I know you are hungry, so why don't we get some food? You'll feel better."

She smiled and wiped the tear away from her cheek with the back of her hand. "Okay."

At the table, it took Piper and Madelyn some coaxing to get Charlotte to join into their conversations. She was still scared. He could feel the tension inside her through their mate bond. It was surprisingly strong, even to him.

He hadn't told her everything he knew about mates. His mother had once explained that such a strong connection so early on could be both a wonderful and dangerous thing. Someday he and Charlotte might be so close they would be able to share thoughts. Their powers would even be shared if they had both been dragons, but Charlotte was mortal. He buried the unwelcome thought that accompanied that fact.

I will die, and my brothers will be left without a protector. Even if a new battle dragon was born to one of his brothers, it would need time to grow up, to train, before it could assume the duties Rurik had held for more than a thousand years.

Rurik glanced at Mikhail and Piper, jealous of their luck. Piper had been a mortal, but she'd almost died trying to save Mikhail's life. But an ancient ruby called the Dragon Heart Stone had allowed Piper to become a dragon. How it worked was a mystery, even to the oldest of living dragons. All they knew was that it had required an act of valor and sacrifice to draw the dragon's spirit out of the stone. As far as he knew, there were no more of these, only stories of those who had been lost searching for them.

No. These are the cards we have been dealt, and we must play them.

He thought of the old babushka from Saint Petersburg, the way she had turned the tarot cards over, her wrinkled face deathly serious. He believed in magic—as a creature of magic, how could he not?—but he'd never given much thought to tarot cards before. It had given him chills to see how accurate the woman had been.

He was silent most of the dinner, preoccupied. Charlotte reached over to clasp his hand, giving it a gentle squeeze. It pulled him away from the distracting path his thoughts had taken and forced him to remember that she was the one who needed him right now.

"So, the Brotherhood," Piper began, taking a hasty sip of her wine. "What's it like to be the little sister of a team of Buffys?" Mikhail and Grigori shared a puzzled look. Piper could tell nobody got the reference. "You know, vampire slayers?"

Charlotte's cheeks pinkened. She laughed nervously. "Uh... Not as fun as it sounds, I can tell you that. But the women hunters are pretty badass."

"That sounds fun." Rurik chuckled. "I'll be keeping you away from all of that danger from now on," Rurik told her imperiously.

"Excuse me? I just escaped two overly controlling brothers. I'm not going to wind up with an overly controlling lover." Charlotte snorted at Rurik's shocked expression.

"I suspect Grigori and Mikhail will be the same way, especially if they have daughters." Madelyn touched her stomach and gave Grigori a knowing smile.

Grigori quirked a brow. "You're only having sons. Daughters would give me gray hairs a thousand years too early."

"Stock up on hair dye," Madelyn said, grinning. "I've been dreaming about a girl. I think that's a sign."

"Fine, have a daughter and watch me age, woman. See if I care," Grigori replied, hiding a smirk as he reached for his wine.

For the rest of the meal, Rurik held Charlotte's hand beneath the table. He could see how it could be...the rest of their lives, full of family, laughter, and love. He was in love with Charlotte, and it made him afraid and excited all at once.

"Well, I think we should leave the new mates alone," Madelyn said. "I recall being unable to focus on much else when we first bonded. In fact, we still have trouble focusing, and it's been four months."

"We should let them be alone," Mikhail agreed, nodding to Charlotte. "You're all right for a mortal, even if your brothers *are* MacQueens." He reached for Piper's hand, and they joined Grigori and Madelyn. They soon made their farewells at the door, and the two were finally alone again.

Rurik kissed her cheek and gave her waist a little squeeze. "See, you survived my brothers after all."

"They are pretty scary." She ducked her head sheepishly as she admitted this.

"Yes, but they understand what it means to be mated. It doesn't matter that you come from the MacQueen bloodline—all that matters is that you're one of us now."

"Am I?" She wrinkled her nose. "I'm not a thunderbird like Madelyn, and I didn't become a dragon like Piper. I'm just me... Charlotte. There's nothing special about me. I'm not—"

Rurik spun her to face him. "How can you say that? You *are* special. You're everything to me. You're a precious gift." He hugged her fiercely, holding her close, suddenly afraid she would vanish if he let go. When she curled her arms around his neck, he relaxed a little.

"Do you trust me, little one?" he asked.

He felt her nod against his chest.

"Good. Now why don't we go to your hotel room and find that vial. The sooner it is in our hands, the more comfortable my brothers will feel. Then we will come back here, and I'll feed you a sinful dessert and make love to you by the fire, though not necessarily in that order."

Charlotte's shy smile made him feel like a god. "That sounds wonderful."

"Then grab your coat." He kissed her again before they headed for the door.

They rode his motorcycle to the hotel and walked into the lobby. Workers were putting up new glass in the front windows of the hotel. It was an awful reminder of how close he had been to losing her, and he hadn't even known then that she was his mate.

"I had a wonderful time today," Charlotte said as they got into the elevator.

"Me too." It'd been years since he'd done something for pleasure besides bed a woman, but today had been different. He had visited his past and had done so with his mate, and it hadn't been as painful as he'd expected. He'd enjoyed sharing the past with her and looked forward to sharing a future.

When they reached Charlotte's room, she caught him, curling her arms around his neck and kissing him deeply, then opened her hotel room door like it was an invitation. His chest was oddly tight, and her kiss had left him dizzy and excited in a way he'd never felt before. Damn, mating was *exactly* like everything he'd dreamed it would be—and more.

Charlotte flicked on the lights in the room. A sudden flash of movement was his only warning. Rurik grabbed Charlotte and shoved her to the ground, covering her with his body. The *phft!* of a silencer cut through the chaos, and his ears picked it up between the shouted commands. He groaned as a wave of nausea hit him.

"Charlotte—run—" he gasped, rolling off her as he clutched his neck. He pulled out a dart as he leaned against the wall by the door. His vision spun, and he saw Charlotte getting to her knees, heard her calling his name as two men dressed in black grabbed her, dragging her away from him. Whatever was in the dart packed a hell of a punch, and the dart had a pure iron tip.

"Run..." he said breathlessly before he slumped to the floor and knew no more.

Charlotte screamed and lunged for her mate but two men pulled her away from Rurik. He collapsed, a red dart falling from his fingertips to the floor.

"Secure him!" a man shouted. The voice was familiar, but...

"Damien?" Charlotte gasped. One of the masked men pulled off his balaclava, and she stared at him in horror.

"Thank God you're okay." Damien pulled her into a tight embrace, but Charlotte didn't hug him back. She shoved him hard enough that he stumbled. The others in the room took their coverings off as the situation stabilized.

"Hey, sis," Jason said with a grin.

Meg came over and clasped Charlotte's shoulders. "Thank God. You scared the shit out of us."

Jason nudged Rurik in the back with his boot. They had already bound his hands behind his back and his ankles together with iron cuffs. Seeing Rurik lying there tore at her. It was because he cared about her that he was on the ground unconscious, because he'd dared to shield her from whatever danger they faced. The entire scene was so sickening, so...

Charlotte rushed to the bathroom, shoving Meg aside. Her palms slapped against the counter, and she dry-heaved into the sink and splashed cold water on her face. It helped, but only a little. When she stopped for air, she saw Damien watching her from the bathroom door.

"Are you okay? He didn't hurt you, did he?"

"Hurt me?" Charlotte wiped her face with a fluffy white towel, wanting to hit her brother. "He didn't *hurt* me. He's done nothing to me."

Damien relaxed. He stopped standing in that alert-soldier way he always did when he was worried.

"Thank God. Then we got here in time."

"In time?" She threw the towel to the ground. "What the hell are you talking about?"

Damien bristled, like a dog with its hackles raised. "We found out what you were up to. You *lied* to me, Charlotte. That's never happened before."

"Yes. I lied. I wanted to do something important for once. I thought if I could do what none of you could do, you'd finally respect me, let me work with you. *I* made that serum, but if I came to you with that, you'd have thanked me and shut me out all over again. So I came here, and now..." *And now I'm mated to the most wonderful man in the world, who my brothers just subdued like some common criminal.*

"You did great," Damien admitted. "You got closer than any of us could to the Barinovs. Now we have one in our custody, and we can get the information we need from him." Damien held up a vial of her serum. The green liquid taunted her as it shimmered in the florescent lights of the bathroom.

"You can't use that on Rurik." She lunged for the vial, but Damien stepped back, slipping the serum into his black jacket.

"Why not? Is there something wrong with the formula?"

"Rurik is a *good* man. He doesn't deserve to be drugged and interrogated."

Her brother raised a brow. "Charlotte... He's a *dra—gon*." He drawled out the word *dragon* into two emphasized syllables. "He's dangerous. You're lucky he didn't seduce you. They can turn women into slaves with their pheromones."

Charlotte advanced on her brother. "Yeah, well, he wasn't the only one using those."

Damien frowned. "Yeah, Meg told us about that. What were you thinking?"

"I was thinking that if we could actually *talk* we might get somewhere, not these crazy roughhouse tactics. Is this how you always intended to talk to the Barinovs? God, Meg was right to be worried about giving you the serum."

"And what would you have us do?"

"Don't treat him like he belongs in prison. I've spent time with him. And he's not dangerous, not to me." She shoved past her brother and ran straight into Jason, who kept her from getting to her mate.

Jason gripped her by the wrists, holding her still while he spoke over her head. "Damien, he's coming around already."

"Shit, that's supposed to keep an elephant out for hours."

"Guess our intel was right—he's a battle dragon."

"Shit!" Tamara hissed and stepped away from Rurik's prone body when one of his arms twitched. "Load another dart."

Charlotte jerked herself free of Jason's hold and rushed to Rurik, kneeling down beside him. She turned to her brothers, fury in her eyes.

"Release him."

"Are you nuts?" Damien and Jason said in unison.

Charlotte turned to Meg, her only ally. "Meg, please..."

Meg shifted, biting her lip. Her gaze darted between Charlotte and Damien. "Charlotte, hon, you're really worked up right now. Once we've got things under control, then maybe we can all talk about this..."

"Oh, for fuck's sake," Damien said. "Nicholas, Jason, take him to the room next door. Inject him again if you have to. I'll join you shortly."

As Rurik was dragged to his feet, his eyes opened and he blinked slowly. Her name escaped his lips in a plea that broke her heart. "Charlotte..."

"Damien, please. Don't do this." Charlotte tried to reach for Rurik, but Damien grabbed her wrist, jerking her away.

"*Listen*. You're clearly under his power. We will break whatever hold he has over you." Damien's hazel eyes, so like her own, were cold and hard now. This was the sort of man Grigori and Mikhail had feared when they learned of her identity. A man who scared *her* now.

"He doesn't have a hold over me. We just—"

Damien called out to one of his hunters. "Tamara."

Tamara stared at him, lips parted in shock. "She's not really—"

"Just do it," Damien snapped.

Something pinched her left arm. She looked down. Tamara was injecting something into her.

"You're *tranquilizing* me?"

"It's a mild sedative mixed with a bit of *verum seri*. We need to be certain you haven't been compromised."

As he spoke, the sedative kicked in and her knees buckled. *Mild my ass.* Tamara caught her and helped her sit in the desk chair by the bed.

"I'm sorry, Charlotte." Tamara pulled out some zip ties and secured Charlotte's wrists to the chair arms.

Charlotte's brain seemed to slow down. Everything was a bit fuzzy, like she'd had too much to drink. She pulled at her wrists, but the zip ties cut into her skin.

"Please... Don't hurt him." Her eyes watered, and she blinked, feeling tears trail down her cheeks. She couldn't help it; she just started crying. It had to be the sedative. It could have an emotionally polarizing effect on some people.

Damien sat on the edge of the bed, a grim look in his eyes.

"I know this is tough, but just answer my questions, and then you can sleep off the drugs. You're safe now, little sis."

But she wasn't. This was her family, and they were treating her like she couldn't be trusted.

"What happened when you got to Moscow? What did you do?"

She tried to bite her lip, but she was unable to control her thoughts as they spun in a kaleidoscope of her mind.

"I went to Rurik's nightclub," she finally said.

"What was your plan?" Damien asked.

"Recon. See the target, watch his habits, get the lay of the land. I thought I stood a chance of getting his attention where your agents had failed."

Damien shared a glance with Tamara. "What happened at the club?"

No. Don't tell him. But her lips moved of their own accord. "I didn't even have to order the wine. He just knew."

"Rurik?"

"The bartender." Charlotte almost laughed. None of this mattered, but she'd tell him anyway.

"The bartender?"

"Yes. He might be a werewolf."

"Okay, and then what?"

"Assholes. They came after me."

"Who?"

"Just some jerks. Human. I hit one...pretty good." She giggled this time, remembered she'd walloped that one guy. But the memories were blurring together, and she struggled to focus.

"So you got into a fight at the club?"

Charlotte's thoughts sloshed around inside her brain, making her dizzy. Flashes of Rurik roaring from behind her...

"*He* saved me. And he asked me to dance."

"Rurik Barinov?"

She nodded. God, she wished she was back in that cage with Rurik. She wanted the whole world to vanish and just be with him.

"You *danced?*" Damien asked, his tone implying he didn't believe it.

She nodded. "It was amazing. I felt so good. For the first time I was enjoying myself. Not looking over my shoulder. Not worrying about you or your agents watching me. And he was wonderful..." It was humiliating to be talking to her brother about this, and it was even worse because he was forcing her to tell them things that were private. What gave him the right? Why hadn't he just asked her?

"Then what happened?"

"Damien, don't make me tell you." If he made her tell him, she would never forgive him. *Never.*

"Charlotte, what happened next?"

She tried to fight, but the story came out. Every detail, every intimate moment—emotionally and physically—that had occurred between her and Rurik.

Damien's hands were curled into white-knuckled fists on his thighs. "He forced you to have sex with him?"

"No! How dare you say that you—you *asshole*!" She shouted the word, even though her head ached. She spoke the one truth she hoped would stop this madness. "He's my mate, Damien. He would never hurt me. Don't you see? He's my *mate*." The truth weighed heavily upon her lips, but it was a relief to finally tell him. Her brother stared at her, his lips parted and eyes wide.

"Mate?"

"Yes. We are mated."

"No. I won't let this happen," Damien argued, his tone cold enough that it made her stomach roil. "You're still suffering some effects of being compromised by him. Whatever bond you think you have with him, it's a lie. He's probably used his powers to bend your will. You're not mated."

"It's true. He is my mate. Matey, matey, you're too latey." She giggled, suddenly feeling completely silly.

"We'll find a way undo it. You won't have to stay with him," Damien vowed.

"But I *want* to stay with him. Don't you understand?" Her voice turned into a screech as she jerked at her bound hands.

Damien looked away. "Dammit. He's got his hooks in you good." He stood and looked at Tamara. "Give her something to help her sleep."

"Damien, you dumb son of a bitch, I will never forgive you for this! I will hate you for the rest of my life. You are not my brother!" Charlotte shouted, her voice breaking as Tamara injected her with another needle. Darkness crept in at the corners of her vision as her brother left the room.

"Tamara. Please, save my mate...I love him." The words came out in a whisper. And it was the deepest truth she'd ever spoken in her life. Tamara had always been nice to her the few times they'd met. She prayed the woman would take pity on her.

"I believe you," Tamara whispered back. "Your brother's not thinking straight. I'll do what I can."

Then the darkness drowned her.

15

> WHATEVER CAN DIE IS BEAUTIFUL—MORE BEAUTIFUL THAN A UNICORN, WHO LIVES FOREVER, AND WHO IS THE MOST BEAUTIFUL CREATURE IN THE WORLD. DO YOU UNDERSTAND ME? —PETER S. BEAGLE, THE LAST UNICORN

"All right, you fucking bastard, talk!" A rough hand shook Rurik in the chair he was tied to. Rurik could feel the tranquilizer leaving his system. If he could delay whatever torture they intended just a few minutes longer, he might be able to break his bonds and then...

"You want me to talk?" he replied with a grin. "What shall we talk about? How about the cowardice of the Brotherhood? You seem well acquainted with it."

The man who'd shaken him cocked a fist, but the door opened and a second man entered. This was the one Rurik recognized—Damien MacQueen. The younger man resembled him so much that he had to be Jason. Charlotte's brothers.

"Stand down, Jason."

"Let me do this," Jason insisted. "Just one little punch."

"I would barely feel it." Rurik chuckled, flexing his hands against the chair arms. "So you're Charlotte's infamous brothers."

"Infamous? Only to some." Damien's expression didn't bode well, but he kept calm, whereas Jason looked ready to explode.

"Guys, I don't mean to interrupt," a dark-haired man in the

corner of the room said, "but he'll be getting his strength back any minute now. Should we dope him up again?"

"Not yet. I'll handle this, Nicholas. Go check on my sister. Tamara's given her something to help her sleep. Make sure she doesn't have a bad reaction to the truth serum," Damien said.

His words filled Rurik with rage. "You drugged your own sister?" he bellowed, jerking violently against the chair. "Where is she? I demand to see her. I want to know she's all right."

"Demand?" Damien laughed. "You don't get to make demands here, Barinov." He pulled out a syringe. The green liquid was something Rurik recognized all too well. "You know, all I wanted was to talk. Russia's got a power vacuum right now. It's a powder keg ready to explode, and you seem to be at the center of it. We tried to talk to you, but you refused."

Rurik snorted. "Talk? Sending your other agents to lure me into a trap? That is how you talk?"

"We don't exactly trust your kind to keep your temper," Damien countered. "And the fact is, you have the advantage over us. So what if we took that advantage away?"

"Don't you fucking dare!" Rurik roared, his body starting to push past the sedative's effects.

"Fuck, Damien. Look at his eyes," Jason said. Damien saw swirls of bright gold starting to fill them. "The tranq's wearing off."

Damien jabbed the needle into Rurik's neck. The serum hit his blood instantly, burning through him. Whatever he had imagined it would feel like to suffer the effects of this drug, he couldn't have imagined it would be like this. It was like his breath had been knocked from his body and someone had sapped all of his strength. It was like half of him was being torn away and locked into an impenetrable safe.

Damien checked his watch. "We'll let it take full effect, and then we'll talk." The brothers moved away from him, consulting quietly by the door.

A few moments ago, his enhanced hearing would have picked up everything they said, but now it was as though he had cotton in his ears. Everything sounded muffled, and the voices seemed tinny. Mortal hearing...and mortal sight. Fuck, he'd never known how good he'd had it as a dragon.

The door opened, and a dark-haired woman whispered something to Damien. Whatever she said made Charlotte's brothers look at him. Then Damien took out a vial, this one with a clear liquid.

"Now let's see what truths we can get out of you."

Rurik remembered Charlotte's story about her brothers drugging her prom date. In a weird way, here he was facing the same fate. It was almost funny. Rurik tensed as the second needle plunged in. A low growl, horribly human sounding, escaped his lips.

Damien and Jason stared down at him, but Rurik had faced worse than them before. They didn't scare him.

"Did you use pheromones to seduce Charlotte?"

"What the fuck is it with you guys and pheromones?"

"But you seduced her," Damien added.

He tried to hold back what he knew would be a damning response, but it came out anyway. "I guess I did."

Jason backhanded him. "You piece of shit!"

"Jason!" Damien caught his arm. "Do that again and I'll have you removed."

Blood trickled down Rurik's chin, and he licked his split lip. His chin and cheek on the left side throbbed. Normally it took a blow from another dragon before he felt pain like this.

"Did you know she was our sister?" Damien asked coolly.

"No. She admitted it to me after we slept together."

"She says you are mates. Is that true?" Damien's hazel eyes lacked Charlotte's warmth. His gaze was stony.

Jason stared at his brother in horror. "*What?*"

"Answer me, Barinov," Damien said. "Is it true?"

"She is mine. My true mate," Rurik said through clenched teeth. "I have claimed her."

For a second nothing happened. It seemed like Damien was

holding himself back. For a moment it seemed like he was reaching for his pistol, but his hand froze as it touched the holster.

"How do we undo it? How do we break the mating bond?"

"How do you undo love? The bond only occurs because the feelings are true. I belong to her and she to me as long as she's alive. When she dies, I die."

Jason frowned. "I thought that was only with other dragons. This works with humans too?"

"Barinov, answer the question," Damien said.

"Dragons mate for life. The bonds are..." He tried to swallow the words, but they bubbled back to the surface. "When a dragon loses its mate, the dragon dies of grief. It always kills the human part of the dragon, because one cannot live without the other." He didn't know how to explain that dragon mythology of his people, largely because so much of it had been lost over the millennia, to the point that no dragon alive knew how much of it, if any, was actually true.

"But does that happen to humans too? If you die first, will Charlotte..." Damien didn't finish the thought, but Rurik knew what he was asking.

"No, at least I don't think so. She isn't a dragon, so I don't think mate grief would kill her."

Rurik sighed heavily. His limbs ached, and the iron cuffs cut into skin that could no longer heal properly.

But he knew the serum's limitations. This would last a day, at most, and then he'd come roaring back to himself, and he could deal out some serious retribution to the Brotherhood. Then he would rescue Charlotte and get the hell out of there.

Assuming they didn't kill him first.

CHARLOTTE LAY ON HER SIDE IN THE BACK OF AN SUV, HER head pounding. She tried to sit up, but her body ached. She blinked, her brain foggy. She recognized the two women in the front seats of the vehicle.

"Tamara, Meg, what's going on?" She didn't immediately remember what had happened, but when her gaze met Tamara's in the rearview mirror, the last few hours came flooding back to her.

"Rurik!" She gasped and scrambled to reach for the car door.

"Charlotte!" Meg spun around in the front passenger seat. "Calm down, okay? Tamara and I are working on a plan. But first we had to get you somewhere safe."

"A plan?"

"Yeah. We both think your brothers are a bit unreasonable at the moment. Damien especially. I know it's going to piss him off, but I know what I saw between you and Rurik tonight. I've seen enough shifters in my day to know what a mating looks like. But the fact is we're never going to get your brothers to calm down by flying off the handle. So just relax, okay?"

Charlotte tried to calm herself, but it wasn't easy. It certainly wasn't helping to have her blood pounding through her head.

"God, what did you guys give me? I feel like shit." She moaned, her stomach churning.

"Sorry," Tamara said. "I had to give you a sedative. Damien was watching. But I didn't give you the full dose."

"Thanks, I guess." Charlotte couldn't keep the sarcasm out of her voice. "Did you see Rurik? Was he okay?"

"He was okay when I saw him. Your brothers were questioning him about your relationship. I swear if anyone else had been involved in this but you, Damien would have reached an understanding by now. It's almost like he doesn't want to."

Charlotte frowned. If they hurt Rurik, she would destroy them. It didn't matter that they were her brothers. Their overreaction was unforgiveable. When Rurik's brothers had found out who she was, they had panicked, sure, but they hadn't drugged her and tied her to a fucking chair.

No, only my family does that.

"What's your plan?" She sat up properly in her seat and buckled herself in. They were driving through Moscow now, but it was clear she'd slept most of the journey because they seemed to be almost out of the city.

"They wanted us to take you to the airport. Don't worry, that's not happening," said Meg.

"We're taking you to a safe house the Saint Petersburg branch has out here," said Tamara. "By the time we get back, they'll probably want Rurik taken to the airport for transport. We'll make sure he ends up at the safe house with you instead. That should buy us some time to talk sense into those numbskulls, give them a chance to cool down before they do something they can't undo."

"Don't worry," said Meg. "We'll get you through this. Even if your brother fires us."

Tamara grinned. "I don't know about you, but I definitely have some serious vacation time accrued."

Charlotte smiled. They were going to help her. Everything was going to be okay—

Twin headlights appeared on the driver's side of their SUV a millisecond before they were T-boned. Everything exploded in a spray of glass. Metal screamed, and the world around her flipped over and over. Charlotte gasped as the car finally stopped rolling. It landed on its right side, smoke billowing from the engine. Something trickled down her nose into her right eye. Charlotte raised a shaky hand, wiping at her face. Her hand came away bloody. She stared at the red smear on her palm, and between her splayed fingers she saw the front of the car where Tamara and Meg were hung like rag dolls, their seatbelts keeping them locked into place.

Charlotte fumbled with her seatbelt, wincing as she fell out of it onto the car roof. She tried to crawl toward the front seat, but two booted feet appeared in front of the shattered windshield. She froze, holding her breath as a man knelt down and peered at her through the shattered window. He had caramel-colored skin, dark hair, and black eyes, like two gleaming shards of obsidian.

The man smiled wolfishly, revealing a set of bright teeth. "*Olá*, chica."

Charlotte didn't move, didn't speak. She slowly looked between Tamara and Meg, not wanting him to know what she was doing, or more importantly, what she was hoping to find.

There. The butt of a Glock stuck out of a holster on Meg's right side. If she could grab it—

"Take her," the man barked. "Before she does something stupid." The car suddenly tilted a few inches as something heavy moved above her. She glanced up to see the left door above her jerk open. Silhouetted against the setting sun, she saw the shadow of a man, his eyes swirling gold as he reached toward her. She shrank away from him, but he grabbed her arms and hauled her up out of the car.

She balled a fist and punched him. Pain exploded through her hand, and the man snarled and tossed her to the ground. She hit the asphalt, biting back a cry of pain. Someone hauled her to her feet. She now faced the man who had greeted her through the shattered window. He was tall and lean, but she could feel the power rippling off him.

"So you are Damien MacQueen's sister?" The man reached up to cup her chin, then trailed a finger down her cheek. "Not exactly my type, but I can see why Barinov broke his vow never to mate." He leaned toward her and inhaled. "You smell sweet."

Charlotte may not have been a hunter, but she'd been trained to protect herself. She pulled her head back and threw it forward, head-butting the man on the bridge of his nose. He let out a string of Portuguese curses and stumbled back, clutching his face. The man behind her smacked her on the back of the head hard enough that white dots burst before her eyes.

"Take her to the car," the man rasped as he clutched his nose. He might have been a dragon shifter, but bone still beat cartilage in a fight.

She was dragged to a black SUV and shoved into the back seat. Three other men climbed in with her. She was almost certain these men were dragons. Damien's voice fluttered up from her survival lessons. *"Stay alive. Do whatever you have to do, but stay* alive. Honor doesn't matter. You breathing is what matters. We will find you."

It was something she'd always remembered. Do whatever it takes. Grovel and beg if you have to. These men knew her brothers were in the Brotherhood and that she was mated to Rurik. It was obvious they wanted to use her for a trap. The man she'd headbutted sat beside her, and his gaze made her flesh crawl.

"You think you are brave?" he asked.

Charlotte studied his cruel smile and swirling gold eyes that had settled into twin black pools. He was definitely a dragon.

Her head ached, and her heart pounded like war drums. "I'm not brave," she replied.

"Good. I don't like my women to be brave. I prefer them screaming for mercy as I take what I want." He gripped her throat, squeezing. "I will take you, and I will extinguish the light behind those pretty eyes. Do you want to know why?"

When she didn't answer, he gave her a rough shake, choking her until she gasped and clawed at his hand.

"You are MacQueen's sister, and that would be reason enough, but you are also Rurik Barinov's mate. We have waited so long for him to show weakness. Now he finally has." The man let go of her throat, and she sucked in sweet, precious air.

"Who are you?" she gasped.

"I am Luis Silva, head of the Silva family of Buenos Aires."

Ahh... That explained the Portuguese at least.

"So what's your plan?" she asked, all too aware that minutes ago she'd asked her friends the same thing under very different circumstances.

Luis laughed. "You say that like I am a Bond villain. Eh, whatever. You will die, and we will convince the Brotherhood that the Barinovs did it, then convince the Barinovs that your brothers killed you to kill Rurik. A sacrifice play." Luis was smug. Charlotte was in no mood to point out that Damien would never do that. Sure, Damien had drugged her—and she was going to throttle him for that—but he would never really hurt her. Still, it didn't matter what she knew, only what the Barinovs believed.

"You're not doing it here?" she asked.

Luis shook his head. "No. No. There is someone who is dying to meet you first. He has waited even longer than I have to see the Barinovs fall. It is he who will choose when you die, though I have claimed the pleasure of killing you myself."

A shiver shot down her spine. "Who are you taking me to?"

Luis's smile grew malevolent. "Dimitri Drakor."

The only surviving member of the other Russian Imperial house of dragon shifters. The one dragon who had come closer than anyone else to killing Rurik.

Oh God...

16

THE COURSE OF TRUE LOVE NEVER DID RUN
SMOOTH. - WILLIAM SHAKESPEARE

Rurik's face hurt like the devil. Jason's one punch had left Rurik feeling agony he normally felt only in battle with another dragon. He spat, the bloody mess landing on the hotel carpet floor. Damien was staring at him, a contemplative look in his eyes, and Jason looked ready to go for round two with him.

"There's really no way to sever the mating bond?" Damien asked, his tone dangerously quiet.

This time Rurik didn't feel like trying to hide his answers. Nothing he would say would change whatever it was they intended to do with him.

"Only death can break the bond." He looked Damien in the eyes. He saw only one option left open to him, even though it would shatter his heart. "Our intention, our *hope*, was to convince you there was another way between our peoples. But if you are so blind that you can't see this, then I have another option."

Damien frowned. "What's that?"

"I will leave her alone. You take her home, and we are done here. You do nothing to my brothers or their mates in retaliation. They had no part in our mating and have caused you no harm, nor do they pose a threat to your kind. You know this. It's the Drakors you have to fear."

"I'm aware of the Drakors, and I know you and your brothers have kept on good terms with humans over the centuries." Damien watched him intently. "What did you mean when you said you'd leave my sister alone?"

"I won't try to keep her. I will stay here in Moscow. You can take her home without fear that I will come after her. It will hurt her to be apart from me, but it's better that she suffer missing me than watching us fight."

Damien and Jason held another whispered conference. Before they could finish, the hotel room door rattled as someone pounded on it. Damien opened the door, letting the one they called Nicholas inside.

"Damien," he panted. "Tamara just called. Charlotte's been abducted. They were leaving Moscow when a car hit them. She and Meg were knocked out, and when they woke up, Charlotte was gone. There's no trace of who or what hit them or where they went."

Panic hit Rurik like a train, but he remained frozen to the chair. His mind worked frantically, absorbing what he'd just heard.

Damien turned to Rurik, his tone now icy. "Was this your brothers' work?"

Rurik glared at Damien. "That's not our way, and you're a fool to think it. We wouldn't put Charlotte's life in danger, nor would we harm your hunters unless they attacked first."

Jason scoffed, but Damien raised a finger. "I believe him. At least the first part. Ramming the car could have killed her, and that would have killed Rurik. It's too risky a play."

Rurik tried to think clearly, but knowing that someone had taken his mate was choking him. He'd never felt so powerless before. There was only one person he knew who would dare to get at him by harming his mate. A growl escaped his lips.

"But I know who took her." He glared at them. "And when I find him, I'm going to tear him to pieces." He jerked his bound hands. "Release me. *Now*." Even though his dragon was gone, he was still fueled by his desire to destroy all those who threatened his mate.

"That's not going to happen," Damien said. "You can tell us where she is, or I will *make* you tell us."

Rurik was silent for a long moment, studying Charlotte's big, bad brother, the man who could snap his fingers and raise hell for dragons everywhere, especially with the new weapon they possessed. He raised a brow in challenge, his tone deadly calm. "Listen to me, *hunter*. Dimitri Drakor has taken Charlotte to get to me. And they know she's your sister, so they intend to use her against you as well. This is not the time to cling to past grudges. We can join forces, like Charlotte wanted, or we can stay here and bicker until they kill her."

Jason turned away from him, but he could still hear him say to his brother, "I don't trust him."

Damien, however, was more thoughtful. He closed his eyes a moment, fingers pressed at the bridge of his nose. "The Barinovs wouldn't risk Charlotte's life crashing into her that way. A Russian warned us when we arrived about the Barinovs torturing Charlotte, but that never happened. He also said the Barinovs were a threat to everyone. He wanted us to take the Barinovs out."

He opened his eyes and raised his head, meeting Rurik's eyes. "We're being played."

Rurik's heart skipped a beat.

"Jason, uncuff him."

"You can't believe—"

Damien looked to his brother. "Did I stutter?"

Jason's lip curled, but he reluctantly obeyed. Soon Rurik was rubbing his sore wrists.

"What do you need from us?" asked Damien.

"Aside from a bottle of aspirin?" Rurik said. "A phone."

Damien nodded to the one called Nicholas, who tossed him his phone.

"Thank you," Rurik said. Calling Grigori's cell, Rurik knew he would have to speak English and on speakerphone so his new potential allies would understand and trust him.

"Rurik, is it done? Did you acquire that third vial?" Grigori spoke in Russian, but Rurik answered in clear English.

"Grigori, we have a problem. I ran into Charlotte's brothers, and while we were having a polite and civil conversation, Charlotte was kidnapped."

There was a short pause. "Drakor."

"That is my guess as well," Rurik said. "We don't have much time. He's not a fool. He won't make the mistake of waiting to kill her in front of us like he tried to do with Madelyn. He will kill her immediately because he knows it will kill me."

"But he hasn't already?"

"No..." It was true, he'd have known instantly if Charlotte died, and though it might take hours or days for him to pass on, that part would be inevitable.

"But why not?"

Damien cut in. "I believe he's going to arrange things to make it look like you did it."

"Who is this?" Grigori asked.

"Damien MacQueen of the Brotherhood."

"Why would Drakor fake Charlotte's death as if we killed her?"

Damien exchanged glances with Rurik. "I think he expects us to exterminate your family in retaliation."

"Which you would do without question," Grigori said, a sting in his voice.

"If it's any consolation, I'd bet money he'd have men in position to take us out afterward," said Jason, edging closer to the phone. "It's what I'd do."

Grigori began cursing, and Rurik heard Madelyn's sleepy voice in the background as she asked what was going on. "What do you propose, MacQueen?" he said at last.

"If..." Damien paused. "If we work together, we need a few agreements in place for what happens after Charlotte is rescued." He met

Rurik's stare, then looked down, as if slightly ashamed. "Look. There's a lot we could argue about right now, I know. Tons of blame to throw at each other. Centuries of bad blood. But that has to wait for another day. Rurik and Charlotte both said that they wanted to be a first step toward us working together, and I believe that. So here's what I propose. We work together, rescue Charlotte, and part in peace. Then, when you're ready, we talk, on neutral ground."

Grigori said nothing for a moment, and when he did speak, his tone had softened. "You're different from your ancestors. You have a dragon's wisdom in you. Agreed."

Jason rolled his eyes. "Great, now that the hug fest is out of the way, would someone explain to me how we find Charlotte?"

"That is up to my brother," said Grigori. "He's the only one who could tell us where she is."

"What? How?" Jason asked.

Rurik stared at the brothers. "The bond between us is already strong. I could sense her wherever she was...until you injected me with that serum."

"MacQueen drugged you?" Grigori's shout made the phone's speakers whine.

"This was before we came to an understanding," Damien said diplomatically. "Let's stay focused on the objective here." Rurik couldn't help but snort at this oversimplification. But for Charlotte's sake, he let it go.

Grigori's voice lost some of its vigor. "Until the drug wears off in Rurik's system, we won't know where she is."

No one moved. Even Damien felt frozen.

"So what do we do?" Jason asked.

Grigori spoke up again. "MacQueen. I need you to listen to me. Drakor will rain fire down on this city. He has nothing left to lose, and once he learns he'll be fighting you as well as us, he won't care about casualties, and the first person to die will be your sister. We know his lairs and his allies better than you. If there is any chance to save her, it lies in trusting us."

There was a tense silence as Damien glanced at the faces of his team, then looked to Rurik and the phone he held.

"What's your plan?"

"Follow my brother to the roof of the hotel. Mikhail and I will pick you up. Five minutes." Grigori hung up, and Rurik gave the cell phone back to Nicholas. He slapped Damien on the shoulder, a serious expression shared between them.

"Don't take it personally, but we're in charge now, hunter boy." Rurik grabbed his leather motorcycle jacket, slinging it on as he strode to the door. "You guys coming?"

The others collected their gear and followed Rurik to the elevators. They had no time to waste, not when Charlotte's life hung in the balance.

17

DRAGONS AND LEGENDS...IT WOULD HAVE BEEN DIFFICULT FOR ANY MAN NOT TO WANT TO FIGHT BESIDE A DRAGON.—PATRICIA BRIGGS, DRAGON BLOOD

"You are Rurik's mate," the Russian dragon mused as he leaned in and inhaled Charlotte's scent. She tensed, closing her eyes as he drew close enough to kiss her. He didn't, but the invasion of her personal space was unsettling.

When he finally leaned away from her, she opened her eyes again. Luis, the man she'd head-butted, leaned against the closed door, watching her with black eyes. He'd brought her to an expensive high-rise structure in Moscow, newly built and mostly empty. She almost fainted at the height when she realized they were more than forty stories up in an empty corner office. She sat in a metal chair, but she wasn't restrained. Why bother? She had no way to escape, except jumping.

Luis's gaze raked down her body. "She reeks of Barinov."

Dimitri Drakor didn't seem nearly as brutish as she'd expected. He was nothing like Luis, who'd so casually talked about using her and leaving her ravaged body for Rurik to find. Instead, Drakor stared at with her with open curiosity, as though she were a strangely shaped puzzle piece that wasn't fitting where he expected.

"He has claimed you." Drakor brushed her hair back from her

neck, his fingers tracing the outline of the still healing bite mark Rurik had left on her.

"That's just a love bite," she said, forcing herself to calm down. They weren't going to kill her, at least not yet.

Drakor smirked. "*Just* a love bite? I think not. You experienced the *dar bogov*, didn't you?" Charlotte looked puzzled, not knowing what he meant. The Russian dragon struggled for words. "I believe in English it means 'gift of the gods.' You could see through his eyes, and he through yours." He reached up and curled his fingers around her throat but did not squeeze.

"Did you know he loved another before you? My son killed her in front of him, before Rurik murdered him. But he never claimed her."

Charlotte swallowed. The suffering he must have endured being so close to her for so long, yet holding himself back.

Drakor growled softly, his eyes glowing a reddish gold as he captured her attention again.

"I'd counseled my son to wait, to let Rurik mate her first, but he was young and impulsive. He got what he deserved, I suppose. But now I will have my wish. When I kill you, Rurik will die. It might take hours, maybe days, but it will happen. And then his brothers, lost in grief over his death, will be easy targets." His fingers pressed a little harder into her throat, but his touch was still loose enough that she could breathe. It didn't stop the panic inside her, however.

"Then why haven't you killed me yet?"

"I have my reasons," Drakor said. "Nothing you need concern yourself about. But then there is this…" He crooked a finger in the air. Luis stepped forward, holding up a set of three vials. Charlotte recognized them with dread. They were early samples taken from her lab. A stronger version of the drug she'd created, a version that she didn't trust herself to use because she feared it might cause long-lasting damage.

"Yes," Drakor said, still watching her face. "Luis recovered these from the hunters and thought they might prove useful. Do you care to enlighten us as to what they are? My instincts tell me that you know. In fact, I feel as though your entire presence here in Russia revolves around them."

Charlotte tried to remember the training she'd had from her brothers, tried to think her way through this. *Stay alive.* That was her biggest concern. Because staying alive kept Rurik alive too.

"It's a drug I created. It has the power to make a shifter's dragon go dormant."

Luis looked like he wanted to throw the vials on the floor and smash them beneath his boots.

"Why would you make such a thing?" Drakor asked, then raised a finger before she could answer. "Ah. Yes. Of course. Control. Your brothers have plenty of weapons to kill us with, yes, but the Brotherhood has never been able to control us."

Charlotte's mouth dropped at the mention of her brothers.

"Oh yes. I know who you are," Drakor replied. "I found great joy in turning the Brotherhood against the Barinovs. If they aren't already killing each other, they soon will be. Your death will be made to appear like the other side was responsible. Blood calls out for blood, and when it is over, I will finish off whoever is still alive. But your drug intrigues me, so we will chat a little longer."

Shit... Charlotte's heart skipped a few heartbeats, the rush of terror hitting her anew.

Drakor finally let go of her throat. "How does it work?" When she didn't answer, his hand erupted in fire. He held the flame painfully close to her face.

"Don't make me ask again," Drakor warned.

"It's an enzyme-reaction-based structure. The enzymes lock onto cells with dragon DNA and paralyze them."

This was, in fact, complete gibberish. The serum had originally been developed by John Dee five hundred years ago, and there was as much magic involved with it as there was science. She could spend years trying to unlock its secrets and trying to explain them in scientific terms. She'd been fortunate that her ability to replicate it hadn't required any magic of her own.

"How long does it last?" he asked.

"About forty-eight hours."

"Could you make a permanent version of the drug?" He moved his flaming hand away from her face a little.

"I don't know. It's possible. I would have to research it more."

Drakor stood and walked over to Luis and took the vials. "Bring one of your men here. I wish to test this."

Luis licked his lips nervously. But then he opened the door and spoke to whoever was outside. The tall, hulking man came in, scowling as he closed the door.

Drakor studied the vial he held, pinching it between his thumb and forefinger. "Does it have to be injected?"

"Yes."

He filled a syringe with contents from the vial and held it out to the Brazilian dragon.

The third dragon looked to Luis, who nodded. Then the shifter accepted the syringe and injected it into his arm. For several seconds nothing happened. The man stood there, staring at them. Then he laid a hand over his abdomen, muttered something in Portuguese to Luis, and then his eyes widened and he started to thrash. He fell to the floor, his body shaking from violent seizures, but eventually they stopped.

For a moment Charlotte thought the drug had killed him, but then he groaned and staggered to his feet.

"Ask him how he feels," Drakor said.

Luis translated the man's reply. "He says he feels empty somehow."

"Tell him to change," Drakor said. "Bend fire, do something with his dragon."

The man frowned and for a moment looked constipated. He shook his head, then looked to his hand and frowned again, flexing the fingers like it might help. Nothing. He began to shake again and started repeating the same words over and over. His entire world was crashing down upon him, and it was making him panic.

"Hearing, sight, he says everything is diminished." Luis let out a stream of furious Portuguese. He raised his hand, and it erupted into flames. Charlotte tried to shield her face, but the attack never landed.

"Silva! Stop!" Drakor growled. "We cannot kill her. Don't you see what she's done?" Drakor held the two remaining vials in his hand, his dark eyes glowing a swirling gold now.

"It's witchcraft is what it is."

"You're right." Drakor grabbed Luis's arm and held him back. "The best possible kind. She didn't just give us a weapon. She gave us a tool." He turned a cold, terrifying smile upon her. "A fate *worse* than death."

Charlotte shrank back in her chair.

"My people lost the Cold War, but we won't lose this one, not with *this*. With this, I will even make the Barinovs my servants." He walked over to her and shook the vials tauntingly. "You are proving far more useful than I anticipated." He glanced at Luis, who was still fuming. "Your men may have her, but they cannot kill her. I need her for the formula."

Luis grabbed Charlotte's arm and dragged her from the chair. "What will you do?" he asked Drakor.

"If the Brotherhood and the Barinovs haven't killed each other yet, they might learn the truth. So we change tactics. I'll make a ransom call and send them on a merry chase far away from us. Buy us some time." Drakor pulled out his phone and dialed as she was hauled away from Drakor.

"Grigori," he said in the phone. "I believe we need to—"

"It's a trap!" Charlotte screamed, praying that Rurik's brother would hear. Luis cuffed her, the blow landing on her temple. Pain shot through her head. She stumbled, hitting the doorjamb hard enough to bruise her right shoulder. Luis pulled her into the hall where his men were standing, and he grinned as he shoved her to her knees. Whatever he said to them made them all laugh.

"Me first, *menina*." He reached down and fisted a hand in her hair, using it to jerk her head up. Charlotte's scalp burned with sharp agony. The sound of men laughing was a haunting, frightening cacophony all around her. Luis jerked her to her feet by the arm and hair. He shoved her into the nearest room, slamming the door shut behind him. Charlotte had a few precious seconds of freedom before he grabbed her again, but she was facing him now, so she kneed Luis hard in the groin. Even dragons felt it there.

"*Puta!*" he snarled. She balled her fist and swung a haymaker at him, but that only hurt her hand. Luis braced himself against the wall by the door, blocking her only way out.

"So you have spirit after all. But not for long." Luis grinned and tackled her to the ground. Her head smacked the thin carpet concealing concrete, and black dots filled her vision. His hands closed around her throat. She tried to scream, tried to fight. She was not going to go down like this.

In that moment she swore she could hear Rurik's voice. She closed her eyes, searching for that veil of snow that she'd seen inside him. The fire hidden within the snow seemed to beat like a heart, and his voice came from it.

Charlotte, let me see through your eyes.

Luis tightened his grip. She clung to life, clung to Rurik, remembering everything she'd felt the moment she'd first kissed him. And then it happened—she felt herself falling into him like a meteor. She was unable to stop falling, even when she got close enough to him.

The flames of his heart enveloped her and she gasped, her body jolting like a live wire. She replayed everything she'd seen after the collision.

Find me, Rurik.

Just as he could see her memories, she suddenly saw his. Her brothers interrogating him, challenging his love for her, and Rurik holding fast, his heart unchanged. Her chest clenched as though invisible fingers had squeezed tight around her heart.

My heart... His words were rough, emotion breaking through like waves on an angry shore.

I won't go home with anyone but you. You are my home. She sent the message to him as clear as a bell. Seconds later, she blacked out.

⚜ 18 ⚜

THE BRAVE MEN DID NOT KILL DRAGONS. THE
BRAVE MEN RODE THEM. - GAME OF THRONES

Rurik stared at the floor number digits, which kept changing in the elevator as he and Damien's team rode it to the top floor, when suddenly his head seemed to clear of the fog that had separated him from Charlotte.

Flashes of what she was seeing came through the bond to him. Drakor's face, the serum in his hand as he talked. Red-gold eyes burning into Charlotte's. Another man standing close behind Drakor...one Rurik recognized with dread. Rurik felt her heart pounding and her terror spiking. He leaned against the side of the elevator, gasping as her strong emotions swamped him.

Charlotte, where are you?

"Uh...guys, the dragon's face just turned green. I think he's going to puke," Jason said, cautiously inching away from Rurik. Meg and the other hunters stepped back.

Damien gripped Rurik by the shoulder. "What's the matter?"

"I know... I know where she is!" Rurik's head exploded with new images. An office building, a distant skyline... She was trying to show him where she was. Then he saw Charlotte being dragged across the floor, hands around her throat, someone choking her...

He replayed the rush of images in his head, particularly the vacant office building only ten miles from where he stood.

"She's in an empty office building not far from here, but we don't have time. Drakor's friends are in town. The Silva family."

"The Silvas?" Damien's eyes narrowed. "They've been killing my people outside of Buenos Aires. I have no problem fighting those assholes."

"Neither do I," said Rurik. The Silvas had wiped out a family line that had been allied with the Barinovs for centuries just so they could expand their drug empire.

"How do you know Silva is there?" Jason asked.

Rurik knew the truth would upset Charlotte's brothers, but he couldn't sugarcoat it. "She's being attacked by Luis Silva, the battle dragon of their family. We have to go. *Now.*"

"How will we get to them in time? Is your brother bringing a helicopter to the roof?"

Rurik grinned. "Not exactly."

Damien and Jason exchanged glances with the rest of their team.

"I'm going to regret this," Damien muttered.

Jason patted him on his tactical vest. "Come on, bro. You're the one looking to foster a spirit of cooperation." The hunters followed Rurik out of the elevator and down a hallway. From there they climbed a flight of steps and came out onto the rooftop. Wind buffeted them, and Rurik stared across the Moscow skyline, searching for the building Charlotte was being held in.

The hunters stumbled back as the massive flat roof suddenly got crowded. Three great dragons landed just yards away from them. They ranged in color from blue, to white, to green, their clawed feet scraping against the concrete.

"Holy shit," Meg gasped.

Rurik laughed. "The blue dragon is Grigori, the green dragon is Mikhail, and the white dragon is Piper, Mikhail's wife. Tie your gear to their legs. Anything you can't hold on to during flight." He glanced at Meg, who stared in awe at the snow-white dragon that was Piper. She reached up to touch her, and Piper bumped her hand with her nose.

"Oh my gosh, she's beautiful."

Damien recovered from his shock quicker than the others and helped Rurik tie their equipment bags onto the beasts' legs.

"We'll have to ride them to the building where Charlotte is being held. Can your team handle that?" Rurik spoke so that only Damien could hear.

"My team can HALO jump from thirty-five thousand feet; they can handle this," Damien answered without hesitation.

"Good." Rurik went next to Grigori, who was pacing restlessly, the blue frill around his neck fanning out with frustration. Rurik understood his brother's mood. Rurik couldn't help his brothers in this fight, at least not in the way he was meant to.

"Meg, Tamara, and Kathryn, you ride on Piper. She is the white dragon. Damien and I will be on Grigori. Jason and Nicholas, you take Mikhail. There are spines on their backs that you can hold on to." Rurik demonstrated as he mounted his brother, showing them a row of spines that extended outward, which they were able to grasp.

"Never considered making saddles?" Jason quipped.

"How often do you let people ride on *your* back, MacQueen?" Rurik retorted.

It had been more than a thousand years since he'd ridden on one of his brothers as a human. Back then he'd been a boy, not yet ready to change, scrambling over Grigori's scaled back. He shoved the memory aside as his brother bent his head and crouched, letting him climb up. At full size, a dragon's body was the length of two buses, and the tail was almost as long. Damien got up behind him, and the others followed suit.

"They'll let us down on the roof. Expect trouble when we land. Once Drakor knows we're there, he won't care about human casualties."

Damien nodded, his eyes hard as he clutched the flared spine between his hands. "Understood."

Grigori stood up to his full height. "Hold tight!" Rurik warned before his brother leaped off the roof.

"*Fuck!*" Damien bellowed as Grigori dropped like a stone. Then his wings fanned out and they were jolted as they caught the air and rose up into the cold Russian sky. Rurik saw Damien clutching his brother's spines for dear life.

Jason, on the other hand, could be heard whooping like a cowboy back on Mikhail.

Hold on, Charlotte. Stay alive. He pushed the thought toward her, praying she could hear him and that they would get there in time.

༺༻

Charlotte woke with a gasp. Rurik's voice still lingered inside her, a whisper, more in her heart than her head. Had she dreamed it? Her lungs burned and her throat was in agony. For a moment she didn't remember where she was, until she saw Luis Silva crouched over her. His hands were no longer wrapped around her throat. Now they were balled into fists at his thighs.

The memories of what had happened before she'd passed out came roaring back. But he seemed to have lost interest in her, which was perhaps the only thing that had saved her life. Luis was staring at something over her head. Clutching her throat, she rolled over and looked out through the tall windows and saw three winged shapes headed straight for them. Their wings flapped in a strange but familiar way, something between a gliding bird and the pulsing frenzy of a bat.

Dragons.

Luis growled, eyes fixed on this imminent threat. Charlotte realized this would be her only chance. She scrambled to her feet and lunged at Luis. She didn't have the strength to hurt him, but she had mass and physics on her side. She tackled him, driving him back into the recently installed window, dropping to the ground as he crashed into it. The glass shattered, and Luis fell out of sight. Charlotte knew better than to assume the fall would kill him, but at least it bought her some time. And time was what she needed right now.

She got up and managed to slip through the door to a supply closet just as the rest of the wall of windows exploded behind her. Luis came crashing back into the building in dragon form. Charlotte ducked behind a set of file cabinets that were partially covered with a white plastic tarp. She covered her mouth to try and silence her panting breaths. There was a roar in the distance, and the building quivered like a tree facing a mighty wind.

Oh God... How was she going to survive this?

Stay alive. Rurik's voice broke through the fear that had rooted her in place.

I'm scared. Too scared to move, to breathe...

Images flashed across her mind. She saw their dance at the Catherine Palace, a moment when she'd felt safe in his arms. Her breathing slowed, and she could feel an inner calm move through her.

She peered around the edge of the cabinets. Luis was nowhere to be seen, but shouts in Portuguese could be heard from other rooms. Seconds later, deafening crashes shook the building so hard the floor tilted beneath her feet before settling back. Her stomach lurched, and she tried not to throw up. For a moment she felt like she was on the world's largest Jenga stack, and someone had just removed a key support brick.

Howls and screams echoed all around her, interrupted by bursts of gunfire. She used the wall for support as she crept to the nearest door and chanced a look out a window. In the sky, dragons were clawing at each other, teeth snapping, jaws closing around scaled flesh. It was unlike anything she'd ever seen in her life. A medieval battle of monsters.

The bark of gunfire made her dive to the ground as shouts echoed from above. She waited, counting the seconds of silence before she dared to move again. The rooms were empty as she slid past each door, but she was afraid she'd run into Luis or Drakor at any moment. They would be looking for her.

She soon found the corner office she'd been in earlier. The two remaining vials of serum lay forgotten on the floor. She had to make sure Drakor didn't manage to escape with them. Charlotte rushed toward the vials and grabbed them, only to be yanked back by her hair.

"There you are!" Drakor snarled. "I'm afraid I don't like Luis's chances out there. But with you, I won't need him. Come." She tried to resist, but it was no use. Already his hands were taking on a clawlike shape. He pulled her toward the window, and she imagined herself being carried off to God-knows-where.

"Back away from my mate," Rurik bellowed as he appeared in the doorway. He was bleeding and bruised, but at that moment he was the most beautiful thing she'd ever seen.

"Rurik!" She cried out his name, and he met her gaze with a smile of hope before he focused back on the threat before him.

"You can't harm me," Drakor said, claw at her throat. "She dies, you die." Drakor and Rurik danced in a slow circle around each other.

"Charlotte, it's okay," Rurik said. "Your brothers are here on the roof, and we will get you to safety."

"I think not." Drakor's nostrils flared a moment. "Your scent..." He closed his eyes briefly, inhaling again. "It's...human. *Only human. Interesting.*"

Rurik didn't acknowledge the awful truth, but Charlotte knew what Drakor would puzzle out. If Rurik was mortal, he could be easily killed, and he'd still have Charlotte for her drug.

Panic shot through her like a bolt of lightning, and everything around her seemed to slow down. Drakor began to turn, his face alight with malice as he finally realized that he had the upper hand.

Have to stop him...but how?

She didn't stop to think her plan through. There was only one way to even the odds. Vial in hand, she rammed her palm into Drakor's mouth, mid-taunt. The glass shattered over his teeth and cut into her hand, which she held over his mouth, keeping as much of the serum inside as she could. Drakor struggled, gripping her hand and pulling it away. He gagged and spat, a mixture of blood, spit, and serum spilling on the ground.

He howled, backhanding his claw at her chest, even as it began to revert to human form. She screamed, staggering over the edge of the building. She grabbed Drakor's hand, desperate to pull herself back up.

Instead, he fell over the ledge with her.

Wind whipped across them in a roar of sound. She couldn't breathe, couldn't catch her breath as she went weightless in the air. Drakor's gaze went wide with terror, seeing the ground rising to meet them, yet unable to do anything about it.

But Charlotte wasn't afraid. Not really. She wasn't resigned to death, it was just that she knew. She knew somehow what she would see as she looked back up into the sky. She knew it before it even happened.

A great black dragon appeared, falling from the building and diving after them, its golden eyes locked onto hers. As it reached her, its giant claws cradled her seconds before they reached the pavement, pulling her back toward the sky...but it wasn't enough.

Rurik covered her with his wings and twisted his body so he was beneath her before they crashed into the street, and everything went dark.

19

LIKE A FRUIT SUFFUSED WITH ITS OWN
MYSTERY AND SWEETNESS, SHE WAS FILLED
WITH HER VAST DEATH, WHICH WAS SO NEW
SHE COULD NOT UNDERSTAND THAT IT HAD
HAPPENED. —RAINER MARIA RILKE

Rurik had fought a thousand battles, but nothing compared to the one inside him the moment he saw Charlotte pull Drakor over the edge of that building. Every nightmare he'd ever had as a boy of having a mate and losing her came true in that instant. The terror, pure and violent, froze him in place, but not for long. His dragon, buried deep beneath the serum, suddenly stirred.

"*No!*" His roar shook the already unstable building around them. He didn't have time to think. He rushed toward the ledge, just as Damien and his team stormed the room. It only took a moment for the hunter to recognize his intentions.

"Rurik, no!"

Rurik leaped from the window, his rage and love blurring together in a swell of emotions that drowned out everything else. His dragon exploded out of him as he hurtled down toward his mate. He tucked his wings flat against his back and shot straight for her. His claws caught hold of Charlotte's tiny form, but he was falling too fast; there was no way he would pull up in time. At the last moment, he turned his body so he was beneath her, his wings covering her, and blackness swallowed him.

Damien rushed to the building's ledge, looking down at the massive black dragon hurtling down toward the earth, toward Charlotte. It had to be Rurik; there was no other explanation. There was a deafening boom, and dust billowed up in a wide circle far below, blocking Damien's view. When the dust cleared, he saw a distant shape on the pavement: Rurik, lying still. Neither of them could have survived that fall.

Grief threatened to drown him, but he buried it fast. The battle wasn't over yet.

Two dragons tumbled from the roof onto the landing he and his team were on—a gray one and a white one, one of the Silva dragons and the one called Piper. The Silva had a grip on Piper's silvery-white neck.

"Eyes and torso!" he ordered his team. "Watch fire!"

He raised his AR-15 rifle, taking careful aim for the Brazilian dragon's head, and fired again and again with marksman-like precision. The rest of the team did likewise, firing pure iron rounds into its abdomen.

The dragon roared, letting go of Piper, blinded in one eye and furious. Piper used the distraction to take the other by the neck and, with a violent thrash, break it. The body of the dragon fell, crashing down toward Damien's team, only to become human before it even hit the ground.

Something in Damien's head clicked. Of course. Nobody ever found a dragon body, because when they died they didn't stay dragons. That meant...

"Grigori!" Damien shouted to the sky, where the leader of the Barinovs hovered, wounded but victorious. "We need to get down there!" He pointed over the edge. The blue dragon nodded and dropped to the platform, letting Damien climb onto his shoulders.

If Rurik was still alive, then there was a chance Charlotte was as well. Grigori leapt off the building and glided down to the ground.

Damien jumped off the dragon's shoulders and stumbled to his knees beside the body of the black dragon, which still lay motionless. Curled in its wings lay Charlotte, her hand splattered with blood, but not moving. Not breathing. Tears stung his eyes as he cupped her face.

"I'm so sorry," he murmured. "I failed you. I—" The rest of his words died upon his lips. They would never reach her, not where she had gone.

Damien stared at the face of the dragon who had dared to love his sister. All he saw there now was the proud, wise, noble heart of a dragon, not an enemy.

He saw Grigori's snout nudge one of Rurik's clawed feet. A shaky breath broke from Rurik's body, but it wasn't one that filled either of them with hope. Grigori made a low, rumbling sound that turned to a keening cry. The dragon bent his head, as if resigning itself to the inevitable. Silver tears like liquid mercury poured from Grigori eyes, splashing onto Rurik's scaled body.

Damien placed a hand on the grieving dragon's leg, feeling the heat of the scales beneath his palm. There were no words to be spoken, none that could ease the pain of their shared loss. Damien felt he understood what the dragons meant when they said they suffered grief so strongly that it could kill them. He scrubbed a hand over his eyes, trying to wipe the tears away.

And that's when he saw flames rise up around Charlotte's body.

***

SNOW...

Snow was falling. Charlotte could feel it on her skin before she opened her eyes. She was there in that realm *between*, feeling Rurik's beating heart. The warm glow was so close, but as she sat up and blinked, she saw the flames flicker and sputter, threatening to go out.

She surged to her feet and pushed through the thick snowfall as the storm became fiercer, wind whipping at her. She had to reach his heart this time, or else the wall of shadows creeping in at the edges of her vision would overtake her.

Charlotte braced her arms in front of her face, shielding it from the icy wind. Shapes moved ahead of her, but they weren't shadows. These shapes were...dragons. Hundreds of them, lined on either side of her path to the dwindling glow of Rurik's heart. Their massive, long-snouted heads bowed, their frills fanning up as they watched her pass by beneath them like giant statues.

"Another comes to the doorstep. Come, brother. Come home. There is so much for us to show you. So much you have never seen..." The words were clear like church bells, sung by unseen voices.

"Keep going, little one. Go!" a lone female voice said from somewhere beside her. *"Go to him before it's too late!"*

Charlotte turned and saw an emerald-green dragon with green-gold eyes urging her forward.

"Who are you?" Charlotte shivered as a new wind funneled down the path the dragons had made for her.

"We are the Barinovs, the souls of the ones long gone, returned to our true home, ready to welcome another," they answered, though their mouths didn't move.

Charlotte somehow knew what they meant by that. They were ghosts...sort of. This was death...maybe. Yet it was like nothing she'd ever expected to see. And somewhere in this snowy world, Rurik's soul was here, his dragon half. The part that needed to be saved.

"I can't lose him. Not now!"

The dragons said nothing.

"Did you hear me? You can't have him!"

The female from before whispered beside her. *"There is a way, but it will not be easy."*

"What must I do?" she asked. "Anything. Please."

"You must give of yourself. Your life must become his, and his heart must become yours."

Charlotte believed she knew what the dragoness meant, so she nodded. "I'll do it."

"Take his heart, hold it close, and don't let go, no matter what. You might yet save him. Go...time is waning, and the shadows are upon us."

Charlotte faced the glowing heart ahead of her, only a little farther, but the path was harder, and it became more difficult to move with every step.

"I love you, Rurik. Do you hear me? *I love you!*" She shouted the words into the blinding snow that tried to hide the heart from her. But she would not stop—she would *never* stop.

She stretched her hand into the flames, curling her fingers around what looked like a giant ruby. Fire exploded around her, burning her hand, her body, her soul. It was killing her, she knew it. If she kept holding on, she would die.

"Don't let go." The dragoness's voice echoed all around her. *"Focus on your love for him."* Charlotte closed her eyes, unable to scream as her body seemed to burst apart, and her life drained away. As her life force left her, something of his came to fill the void. Something strange. Something alien. Something...Rurik.

With a powerful burst of light, she fell to the ground, her fingers still clutching Rurik's heart. When she dared to open her eyes, she saw snow everywhere, but it wasn't the between-world she'd just been in. Gone were the Barinov ghosts, the shadows, and the storm.

Wherever she was now, the snowflakes were suspended in midair, as if time itself had frozen over. She tried to stand and jolted when she realized she was not herself any longer. Her arms were covered in obsidian scales, and her fingers ended in razor-sharp claws. Her nose had lengthened into a lethal snout. A sense of something—or rather *someone*—else sharing her body was eerie but not unwelcome. It was the dragon. It was part of her now. It was also part of Rurik. Rurik was part of her.

Her dragon-self stirred, managing to stand, and she turned to see a beautiful black dragon lying in the snow, still as death. In that dragon she saw her mate, and she saw herself.

Rurik. She moved forward on shaky new legs and nuzzled his chest, huffing warm breaths across his throat. He didn't stir.

"*My mate...*" she crooned, singing a dragon song buried deep within her.

"*Little rose?*" The response was like a faint echo, but she kept singing. The dragon part of her knew there was magic in dragon song. The sweeping notes spun spells in the air, and her mate lifted his head weakly, his golden eyes fogged with pain.

"*Come back to me, Rurik. Don't be afraid to live. I love you.*"

This time when he lifted his head, she saw the gleam of returning strength in his gaze.

"*You've changed. How?*"

Charlotte nudged him, urging him to stand. She and her dragon needed to see him up and moving before they could relax.

"Ho-ly fuck," someone said behind her. She turned and saw someone she recognized, but her dragon also felt him to be a threat, and she bristled defensively.

Damien. The name was there, along with the memories, but her dragon growled, forcing her brother to stumble back. He fell into the snow next to a large sapphire-blue dragon. Rurik chuckled inside her head, and the sound filled her with joy.

"*Let the dragon go, little one. She'll slide back beneath your skin, and then you'll be all right.*" She turned to Rurik and watched him change, his dragon morphing into the beautiful, battle-scarred man she loved.

Her need to be with him was so strong that she collapsed into the snow, trying to get to him, her body doing just as he suggested. The dragon sank back into her, present but hidden. She fell on top of Rurik, and he curled his arms around her. Tears crept from the corners of her eyes.

Rurik kissed her temple and held her close. "It's all right to cry." With those words she gave in to the outpouring of emotions that had been bottled up.

"Is she okay?" Damien rushed over, but his voice made her bury her face even deeper into Rurik's neck.

"She's overwhelmed. Mikhail saw this with Piper when she first transformed," Grigori said, having changed back to human form. "What I don't understand is *how*. We have no dragon stone."

"I am not sure what happened—or how," said Rurik. "But I recognized the dragon I saw just now as my own."

"What do you mean?" Grigori asked.

"I can't explain it other than that. My dragon and Charlotte's... are the same dragon but shared between her body and mine. I think we now share the same dragon soul."

Charlotte listened to the men talking around her, but she wasn't ready to face them, not yet. She felt vulnerable and exposed and weak. She didn't want to open her eyes or let go of Rurik. He was the only thing she could cling to in that moment.

"Um," Damien stammered to Grigori. "Do you guys need clothes? I...just realized that everyone here but me is completely naked."

"I'm naked?" Charlotte said weakly. "And *Damien's* here? Oh God..." She'd survived a fall from a skyscraper only to die here now of embarrassment.

Rurik's body rumbled against hers with laughter as he stroked her back. "It's all right, Charlotte, my mate. Everything will be all right now." Charlotte raised her head, slowly opening her eyes. Her gaze locked on Rurik, and she knew nothing would ever be the same again. And she couldn't be happier about it.

"It's time for us to face the future," he whispered. "I love you."

"I love you too." That was all that mattered. The love that even in death had kept them together and saved them, because love was the strongest magic, the oldest magic. Even death couldn't stop it. "Now, get me some clothes before I scream."

EPILOGUE

ABOVE US, OUTLINED AGAINST THE
BRILLIANT SKY, DRAGONS CROWDED EVERY
AVAILABLE PERCHING SPACE ON THE RIM. AND
THE SUN MADE A GOLD OF EVERY ONE OF
THEM. —ANNE MCCAFFREY, NERILKA'S STORY

The sound of the door chime at Rurik's apartment made Charlotte tense. Madelyn and Piper both giggled at her, but Charlotte wasn't laughing. After she'd almost died the day before, everything had become a chaotic blur. She'd been staying at Rurik's apartment while her brothers and Rurik's had seen to handling the cleanup of the dragon battle. She hadn't been sure if they would agree to come when she and Rurik had invited them over today.

"It's going to be fine," Madelyn said. "They fought together against Drakor and the Silvas."

"And your brother saved my ass," Piper added. "That counts for something."

Charlotte bit her lip, studying her future sisters-in-law. Behind them in the kitchen, Grigori and Mikhail were teasing Rurik about being mated, just as he'd predicted. He'd put up with it long enough, it seemed, because she heard him hiss in warning and saw his brothers jump back, though still smiling.

The doorbell chimed again. "Go on, answer it." Madelyn nudged Charlotte toward the door.

She paused at the entrance, her hand settling on the silver

knob. It had been only a day, but already everything felt...different. Her human body had changed, with eagle eyesight, intense olfactory senses, and greater strength. And beneath all that, she was a dragon. A creature her brothers didn't trust.

Open the door, little rose. Rurik's reassuring words came through their bond. He stayed back, letting her greet her brothers privately, hoping to show respect and also to show that he wasn't controlling her, though the truth was even harder to understand.

She turned the knob and pulled the door open. Damien and Jason as well as the rest of their strike team stood there in civilian clothes. That boded well for this official meet and greet.

"Hey," Damien said, a bashful look on his face that Charlotte had never seen before.

"Hey," she murmured and stepped back. "Come on in. We have food and drinks..." She trailed off, suddenly feeling incredibly shy.

Am I still his little sister to him? Will he still call me family? Her worries knotted her stomach. She laid a hand over her belly, trying to quell the anxiety.

Rurik and his brothers remained at the edge of the kitchen as the hunters entered the spacious apartment.

Madelyn came forward, Piper right behind her as they filled the awkward void. "Welcome! I'm Madelyn, Grigori's mate, and this is Piper—she is mated to Mikhail." Madelyn held out a hand, which Damien shook.

"Damien MacQueen. This is my brother, Jason, and my team—Tamara, Nicholas, Meg, and Kathryn." He pointed at each in turn.

Finally, Rurik stepped forward, his brothers close behind him. The moment of truth.

"Glad you decided to come," Rurik said, locking eyes with Damien. "Hopefully we can avoid the handcuffs and drugs this time."

Silence fell over the room. Charlotte's eyes widened in shock, but her brother's impassive face slowly cracked a smile. It was Jason who broke the tension, however.

"In Vegas you'd have to pay extra for that."

Rurik cracked a grin. "Indeed." He then gestured to his brothers. "You haven't been formally introduced. This is Grigori, and this is Mikhail."

Grigori held out a hand to Damien just as his mate had done. "Mr. MacQueen." Damien hesitated only a moment before placing his hand in the dragon's.

Beside Grigori, Mikhail stood with his arms crossed. "I never thought I'd be in the same room as the Brotherhood, let alone offering them our hospitality, but I believe it's time for things between us to change."

"I agree. This is long overdue," Damien said. Charlotte could smell her brother's tension, a soft dark scent with just a hint of fear. It was so peculiar to be able to smell things like that now. There was so much she could pick up from sight and scent alone.

"Please, sit. My mate has insisted we serve refreshments." Grigori waved a hand at the dining room table, which was laden with trays of sandwiches and other snacks.

"Food goes a long way in peace talks," Madelyn announced. She touched her belly absently before she came over to Grigori and hugged him from behind.

"Woman, don't remind them we used to be enemies," Grigori growled, but there was a playfulness in his tone.

"Are you kidding? I had to face way worse back at Elwood University. Gun-toting monster hunters don't scare me. Try dealing with angry professors who have tenure! So let's sit and talk like rational creatures."

Meg grinned at Rurik. "Sounds good to me. First, I have some questions."

Rurik linked his fingers through Charlotte's. "Ask away."

"You love Charlotte, right?"

Damien shot her an angry glare. "I wasn't planning to lead with that, Meg."

Meg shrugged. "Hey, I've been her chaperone most of her dating life. I'm entitled to ask a few personal questions."

Rurik nodded. "I do."

"But how? You've only known her a few days," Damien said.

"And in those days, I have lived with Charlotte in ways I haven't in a thousand years. I love her for her intelligence, her compassion, her bravery, as well as her beauty. I've shared some of her memories; I have seen into her heart. It would be impossible not to love her after knowing her the way I do." The myriad emotions in his eyes filled Charlotte's soul with pure joy.

Damien looked to Grigori and Mikhail. Charlotte went rigid as he spoke.

"You're okay with him mating my sister?" Damien's voice rose in volume, and the tension around the table resumed.

"A mate is a mate," Mikhail said. "Love is love. And for us, it is destiny." He kissed Piper's hand, making the woman blush. "The bond is one that can be sensed, just like sight or smell. It is impossible not to recognize it for what it is. And our kind would never deny a mating, not when it's a gift from the gods. Charlotte is a part of our family now."

That was the wrong thing to say. Charlotte already sensed the old protectiveness rolling off of Damien. "She's not yours. She's a part of *my* family."

Meg stepped in front of her boss and placed a hand on his chest. "Uh...Damien, remember what we talked about? This is what drove her away in the first place. You keep talking about keeping an open mind, about the Brotherhood changing its ways. Well, that attitude has to start at home."

Damien locked eyes with his subordinate, ready to challenge her. Instead, he took a deep breath and nodded. "You're really okay with all of this, sis?"

Charlotte got up from her chair. "Yes. I love him. I'm part of him. And he's part of me."

Damien was still silent, uncertain, but Jason came over and pulled her into a fierce hug. "He'll spoil you, right? He'd better, if he knows what's good for him."

"Yes, he will—too much, I suspect!" She laughed and let him go. After that, everyone began to relax, even Damien.

Mikhail opened the bottles of beer and wine and filled a glass for everyone. Meg wasted no time in catching her friend up on events. Part of her couldn't believe that she was here in Rurik's apartment, the Brotherhood and the Barinovs partying...*together*.

"So this whole dragon thing...does it make you less afraid of heights?" Jason nudged her with his elbow in the way he'd always done when he'd teased her as a kid.

She considered the question. "The dragon isn't afraid when she's in charge. I trust her to keep us safe."

"She?" Meg asked. "I'm a little confused. Someone said that you and Rurik share the same dragon soul. I mean, let's back up and get to the question everyone really wants to ask: *What the hell happened to you?*"

Charlotte frowned. So much of that other world had faded from her memory, like she wasn't supposed to remember. Snow, dragons, shadows, fire... Was it real or some kind of dream realm between worlds?

"It's hard to explain. I was...somewhere else. Rurik was dying, and the only way I could save him was by giving my life to him. To fill the void left behind, some of his dragon came into me. We are the same dragon."

"Then how is your half a she?"

"Any psychologist will tell you that we all have a masculine and feminine side," said Madelyn, leaning in. "My guess is that the soul divided along those lines."

Sitting on another sofa with Piper, Mikhail spoke up. "It's true. Charlotte's dragon did not just look feminine, she looked *supremely* feminine." This got him a glare from his mate. Mikhail coughed. "Perhaps I should have said *too* feminine."

"Perhaps you should have."

"Yes, and Rurik looks more masculine than ever," said Madelyn, which earned her an equally harsh glare from Grigori. Dragon shifters and jealousy seemed to go hand in hand.

"That's so crazy." Jason sipped his Russian beer.

Damien, on the other hand, looked at Charlotte with a sad smile. "Do you guys mind if I have a moment with Charlotte?"

"Sure." Jason gave her another quick hug and then went to join Grigori and Kathryn, who were already in animated conversation. Kathryn was spinning her hands to weave a small spell for the oldest Barinov dragon, which he seemed to find fascinating. Charlotte turned her focus back to Damien, and her eyes, so much sharper now, didn't miss the lines of weariness around his eyes and the sorrow in his gaze.

"I fucked things up royally, little sis." He rubbed the back of his neck with his hand and ducked his head. "I came into Moscow guns blazing, ready to kill for you, and that wasn't the answer to the problem."

Charlotte stiffened. "Problem?" He thought she and Rurik being mated was still a problem?

"Yeah, the problem of your unhappiness. It's my fault. I kept you caged your entire life. I didn't trust you to be strong like I know you are. I tried to convince myself you were helpless and that you needed me. I guess losing Serena made me half-crazy when it comes to protecting those I love."

"Just half?" Charlotte tried to tease, but her throat was tight.

"Okay, completely crazy." His rueful smile tore at her heart. "My point is, I was wrong, Jason was wrong. We shouldn't have shut you out of our lives, even the dangerous parts. You are strong enough—hell, *more* than strong enough—to handle it all on your own. And it's our fault we didn't want to acknowledge that." His gaze met hers before his focus flicked over to Rurik.

"I love him, really love him, Damien." She touched her brother's arm. "But just because I'm a dragon shifter now, it doesn't mean I'm not your baby sister anymore."

Damien chuckled and let out a long sigh, looking sideways at Rurik out in the living room with the others.

"As much as I want to punch him, I have to give him credit." Damien's smile was rueful. "I watched him leap out of that window, not knowing if he would be able to save you. It's not what I expected from a dragon, but he did it because he loves you."

Charlotte blushed at Damien's words. It was always awkward to talk to her brothers about love, but especially Damien because he was more like a father to her than a brother.

"And I have to apologize to him too." He scrubbed a hand over his jaw. "What we did to Rurik and to you... I'm just so sorry. Jason and I were completely overreacting assholes." The pain in his hazel eyes filled her with an echoing sympathy. "I've tried so hard to make the Brotherhood different from the old days, and yesterday... yesterday I almost took us down that same path."

"I was so mad at you," she whispered. "But when you love someone, you do crazy things to keep them safe."

Damien looked down at the floor, defeated in a way she'd never seen before. She flung her arms around him, squeezing him tight.

"All is forgiven," she promised. "But you have to let me go. I'll always be your sister, but I'm my own woman. I always have been."

"I know. And you're part of Rurik now. You need him as much as he needs you. And he's good to you."

"He's good *for* me," she corrected gently, letting go of her brother. "With him around I don't just live, I feel alive. Does that make sense?"

Damien nodded, looking back to Rurik, who was laughing at whatever Meg and Tamara were telling him.

"So you stay with him," Damien said. "A dangerous battle dragon. He better not put you in any more danger."

She couldn't help but grin. "You don't get it, do you? I'm a battle dragon now too."

"I know, but—"

"And it's more than that. We're the same dragon, just different parts. We're like two arms of the same body. Can you imagine how much more dangerous that makes us?" She smiled at him, feeling a power and confidence she'd never had before. "You won't have to worry about me, Damien. Trust me."

"The Barinovs have enemies," he countered.

"And so does the Brotherhood." She touched arm. "But as of now, the Barinovs and the Brotherhood are on the same side. And with luck, maybe we'll get some other factions out there to see the light too. This shadow war that's existed for so long between humans, shifters, and the corruptions like werewolves and vampires? It all stems from a lack of communication. You know that."

"Who knew my sister would end up being wiser than her big brother?" Damien chuckled, looking back at the ongoing party. "Or that my in-laws would be fire-breathing dragons?"

"This is going to change everything. Between our families, we can stop the Silvas and the Drakors out there. The ones who don't believe in coexistence, only control."

Her brother nodded. "The world needs a safer path, and we will make it." He leaned in and kissed her forehead. "Just promise me you'll be happy with him."

"I promise." Life with Rurik was everything she'd dreamed of having.

"Good. Now let's get back to the party before Jason finds a way to embarrass himself."

Charlotte smiled. "Sure. But, Damien…" Her older brother—a man who carried the weight of the world on his shoulders—deserved that happiness too. She only hoped he would be brave enough to let a woman back into his heart.

"Yeah?"

She wiped her eyes. "Don't be afraid to love again. Serena can't be the only woman out there for you. You can find someone else who will love you as much as she did."

He chucked her under the chin like she was a little girl, and with a sad smile he said, "It's too late for me, sweetheart."

She watched him join the others and closed her eyes, thinking of the land of snow where her lover's heart had been guarded. But the storm was gone. The snow fell softly around her. In her mind, she touched the fiery heart. *Their* heart.

"Charlotte?" She opened her eyes. Rurik was at her side, arms wrapped around her waist. The scar down his cheek was a thin pink line that she barely noticed. Somehow it had healed more since she'd shared her life with him. She focused on the crinkle of laughter around his eyes and the way he said her name with a gentle reverence.

"Hi," she whispered, biting her bottom lip.

He cupped her face in his hands. "Hi," he echoed. She reached up to curl her fingers around his wrists as he held her face. There was something she'd been waiting to tell him since she'd woken up. Now felt right.

"When I was trying to save you…" She sought the words to explain what she'd seen. "I was in a snowy world, and I saw your beating heart, like a living flame. I don't remember much, but there were dragons all around me, welcoming you home. But one was urging me to reach you, to save you. She called me *little one*."

Rurik's gaze sharpened. "She called you *little one*?"

Charlotte nodded. "Just like you do. She was green, like your eyes."

His eyes softened, the jade color turning into a delicate seafoam green. "Mother," he mused. "It must have been."

"She told me to hold your heart and never let go." She curled one arm around his neck, pulling his head down to hers. "And I don't intend to."

She tasted a smile upon his lips, the kiss they shared full of an inner fire that they had felt from the moment they first met. When their lips finally parted, she glanced back at the party, which seemed to be going better than either of them had expected.

"The Capulets and Montagues will survive together after all," she said. "Thank God for that."

Her dragon grinned back at her. "Thus, with a kiss, we live." And with that, his mouth captured hers.

Wait! Don't turn off your e-reader! I have some awesome news to share with you super quick plus a 3 chapter

preview of *Grigori: A Royal Dragon Romance* which is the first book in the series!

Don't worry this isn't the end! I promise more sexy dragonshifter romances are on the way! Stay tuned to the very END of this book to see the cover for the *The Lost Barinov Dragon*!

I give away 3 FREE romance novels! Fill out the form at the bottom of this link and you'll get an email from me with details to collect your free read! The free books are *Wicked Designs* (Historical romance), *Legally Charming* (contemporary romance) and *The Bite of Winter* (paranormal romance).

Claim your free books now at:
http://laurensmithbooks.com/free-books-and-newsletter/
Here's were you can find me on social media!
My Main Website
Facebook
Instagram
Twitter
Private Facebook Fan Group
Wattpad
I share upcoming book news, snippets and cover reveals plus PRIZES on all of the above places!

NEVER MISS A NEW BOOK OR A DISCOUNTED BOOK! FOLLOW ME HERE FOR ALERTS:
Amazon
Bookbub

Turn the page to read 3 chapters from *Grigori: A Royal Dragon Romance* now!

RURIK: A ROYAL DRAGON ROMANCE

GRIGORI

LAUREN SMITH

BROTHERS OF ASH AND FIRE

GRIGORI: A ROYAL DRAGON ROMANCE

CHAPTER 1

"*Here there be dragons.*"

—Note on a map from the Age of Exploration, regarding Terra Incognito.

Blue and silver scales whispered against grass as the giant beast crawled across the field toward Madelyn Haynes. Rain lashed her skin and lightning laced the skies. Smoke billowed from the beast's nostrils, and his amber eyes narrowed to dangerous slits as it crept closer. There was no escaping. The creature had finally found her and would destroy her. It had already killed tonight and would kill again. Ash infused the air, the scent of smoke choking her. Fear and rage filled her, drowning her with the overwhelming sensations until she was torn between two instincts: fight or flight. Her skin tingled, the feeling building until it felt like she was on fire.

A man was shouting . . . *"Run!"*

The beast turned away from her, searching for the person who'd cried out a warning but it was no use. The creature would kill her too once it found her.

There was no way she would survive. She was going to die . . .

"*No!*" The word was a silent scream upon her lips as she tried to run.

Boom!

Madelyn jolted upright, her mouth open in a strangled shout. The covers of her bed were wrapped around her legs, and she kicked out trying to free herself. Panting, she clutched her head as a dull throbbing ache beat behind her temples. She breathed in and out, focusing on each breath and the tranquility it gave her before the headache subsided and her heart stopped pounding against her ribs.

Then she turned on the light by the bed in her small hotel room and reached for her sketch pad and pencil. Using pillows to prop herself up she flicked to a fresh page and began to draw. The lines came easily, as they always did when she had the nightmares of the beast. It left such a vivid image in her mind that she had no trouble bringing it to life on the page. As the sketch began to develop, she knew what she would see. A serpentine creature with an elegant snout, two large wings and a long tail that could snap back and forth like a whip.

A dragon.

For as long as she could remember, whenever it rained, she dreamed of that same dragon. Rain, scales, lightning, and a crashing sonic boom that rattled her awake.

Madelyn studied tonight's dragon. It was blue and silver with a deep sapphire underbelly. The webbing of its wings was a fainter, almost icy blue. It had a large, almost lizard-like frill that fanned up around its head like a lion's mane which was that same glacial blue as its wings. It was an eerily beautiful creature with fierce eyes and sharp talons and was in a predatory crouch as though ready to hunt her down. Madelyn's hand trembled as she set the pencil down and stared at the dragon. A part of her had hoped that leaving the United States—and changing her surroundings—would make her feel less trapped, less hunted. But the nightmares had followed her.

She was still being hunted.

She'd come all the way to Russia to save her career. As a professor in medieval mythology, she had been reading and researching dragons for the last five years. But lately she'd become convinced, as insane as it sounded, that dragons might have been real at some point in history. She was hoping to prove that some remnants of dinosaurs had remained alive into the time of humans, and that could explain the unique collection of global mythology around dragons. How else could dragon myths around the world have such eerie similarities? Something told her there was a kernel of truth to each myth she'd come across, but she had to find a way to prove it.

Or else I'm fired.

Ellwood University had given her a three-month sabbatical to either pursue her theory and prove it, or drop it and attempt to tie her research to more traditional projects. Madelyn had collected her meager savings and rented this hotel room by the month in the Tverskaya district of Moscow.

Outside her window she could see the distance lights of the city and hear the low steady hum of traffic. Moscow was so different from her small town of Shelby, Michigan. Instead of a Russian concrete jungle and tangle of complex cityscapes and police sirens at night, the Midwestern air was filled with the hum of crickets and the throaty songs of frogs in the ponds. Some nights the breeze from Lake Michigan would slip through the windows and soothe her as she slept. Even the winters in Michigan felt pure, clean, not like the dark, dirty snow-covered streets of post-soviet Moscow.

With a shiver of longing for home, Madelyn set the sketchbook aside and glanced at the clock. It was 6 AM. There was little point in staying in bed for another hour. She had to visit the Russian State Library and a few small antiquarian bookstores which could take up most of the day. She'd been here one week and had settled into a routine. *Sleep. Research. Eat. Research. Home. Sleep.*

She had come to Moscow alone and was hesitant about going

out on her own after dark. She spent most of her evenings cuddled up in the armchair by her bed, reading. It was certainly safer than going out. Madelyn needed to feel safe. She feared the unknown, and what might be around the corner.

A therapist had once diagnosed her airily with a generalized fear of the unknown, citing trauma from her parents' deaths. She had been two years old, too young to remember the details though she'd been with them when they'd died. Too young to know her own name or where she came from. Neither of her parents had IDs when the police found her in the wrecked car that had rolled into a ditch during a storm. Her name, "Madelyn", had come from the name stitched onto her baby blanket. Her adoptive parents, the Haynes's, had wanted her to keep that name.

Thoughts of her birth parents always made Madelyn sad and oddly helpless. She wished she could have done something to save them from the car crash. She knew that there was nothing a baby could have done, but it didn't erase the helplessness. For a long moment, Madelyn watched the rain outside and rubbed one hand absently on her chest where her heart ached. And then, she did what she'd always done. She buried the memories and the pain and turned her thoughts to her research. It was the best distraction. There was nothing like wandering through the stacks of a library and letting the musty scent of ancient books overwhelm her. It was one of the reasons she'd been drawn to history when she was in college. Surrounding herself with the past, she knew what had happened, and couldn't be shocked or surprised . . . was comforting.

Madelyn crawled out of bed and stripped out of her clothes before she jumped into the small shower, cringing as she expected the icy blast of the spray. There was only so much hot water before it turned cold she couldn't stand a cold shower in October in Russia.

Two hours later, she was dressed and had filled her backpack with notebooks and other research related materials. When she stepped out on the street in front of her hotel, her nose twitched as it picked up the harsh scents of the city. People bustled past her in a frenzied haste to reach their jobs, and for a strange moment Madelyn felt rooted in place as humanity flowed around her. An eerie sense of being watched made the tiny hairs on the back of her neck raise up.

Of course she was being watched. This city was home to millions of people; someone would always be looking at her no matter what. The uneasy sensation inside her didn't disappear, even when she hailed a cab and headed for the Russian State Library.

The State Library was a beautiful architectural cross between Soviet era design and classical design, which called back the days of the Czars. The smell of musty texts and recently cleaned marble steps were a welcome mix of aromas that always calmed Madelyn.

She walked up the white stairs to the upper decks of the library, her eyes dancing from the blue marble columns to the endless shelves.

17.5 million books were here . . . Her heart sped up at the sheer thought of having a world of infinite stories at her fingertips. But she wasn't here to see their vast array of novels. She was here for one book. A heavily guarded tome that required supervision whenever it was handled.

She kept walking and left the modern rooms behind before reaching a wing of the library that housed antiquarian collections. One of the collection areas was a beautiful two-story room with gleaming walnut bookcases illuminated by hanging golden globes of light. A slightly domed ceiling was painted with scenes of Greek mythology, the gods on Olympus displaying their power and might.

A security guard stood at the back of the room by a small reception desk and he waved her over. He greeted her with a warm smile and spoke something in Russian which she thought sounded like hello. She was still listening to her Russian audiotapes and hadn't picked it up as quickly as she'd hoped.

"Good morning," she greeted back. He was different than the guard from yesterday.

"Ahh, English, I help you?" he asked in with a heavy Russian accent.

Madelyn smiled. She'd been relieved to discover that many of the guards were fluent in English to a degree. She knew enough of modern Russian to get by but her specialty was the rare dialect East Old Slavic which she used to read older Russian primary resources.

"I'd like to check this book out please." She retrieved a small piece of paper with the name of the edition in English and Russian and its location on the shelves. The guard read the card and then his brown eyes looked from it to her face, studying her.

"This volume? You are sure?" he asked, his voice was oddly hushed and his face drained of color. He stroked his security badge on his chest with one finger as though he'd done it a thousand times when nervous. He glanced around the room, which was almost entirely empty save for another researcher, an elderly man, who was buried in a stack of what looked to be medieval texts. The man glanced up at them, squinted, and pushed his glasses up his nose before returning to his work. The guard stared at the man for a long moment before he turned his focus back to Madelyn.

"Please, miss, I could get many other books for you, but this one... Are you sure?" It was the second time he'd asked that question, and it made her skin prickle.

"Yes. That one." Madelyn assured him. Why was he so protective of this one? This entire room was filled with ancient texts that with proper care could be viewed by researchers. The guard sighed slowly, his face turning red as he nodded to himself and muttered in Russian.

Now she was feeling really anxious. She'd checked out several tomes yesterday but hadn't discovered this particular text until she was pouring over the ancient collection of card catalogues that looked as though they'd been written half a century before. There on the yellowed paper of the cards, in ink that was turning brown, she'd read the name of the volume *My Year With Dragons*. The library had been about to close and she only had time to scribble down the book's information before a guard politely escorted her out of antiquarian collection area. Surely today this guard would let her check it out . . . it was just a book after all.

The guard stared at the card again and then nodded. "*Dah*, okay, we get you this one. Sit, please." He pointed to a small research table near one of the vast glass windows. Then he took a card and walked over to the shelves on the opposite side of the room.

While he retrieved the book, Madelyn set out her notebook and pens with shaking hands before she donned a pair of library approved white gloves to handle the books safely. Why was the guard so hesitant to give it to her? From the text's description in the card catalogue that she'd be able to translate, it was a memoir of an English man who had spent time in Russia. There was no political or social discourse in it that could prompt a Russian security officer to be concerned . . . But he had been. The man had looked ill at the thought of fetching that tome.

She peeped at the guard from the corner of her eye. He unlocked a glass case on one of the shelves, his head cocked to the side as he squinted at the titles on the spines. Then he used his index finger to gently tug a shorter leather-bound edition free of the case. Once he had it in his hands, he didn't immediately come over to her. For several seconds he stood there, holding the book and staring at her. His lips were pressed tight in a grimace as he finally walked over to her.

"Please be careful. This is special book." He held out the leather bound tome and Madelyn accepted it. Her skin tingled again as she felt the smooth leather in her palms but she hid her reaction. The guard nodded at her again and then walked back to his station.

Madelyn's skin continued to tingle as she lifted the leather tome to get a closer look. The cover was made of thick leather, bare of any titles or identifying marks except the initials *J.B.* in the bottom right corner. Madelyn smoothed her fingertips over the initials and opened the front cover. The title was written on the front page in pen and ink. Not in typeface.

My Year With Dragons—A personal collection of observations about my time spent with the Barinov family, by James Barrow. Dated 1821.

Madelyn whispered the words. It was written in English, and James Barrow could be English or American. She held the text in one hand and made a note in her notebook before she turned to the next page.

Her heart stuttered to a stop in her chest.

Three pencil sketches depicted the faces of three different men. Names were scrawled beneath each intimate portrait.

Mikhail, Rurik and Grigori. The Barinov Brothers.

The first man, Mikhail, seemed more brooding, his hair dark and his eyes almost black. He seemed worried, but he was attractive and even the shadows that haunted his eyes were enchanting. In the second drawing, the man named Rurik had dark hair and mischievous eyes, with a playful, charming grin on his lips that outshone the white scar drawn from above his right eyebrow down to his cheek as though he'd been slashed. He looked like a bit of a troublemaker but the thought made her smile.

Her eyes lingered longest over the sketch of the man named Grigori. Something about him stilled her, like the moment she stood outside on the first snowfall of winter. There was a strange whispering at the back of her mind, a collection of hushed voices that she couldn't seem to hear clearly enough to understand. She was fascinated by the man's handsome face, the pale hair and light eyes. There was a melancholy beauty to his lips, and an almost rueful smile barely hinted in the drawing—as though he had sat still long enough to assist the artist but as soon as he was able, he'd move again.

While all three men were intriguing, it was Grigori that Madelyn's eyes came back to over and over. Something about his face . . . Like a half-remembered dream. Deep inside her, there was a stirring, as though a part of her she never knew existed had awoken. The voices didn't stop that whispering and Madelyn couldn't help but wonder if she was going mad. Between the dreams at night and now this . . . She drew a deep breath in and let it out, slow and measured, calming herself.

Stay focused on the research.

"Grigori," she test his name upon her lips, finding she liked the way it sounded, the syllables strong and yet soft.

She wanted this sketch. The compulsion to possess his likeness was too strong. She glanced about the room and saw the guard was on his phone, texting and not looking her way. Sneaking her cell phone out, she flicked on the camera and snapped a hasty picture of each of the brothers before she put it back in her purse. Hands trembling, she turned the page again, forcing herself to look totally calm and not like she'd been taking photographs of a protected manuscript.

The next page was a diary entry dated March 16, 1821.

"Dragons are real . . ." The first words of the entry made her body shiver and a sudden chill shot down her spine. She forced herself to keep reading and couldn't help but wonder what James Barrow meant. Dragons weren't real, at least not in the fire and brimstone sense. She was convinced that some extinct reptile species were behind the legends, but there was no such thing as *real* dragons.

"I met the Barinov brothers in Moscow and learned they were not mortal men . . . they were possessed of strange abilities. The touch of fire, the breath of smoke, the eyes that glowed . . ."

What the hell? Madelyn reread the last few sentences. What was Barrow saying? She'd expected the volume to recount tales of large serpents or lizards that Barrow must have encountered on his journey. As a naturalist, he would have been out in the field exploring different species of animals, and he could have easily glimpsed an ancient breed of reptile that looked dragon-like. The Komodo dragon was a modern example of what many rural cultures still believed were the descendants of dragons. It was part of her theory for her research. But Barrow wasn't talking about Komodos or any other type of reptile. He was discussing men . . .

Men who had powers. Perhaps the word dragon was simply a metaphor Barrow was using?

She glanced down the page and saw a smaller drawing of a man's hand and what looked like an elaborate ring. When Madelyn peered at it more closely, she recognized the style. The metal of the ring had been formed into the shape of a serpent biting its own tail, the symbol for eternity or the cycle of renewal. An *ouroboros*. Another dragon connection, but still not the type of dragon she was searching for.

Rather than read the rest of the journal entry, she turned the next several pages and paused when she came across a full page sketch. The drawing of a sleek, serpentine beast perched on a rock outcropping overlooking the sea made her breath catch as much as Grigori's portrait had. The beast sat back on its haunches and its large wings were flared wide, the clawed tips arching outward as though it was ready to fly. A barb-tipped tail curled around its legs. It was both a beautiful beast and a creature of nightmares, with gleaming teeth ready to snap. Reptilian slitted eyes stared straight ahead at her. The beast in her dreams came rushing back, the hiss of smoke escaping the nostrils, the puffs of breath as he prepared to spew fire, the lashing tail . . .

Beneath the sketch was one word. *"Grigori."*

But the sketch was of a man, not a dragon . . . Was this one of the men with supposed powers?

Whatever this journal was, it was clearly the workings of a man prone to flights of fancy and not a real naturalist. Disappointment made her heart drop to her feet and her shoulders slump. She'd been so hopeful to find a book that could show an anthropological connection to the dinosaurs or explain the worldwide dragon mythology. But this journal was not the answer.

Even though she wanted to keep reading, it wasn't a good idea. Many a good scholar who lost their way down a strange research rabbit hole had to find their way back to good solid research. She refused to let this one odd little book stump her. Better to put it back and move on. Still . . . she wanted just a few more photographs of the book; it couldn't hurt to read it over as long as she didn't use it for her research.

She surreptitiously took pictures of the next twenty pages before she hid her cellphone back in her backpack. Closing the book, she started at the leather surface, wishing she didn't have to give it back. Indecision flitted through her, but there was no real choice. It wasn't hers, and she couldn't keep it. With a sigh, she rose from her research table and walked back over to the security station and held the book out the guard.

"Finished?" he asked, his eyes fixing on the book rather than her as though he was anxious to snatch it out of her hands.

"Yes, it wasn't what I was looking for." She almost didn't let go when he tried to pull the book away from her. Finally the leather journal slipped through her fingers.

"Thank you," she said to the guard. With a heavy heart, she returned to her study station and collected her notebooks and papers before removing her gloves and tucking them back in her bag. Each step away from Barrow's mysterious journal left her feeling cold and distanced in a way that made little sense. A soft feminine voice, like the hum of a murmur from a dream teased her mind.

He has the answers but you're too afraid to see...

Madelyn shook off the thought. The notes in Barrow's journal were impossible to believe. He clearly didn't know what he was talking about. He was rambling on about men with powerful abilities and drawing beasts more suited to a role-playing fantasy computer game than he was about creatures that tied to real mythology.

She would have to start back at the catalog again, but she had no energy to hunch over the little metal filing cabinets squinting at poorly scribbled titles and book descriptions the rest of the day.

Maybe I could take a day off. Wander around the library a bit and explore.

The architecture was beautiful and she hadn't really had a chance to examine it before. As she exited the antiquarian room she glanced back one last time. The security guard was holding the journal, and he was speaking into his cell phone. He was also staring right at *her*.

That sense of being watched and being talked about was too strong this time to ignore. The guard said something into the phone and rather than put the book back on its shelf, he set it down and put a hand on his gun holster at his hip.

"Miss, please come back," he said, taking a meaningful step in her direction. "My superior wishes to speak to you. You cannot leave."

"He does? Why?" she asked, her muscles tensing and her hands tightening on her bag.

"The book you chose, he has questions . . ." The guard said, his gaze darting around her as though expecting someone to come and help him. "Sit down, now." His tone was more forceful than before.

Madelyn knew she should stay put, talk to him . . . but her instincts suddenly roared to life and the only thought that flashed through her head was *run . . . run fast*. Body shaking, she stumbled on trembling legs to flee.

She shoved open the door and sprinted down the hall, hitting the top of the long set of stairs at a brisk run. Everything around her seemed to blur, and her heart was pounding hard enough to explode from her chest. Covering the steps in seconds, she forced herself to slow when she realized people were staring at her. That was the last thing she needed, people seeing a panicked woman fleeing a Russian library like a crazy person. It was a conspiracy theory in the making.

Her breath was labored and her body was shaking with a surge of adrenaline as she tried to walk calmly out of the library. The crowded streets were a blessing as she melted into the flow of people. She only looked back once and caught a glimpse of the security guard from the collections room. He stood at the top of the Russian State Library steps, his gaze scanning the crowd. He was still on his cell phone, talking rapidly.

Lowering herself by hunching over, Madelyn slipped down a

side street to catch her breath. What the hell just happened? Sure, she'd snuck a few pictures of a text, but why would he chase her? She hadn't seen any rules about no photography in that section of the library. Why had the guard chased her?

What about James Barrow's book was so dangerous that men would look for her?

Grigori's face and the body of the fierce dragon like beast flashed across her mind. *What have I stumbled onto?*

CHAPTER 2

"PEACE, KENT! COME NOT BETWEEN THE DRAGON AND HIS WRATH." —WILLIAM SHAKESPEARE, THE TRAGEDY OF KING LEAR

Grigori Barinov stood in front of the floor-to-ceiling windows in his executive office, staring out over the city of Moscow. Body alert, every muscle rigid, the expensive gray wool suit he wore felt tight as he shifted. Below him, people were passing on the streets. A flash of silver caught his attention. It was the wink of a diamond earring dangling from a well-dressed woman's ear. With eyes that were ten times as powerful as a mortal's, he scanned the streets, absorbing every detail.

Searching...

For the last few days, his senses had picked up on something in his city. A creature he didn't recognize. It made him restless. Moscow was filled with supernatural beings—werewolves, vampires, shifters of all kinds, and magically gifted humans were all present—but none of them fired up his instincts. No, he'd never felt this before in his life, but he knew in his gut what it was. An enemy was in his city, a creature that posed a threat to him. As a dragonshifter, few creatures in this world could give him pause and put him on his guard. He only wished he knew what sort of beast it was so he could hunt it down and remove the threat.

The sapphire dragon tattoo on his forearm itched, but he

didn't scratch it. He knew the dragon inside of him was trying to warn him to stay on his guard. The phone on his desk buzzed and his personal assistant, Alexis spoke.

"Mr. Barinov, you have a call from the Russian State Library."

Every muscle in his body tensed. There was only one reason anyone from the Russian State Library would be calling him. That damn book by James Barrow. He'd been too softhearted and Barrow had been so earnest. He'd gone against his better judgment and allowed the Englishman to spend a year studying him and his brothers. And he'd been paying for it for the last 200 years. He'd been lucky Barrow's heirs had sent him the journal. Thankfully, it had never been sent to a publisher; Barrow had kept his word about his writings remaining a secret.

I should've burned it. But he hadn't been able to. Barrow had become a friend and Grigori hadn't wanted to destroy the memory. There was also something fascinating about reading an insightful human's observations about him and his brothers.

He couldn't leave it at his office or his home in the country. His enemies had frequently broken into both places more than once, searching for anything they could use against him. He'd thought he'd be clever and tuck it away in a library amid other obscure texts that no one ever looked at in a guarded collection. It had been safe all these years, hiding in plain sight. Until now.

"Mr. Barinov?" Alexis queried again.

"Put the call through." He turned away from the window and walked over to his mahogany desk just as the phone rang.

He answered. "Yes?"

"Mr. Barinov, my name is Yuri. I'm a guard for antiquarian book room at the Russian State Library." A man spoke, his voice hushed and anxious.

"Yes." Grigori waited, his patience on a razor's edge.

"When I first took over security for this room I was given strict and confidential instructions to call you if anyone ever came asking about a certain title in the collection. Someone checked out the *Barrow* book, Mr. Barinov."

Grigori closed his eyes, holding his breath for a moment. "And?"

"I followed protocol. She did not leave the library with the book. But . . ." The guard hesitated. "She was taking pictures. I have no instructions regarding pictures." The phone cracked as Grigori's temper flared.

"Pictures?"

"Yes. She was using her phone." The guard's voice wavered as though he sensed Grigori's building rage.

Pictures. Fuck, if any evidence of his existence was discovered and exposed in the world of mortals it would put a target on his back and that of his two brothers. The magical world knew of his family, the last three brothers in ancient bloodline of Russian Imperial Dragon shifters, but the rest of the world didn't know . . . *Couldn't know.*

"Can you detain her until I arrive?" he asked the guard.

"But she's leaving now—"

"Stop her!" Grigori barked. The other end of the phone was full of panting, the flapping of rubber soled shoes on marble, a muffled shout for someone to stop. Grigori tried to picture the library in his mind, wondering why the guard couldn't catch up with this woman. Finally the footsteps stopped, and Grigori heard the sounds of streets of the city muted beneath the guard's gasping for breath.

"She ran—I couldn't catch her before she left the library. She's gone. But I have the book."

Grigori sighed. "I will come to collect it. When I do, I want every detail you have about this woman. Her name, where she's from, *everything.*"

"Yes, Mr. Barinov," the guard replied, still breathless.

Grigori slammed the phone down and cursed. His hand was white-hot from his temper and he'd left burn marks on his expensive new phone. With a growl, he pressed the intercom button

"Alexis, please have someone replace my phone in the office. This one met with an unfortunate accident."

A second later his receptionist opened the door, leaning against it to look at him in concern. His dragon perked up beneath his skin at the sight of the woman's killer legs. She was staring at him, the perpetually hungry look in her eyes always an open invitation to share her bed, but he'd never once been tempted. Sure, he'd noticed, and his instincts, so close to the surface, never let him ignore a beautiful woman. But things had changed over the last hundred years. His skin didn't prickle with awareness and excitement. His dragon didn't growl with arousal the way it had in his youth.

No one had truly tempted him enough in a long time to let his bestial urges run free. Had he been in a better mood a smile would have curved his lips. As a younger dragon, he would have bedded several succulent mortals in a day, breaking bed frames as he gripped the wood to keep from harming the females while he fucked them into oblivion. Now his bed was empty of companions, but he wouldn't sleep with just any woman. Not anymore.

"Another accident Mr. Barinov?" Alexis purred as she approached his desk.

"Yes, please order me a replacement."

"Of course." She held out a hand and he handed over the destroyed phone.

Her expensive perfume rolled off her in thick waves. The decayed floral aromas made his nose twitch even as she walked out of his office and closed the door behind her. He never liked perfumes. A woman's natural scent was a heady thing and shouldn't be ruined with perfumes.

He could almost hear his younger brother, Rurik, teasing him. *"As if you know anything about women anymore. You haven't had a woman in over a decade, brother..."*

It was true. He found women less and less appealing these last few centuries. His urge to mate, to find the one female in the world that was truly his, had started to drive him mad with frustration. When a dragon reached a certain age, they stopped running wild and craved the closeness of a long-term companion. Most dragons never found their true mates and settled to simply breed with other dragons for the sake of children and to cure loneliness.

His gaze dropped to a framed photo on his desk. It was one of the few of his parents in existence, from thirty years ago, just a few years before they died.

If I could be as lucky as them and find a true mate...

No mere woman would suit him. It had to be the right one, one chosen for him by destiny. He would know her by her addictive scent that would send his pulse racing and his blood pounding. If he kissed her, he would catch glimpses of her memories and she would see his. A bond would form the longer they spent together, making them inseparable.

I want that more than anything...

He was not going to be tempted by Alexis or any other woman. They would only pale in comparison to a woman who would truly belong to him. He wanted a woman of his own, one to share his heart and soul with. Despite being alive for almost three thousand years, he still hadn't found the one woman that was meant to be his.

The sad fact was he couldn't wait any longer. His once great family, the Barinovs, had included almost a thousand dragons.

Now we are only three. We are a dying breed.

The loneliness he was facing was slowly killing him, an immortal creature. The idea was almost laughable but it was true. A longing for a true mate had haunted him to the point that he was dreaming about her and waking up in the dark, his arms aching for a woman who was never there. He might never find the woman destiny had made for him. It was time to settle, and find a dragoness who could bare him children and continue the line, even if it meant he'd never know true love and completion.

"Mr. Barinov, is there anything else I can do for you?" Alexis asked, her suggestive tone telling him in no uncertain terms that she was offering herself to him if he was interested, which again, he wasn't. She wasn't his type. He liked his women with soft curves, a little petite with sunny smiles and warm hearts. He hadn't met a woman like that in Russian in over a hundred years . . . He was tired of Alexis throwing herself at him when he continually turned her down.

"No." He almost growled the word. Frustration slithered beneath his skin making him irritable enough to snap at her.

Alexis blinked, her face pale as a sheet as she backed out of the room. Smart woman. Dragons tempers were nasty things and it was best to stay clear when a dragon was fuming.

He pulled out his cell phone and dialed one of the few numbers he called with any frequency.

"Grigori? What's up?" His younger brother answered, his voice half-laughing as though he'd been chuckling when he'd answered the phone. The thought made Grigori's temper deflate somewhat as affection for Rurik swelled in his chest.

"Rurik, we have a situation."

"What is it? The Drakor family again?" His brother's tone turned gruff and serious.

Grigori stroked his chin as he replied. "No. They are abiding by our current treaty and staying to the eastern half of Russia." It was true enough. The Drakors were notorious for their egos, and if they had been causing trouble in his territory, he would have heard about it.

Rurik blew out disappointed breath. "I miss the battles. What I wouldn't give for the Drakors to put one foot on our soil . . ."

"You battle dragons," Grigori was torn between groaning and laughing. "Always wanting to start a fight." He loved his little brother, but he was the first to jump without looking—which often put their family in tense situations when it came to matters of diplomacy with other dragons.

Rurik was the family warrior, the one best suited for battle and to wage single combat against other dragons when territorial disputes arose. The Drakors were the other Russian Imperial breed of shifters that vied for dominance of Russia against his family. The Barinovs and Drakors had been enemies for centuries.

"So if it's not the Drakors, what's the matter?"

"Remember James Barrow?" Grigori turned back to his window once again, searching in vain for the creature he sensed but could not see.

"Of course. The Englishman who visited us in the Fire Hills. He was always drawing and scribbling away in that leather journal."

"Yes. A woman was taking pictures of his journal today at the Russian State Library."

"Fuck. That can't be good . . ."

"My thoughts exactly," Grigori affirmed. The journal was almost a handbook on dragons—their powers, their weaknesses—and it had dozens of pictures of the three of them specifically. They might as well have put a neon sign above his building saying *"Real Dragons Inside!"*

"Do you think she believes what he wrote down about us is true?"

"I have no idea, but no reason she has could be a good one. I'm going to the Library to collect the book now and learn everything I can about the woman who took the pictures. I want you to help me track her down."

"Meet me at the club once you have the book." Rurik hung up and Grigori slipped his phone back into the pocket of his trousers before he turned away from the window.

As he left his office, he ignored Alexis's hopeful wave and he took the elevator down to the first floor. Barinov Industries, the family company he created a hundred years ago, had withstood wars, famine, and the many regime changes of Russian governments over the years.

He was not going to let one woman with a cell phone camera destroy his empire. For the last eighty years especially, Grigori had suffered the charade of "retiring" every thirty years and leaving the company to his son, also named Grigori. He'd spend the next few decades pretending to age, dying his hair silver and having new passports and forged birth certificates. The intricate lies he laid in place to keep the company going had cost him time and energy. He would not let his work be ruined by some overly curious human female.

His car was pulled out in front with his driver ready to take him anywhere he wished.

"The Russian State Library," he ordered as he settled in the black leather seat of the sedan.

"Yes, Mr. Barinov." The driver pulled out in traffic and began to head towards the library.

Grigori barely looked at the passing scenery of Moscow, his entire being focused on this mystery woman. Why was she researching dragons, and how had she found out about Barrow's journal? She shouldn't have even been allowed to take it off the shelf. Grigori acquainted himself with the new library director and informed him that should anyone ask for the book he must be called immediately and they were not to check it out. The guard had clearly failed in his duties and Grigori would make sure the library director would have him fired.

The time had come to take Barrow's book home and destroy it once and for all. While he had fond memories of Barrow, the details and personal histories of him and his brothers must be protected and that meant burning the book to ash. And dealing with this woman.

The only mortals who knew of his existence, aside from the ones in service to his family, were supernatural hunters. Namely the international organization called the Brotherhood of the Blood Moon. Pesky creatures, hunters. They rarely came into dragon guarded territories; it was simply too dangerous. Maybe this woman was a hunter, or they had hired her to find and retrieve any info she could on his family. If that was the case, he had a very nice dungeon she could rot away in for the next fifty years.

"Here we are, Mr. Barinov."

Grigori climbed out and told the driver to wait for him. Then he quickly ascended the stairs and entered the library. The guard, Yuri, was waiting for him at the security desk.

"Mr. Barinov?" Yuri held out the faded leather bound journal and Grigori took it.

The leather was warm to the touch and he lifted it to his nose, inhaling. A lingering scent teased his nostrils, the feminine aroma inviting and enticing. For a long second Grigori simply drank in the rich smell . . . it was *pure*. The pheromone sweet, like ripe dragon fruit. He had not smelled something like that in some years. The woman was a *virgin* of childbearing age.

Must have her . . . Need to find her.

His body went rigid as the scent continued to plague and torture his nose with irresistible sweetness. If there was one thing besides a true mate that a dragon couldn't deny himself, it was a virgin. A growl began to rumble at the back of his throat as he pictured himself finding this woman and curling his arms around her and breathing in her scent before he seduced her.

The old Grigori, the wild beast he thought had vanished this last century, was roaring back to life. His dragon was pacing inside him, ready to be unleashed. He wanted to sink his teeth into this woman's neck and hold her still while he thrust into her over and over until she screamed with pleasure.

"Mr. Barinov?" Yuri interrupted the sudden lust and hunger in Grigori's thoughts.

"Who is she?" he demanded in a low growl.

Yuri swallowed hard and held out a photograph, a print of a security camera photo of a woman.

"She is American. Her name is Madelyn Haynes. She's a professor at an American university."

Grigori stared down at the colored photo. It was slightly blurry, but he could tell that the woman had long strawberry blond hair and soft features. An ordinary woman, yet there was something about her face that he found fascinating. The lush curve of her lips, a slightly upturned nose and eyes framed by dark lashes. He lived in a city where beauty was praised and often the only way to survive. This woman would not have been considered pretty by such standards, but Grigori liked her full curves and romantic features more than he did the harsh, bony runway models that populated the Russian nightclubs.

Yes, she would be quite a delight to lock away in his dungeon.

He turned away from the security booth and exited the library. Back inside his car, he texted Madelyn's information to his brother. Within a few minutes Rurik sent the address for a hotel near the Red Square. He texted Rurik to meet him at the woman's hotel. He had a plan to trap their cunning little virgin and he was not going to let her escape.

※

Alexis Petrov slipped into the ladies restroom close to her office in Barinov Industries. Flipping the lock on the door so no one else could come in, she checked beneath the stalls to make sure she was alone. This was one of the few places she could make a call without being seen on surveillance videos. She dialed a number on the screen, hit call and waited, her heart pounding.

"Drakor here." The deep, growling voice sent shivers through her.

Dimitri Drakor was a veritable god, much like her own boss Grigori Barinov, but Drakor had promised her things Barinov never would.

Sex and power.

It had been too tempting to agree to spy on her boss the moment Drakor had taken her to his bed and promised her the world. All she had to do was tell him what Barinov was up to. It was her boss's fault—if only he hadn't ignored her! She was a former model and she knew she was gorgeous.

How can he ignore me? Me? I walked runways in Milan and Moscow! Resentment prickled her beneath her skin and she scowled.

"Barinov just left his office. He received a call from the Russian State Library."

Drakor breathed softly on the other end of the line before replying.

"Do you know what he was going there for?"

Alexis flinched. "No. Only that the moment he hung up, he left. That means it's important, right?"

"Yes, perhaps," Drakor mused. "Call me immediately with any more news." Then the phone connection went dead.

Alexis stared at her reflection the mirror for a long moment, her eyes haunted and her face suddenly showing her age. All of the parties, the drugs, the nights with powerful men who never called the next day had been a waste. She was past her prime.

Desperation drives us all. She forced a false smile on her lips, unlocked the bathroom door and stepped outside. She needed to be ready for when Mr. Barinov returned.

CHAPTER 3

"I DO NOT CARE WHAT COMES AFTER; I HAVE
SEEN DRAGONS ON THE WIND OF MORNING."
—URSULA K. LE GUIN

No one followed me.

Madelyn sighed in relief as she peered around the corner of the next street and watched the tourists mingling by the entrance to the Red Square. After two hours of dodging through streets and ducking into shop doorways, trying to look too interested in cheap touristy knick-knacks, she was fairly certain the guard from the library hadn't come after her. Her heart was still beating hard, but the panicked quick breaths had slowed.

"You're fine, everything's fine," she whispered. She smiled at an old man who pointed at some Lenin-shaped figurines, and she politely shook her head and walked away from his shop.

A young man selling food from a cart on the street caught her eye. She dug her travel wallet out and bought a bottle of water and a meat and cheese pie called a *pirozhki*. Her stomach grumbled as she took the pie and inhaled the tasty aroma. She'd been so focused on running she hadn't realized how hungry she was. As she ate, she kept her gaze alert for the guard, even though she was fairly certain he hadn't followed her. Even if he could find out her name from the library system, she hadn't had to supply any other information. The hotel would be a safe zone.

I hope...

Madelyn licked her fingertips as she finished the last bite of her *pirozhki*. She crumpled the wrapper of her pie and tossed it in trashcan before she sipped the last of her bottle of water. Then she followed the crowd across a busy street to her hotel. She was still a bit on edge, but if she got into her room, she'd feel more secure.

The hotel was a bit shabby on the outside, with a grey stoned façade. The faux glass windows of the lobby were slightly fogged with age, but she had a budget to live on and couldn't afford anything more expensive. She wasn't sure how long she'd need to stay in Moscow for her Russian dragon research. She would have been lying if she hadn't glanced at some of the more beautiful five star hotels when she'd been making her travel plans. They had taken her breath away with underground pools and fancy suites with endless amenities. It had been fun to dream about them, but she could never stay at a place like that, even for one night—no matter how incredible it would be to live like a princess in a king-sized bed and look out across the city from a deluxe room's balcony.

She pushed the doors to the lobby open and stepped inside. A faint tingling started beneath her skin, the fine hairs rising on her neck and arms in response. The air around her felt charged with energy, like the moment before a storm broke out. Madelyn paused, trying to assess the feeling inside her body as it responded to the sudden change in the air . . . A queer pulsing sensation began to build inside her, and a headache started to beat against her temples. She'd been fine just moments ago . . . Was her fear from earlier just now getting to her and her body was crashing from the adrenaline high she'd been on?

Maybe I just need to go take a quick nap in the room and take some Tylenol.

A man in blue jeans and a dark gray T-shirt was leaning against the wall by the elevators, his head down as he texted on his phone. Was he waiting for an elevator? He hadn't pressed the button . . . Madelyn tried not to look directly at him, as some men viewed it as an invitation. Her backpack was still full with pamphlets her mother had sent her about how to travel safely in Russian alone.

She couldn't help noting his muscled arms and the general attractiveness of his body. When she joined him at the elevator, she glanced down at her shoes, staring at the scuffed black boots peeking out from her own jeans.

A little flush heated her cheeks as she realized how boring she must have looked. Not that she wanted this man's attention. She didn't, but she'd been all too aware in the last week how unremarkable she was. So many women here wore bright sexy clothes or sleek business suits. She didn't fit into either group with her jeans and a cream colored Cashmere sweater. Not to mention she was a bit on the curvy side and Russian women her age were rarely curvy. They all seemed to be rail thin and ready for the runways and catwalks.

The metal elevator doors swished apart. She and the man both entered the tiny metal cubicle and she hit the button for the fourth floor. He continued to text and didn't hit a button.

Maybe we are on the same floor?

The second the doors slid closed her headache got worse. It was like two invisible spikes were being driven into her temples. She leaned against the side of the door farthest from the man, struggling to breathe. It was as though something inside was trying to claw to the surface.

What is happening to me? Fear clouded her rational thoughts. *Am I sick?* Was there something in her water from the vendor? Had she been drugged?

The man lifted his head a few inches, the fall of his brown hair still shadowing most of his features from view. The door opened to her floor and she stared at him. Was this his floor too? He still hadn't pushed a button for a different floor.

Something was wrong. She swallowed and tried to stay calm.

"Excuse me," the man waved her to go. "Please, go first," he said. His voice low and soft with a musical accent.

"Thank you." She took two shaky steps into the corridor before she realized that something was off. He knew she spoke English? How—she turned around to see him getting out of the elevator behind her.

Oh God... was he following her? She'd been warned before going to Russia that human trafficking was a risk and she had to be careful. She struggled to find her key, cursing as she walked to her door and trying not to look too panicked. Shooting another glance behind her, she saw the man was walking the opposite way down the hall.

She exhaled and sighed in relief against the door just as her hands closed around her keys. But she was still shaking and her legs were unsteady. The invisible knot of tension inside her was thrumming hard now, and every fiber of her being was on edge. That old instinct to run was whispering at her.

The key stuck in the lock and she had to jiggle the keys two times before the deadbolt slide back and she was able to get inside. The apartment was dark. Hadn't she left the curtains open? *I know I did...*

The door clicked shut behind her and she set her backpack down on small desk. She took a moment to catch her breath, and let the last few seconds of fear subside. She was safe inside her hotel.

I just need to chill. Everything is fine.

Seconds later, the light next to her bed switched on. A man sat in the chair by her bedside table and lowered his hand from the lamp back to the arm rest.

Madelyn jumped, clutching her purse to her chest. Her throat worked but no sounds out. There was a man in her room. *Oh God..*

The light washed over his pale gold hair and the three-piece gray wool suit he wore. Her eyes tracked up his expensive shoes to the beautiful, masculine hands resting on the chair's arms. A thick gold ring wound around the little finger of the man's right hand. She squinted at it and then her heart leapt into her throat. The ring was molded into the shape of a serpent biting its own tail. It looked exactly like the ring in James Barrow's book . . .

"Ms. Haynes, we need to talk." The man spoke, his rich accented voice pouring over her like cognac.

She lifted her gaze to the man's face and her heart stopped beating.

It was him.

The man from Barrow's book.

Grigori Barinov. The melancholic look of an ancient king whose time of ruling had long since passed into the mists, like a Russian King Arthur. With blue eyes and blond hair, he was not what one expected of a Russian man. Most of the men she'd seen in Moscow had dark hair and dark eyes. Strength and virility rolled off him in waves with a dominant air of calm and control that came from years of mastering oneself. Something about that made her shiver deep inside.

"Who are you?" she whispered, her voice catching. Had she passed out in the elevator? Was she dreaming? There was no way this was happening.

He couldn't be Grigori Barinov. Grigori was a man who had lived and breathed and died over two hundred years ago. There was no way he could be sitting in her hotel room looking like an intimidating fantasy. She wasn't sure if it was a fantasy born of secret desires or a nightmare. He had broken into her hotel room whoever he was and that wasn't a good thing.

The man reached up to remove the leather bound book from his jacket. *Barrow's journal.*

"I believe you already know who I am." As he spoke his blue eyes seem to turn to yellow, then to red and then they glowed white hot.

"But . . . You . . . It's not . . ." She couldn't wrap her mind around what he was trying to tell her. It was insane. It wasn't possible.

"Possible?" His full, kissable lips curved into a slow cold smile that sent fresh shivers through her.

"How . . ." she struggled for words, picturing the massive dragon perched on the edge of a cliff by a sea.

Her skin was almost on fire now, the pain making her want to scream but she didn't dare move or speak.

"'How' is not a question I will answer, at least not here." He rose from the chair and she stumbled back a step. He was too tall, at least six foot four. So much taller than her own five foot five. His height made her feel too small, too vulnerable. He could easily overpower her if she couldn't find a way to get out of here . . .

His perfectly cut suit molded to his muscled form like a second skin and his throat above his collar was sun-kissed. How could he be even slightly tan in the middle of a Russian October?

"Look, I don't want any trouble." She backed up another step, glancing around. She needed to find her phone. It had some international minutes . . . but she had no clue how to call the Russian police. Never in life had she felt so foolish than she did in that moment. Why hadn't she learned how to contact the police? Would it even matter? A panicked despair battled with her determination to survive.

"We are past that, Ms. Haynes. You're a liability now."

A liability? "But I don't even know what was in that book that even matters—" She swallowed hard and took another step, praying she could get to the door, but then she'd have to beat him to the stairs, because the elevator was out of the question.

"Unfortunately *everything* in that book matters. You must come with me," he said, taking another step.

Madelyn tensed, her hand searching for the doorknob behind her. When she found it, she wrapped her fingers around it and turned. The door opened with her body weight against it. Rather than fall into the open hallway, she bumped into something warm and hard.

"Going somewhere, *malen'kiy tsvetok?*" someone said from behind her.

"Ahh!" She screeched but the man behind her grabbed her

around the waist with one arm and covered her mouth with his other hand.

"Little flower?" Grigori asked the man behind her.

"She smells sweet," he replied gruffly.

Madelyn screamed against his hand but the sound was muffled. She kicked out her legs, knocking Grigori back a few steps. He clutched his chest and sucked in a breath, then lifted his head, scowling at her. She thrashed in the second man's arms, but there was no getting free. Blood roared in her ears. Grigori's eyes were blazing and he licked his lips before he spoke to the man behind her.

"Do you have her or not?" Grigori growled.

The man holding her tightened his grip and dragged her away from Grigori. How could he be a man from the past?

Grigori's eyes were back to blue, a pure, unfaceted color that glowed like a lake reflecting the summer sky. Madelyn stared into the blue depths and her limbs became too heavy to move.

"That's it, little one, let go," Grigori breathed, never taking his eyes off her. The hand around her mouth disappeared and yet she didn't scream or cry out. She was lost in his mesmerizing gaze.

"Let your mind go . . ." Grigori's voice wrapped around her, and she suddenly was falling through space and time. As her eyes closed she saw a distant horizon, a memory so old she never knew she had it . . .

The grass was as soft as velvet as she toddled over toward her parents. They were sitting beneath a tall redwood tree. Her father had his back to the tree with his legs spread so her mother could lay back against him in the cradle of his body.

"She's growing so fast," her father said, smiling, but a tinge of sadness colored his gray eyes.

"Not too fast." Her mother held out her arms to Madelyn. "Madelyn, come here."

Her legs wobbled as she walked over the spongy grass. When she reached her mother, the feeling of being warm and safe made her sigh and nuzzle her face in the crook of her mother's neck. Her father circled his arms around them both, holding them in an unbreakable trinity.

"Why can't we stay here?" her mother asked wistfully.

"It's too dangerous. We must keep moving."

Madelyn didn't fully understand the words, not as a child. She'd only known that they'd meant leaving the sunny fields and ancient redwoods.

"I wish she didn't have to grow up on the run like us." Her mother's voice was soft with quiet grief.

"I know, honey, I know. Maybe someday she won't live in fear as we do."

The memory started to fade and Madelyn sank deeper and deeper into a dreamless sleep, Grigori's face following her into the depths.

"Give her to me." Grigori held out his arms and his brother handed him the unconscious woman. The feel of her completely in his control, made him relax as they left the hotel room. From the moment he'd picked up her scent on Barrow's book earlier that afternoon, he'd been possessed of a wild need to find her. It hadn't helped that once they found her, his brother had been the one to grab and hold onto her. His dragon had hissed softly inside his head.

"How was she able to stay awake for so long?" Rurik asked. "You used to be able to knock out mortals in mere seconds. That took nearly two minutes." He stroked his chin thoughtfully as he eyed the woman in Grigori's arms.

The uneasy thought struck him too. A dragon shifter's gaze could mesmerize and short-circuit a human's mind and knock them out. But the little American woman had simply looked dazed at first. It had taken too long to affect her.

"Something isn't right about her," Rurik muttered as they entered the elevator and rode it down to the lobby. "She makes my skin crawl whenever I get too close. But she smells divine and I just keep thinking about how much I want to take her to my bed . . ." He leaned over and inhaled her scent deeply.

Grigori almost growled at his brother. This was *his* woman, and he had no intention of sharing her. Rurik was a charmer who never slept with the same woman twice. He had no right to bed this singular beauty and move on.

"What you're smelling is her purity."

"Her what?" Rurik crossed his arms, scowling in open confusion.

It was easy to forget sometimes his younger brother was so young compared to him. There were things Rurik didn't know about their other halves, the dragons within.

"She's a virgin. You've probably never been around one of child-bearing age. They put off the most enticing sent. It's irresistible . . . to some." He didn't want his brother to know just how intoxicating the scent was to him. Just a hint of it clinging to Barrow's book had captivated him. Now that he held the female in his arms, her aroma enveloping him completely, he was addicted to it.

"A virgin?" Rurik practically choked on the word.

Before either of them could speak, the elevator doors chimed and slid open. They walked through the empty lobby and headed for the sleek black sedan parked outside. Rurik and the driver helped him get Madelyn inside. Only a few people in the streets dared to stare as they left. Most humans knew when to avert their gazes when in the presence of dragons. Some instincts were still strong in them, and they sensed that Grigori and Rurik were not to be trifled with.

The entire ride to Grigori's apartment building he held Madelyn his lap, overcome by a possessive urge to never let her go. She was like a jewel, precious piece of gold that he wanted to secure in a safe haven and guard, even sleeping with one eye open. He smiled as he drank in the sight of her face. She was even lovelier than he'd expected. The glimpse from the security camera photo hadn't done her justice.

"Why are you smiling?" Rurik demanded suspiciously. "You *never* smile."

Despite his frustration with his brother, Grigori didn't stop smiling. "I don't know, I can't seem to stop it. But she's mine. Do you understand? You're not to touch her. Are we clear?"

Rurik's brown eyes blazed to life. "Is that a challenge?" If he had been in his dragon form, the ruffled frill about his neck would have stood up in an opposing way to make him look bigger, fiercer. As a battle dragon, it would have been a deadly warning to anyone save close family.

"It's not a challenge." Grigori returned the warning with a growl of his own. "She is mine, end of discussion. You have an entire city of women who worship you. You do not need this one."

Rurik huffed, the sound so similar to the disgruntled noise as he made in dragon form that Grigori laughed softly.

"It's not as though I know what to do with a virgin anyway," his brother muttered.

Grigori's smile only widened. Rurik may not know what to do with a virgin, but Grigori definitely did. It had been so long since he had the pleasure of making love to a woman and introducing her to the sensual world that awaited her, but it wasn't something a man forgot.

In that moment, he decided it didn't matter what Madelyn's plans were in regard to James Barrow's book. He would discover that soon enough, but he was going to seduce her and possess her. While he had the strength to force her, he'd never done that to any female. Any man could take a woman's body, but only a master could make them surrender to passion of their own free will. And he wanted Madelyn to surrender to him.

When they arrived at his penthouse, Grigori carried Madelyn to his bedroom and set Barrow's journal on the night stand beside the bed. She was still unconscious and would be for several hours. It would give him time to make arrangements. He was going to take her home, to his house in the country. It was a place he could be himself and not worry about the city or the restraints it placed on his dragon half.

Grigori removed Madelyn's coat and slipped her boots off before he placed a pillow beneath her head. Her hair was soft, like silk beneath his hands as he brushed it away from her face. Even just an innocent touch made his body tense with hunger. He had to regain control.

He retrieved a white mink fur blanket and draped it over Madelyn's sleeping form. Impulsively, he leaned over to brush his lips on hers before he turned off the lights and closed the bedroom door.

"You're acting very strange, brother," Rurik noted. He was leaning back the doorway to the bedroom.

Grigori bristled. "I am not acting any differently." He used the tone that Rurik would recognize as a warning to drop the subject. But Grigori knew he was acting differently. The little human was bringing out old instincts in him, ones he thought he'd mastered long ago.

As the eldest of their family, his duty was the preservation of their lands and its protection. It was also his duty to carry on their line by either finding his true mate or by breeding with an eligible dragoness. He couldn't afford to let himself become entangled with a mortal that would leave him open and vulnerable. The pressure of his duties had left him cool, aloof, and in many ways unchanged over the years. But he was willing to let that part of himself go in order to seduce Madelyn.

"Come into the kitchen with me," Grigori closed the bedroom door and they headed into his kitchen.

His brother trailed a fingertip along the onyx granite countertop. "You aren't considering starting a relationship with a mortal. You know that doesn't end well, at least not unless you promise to keep it to only one night. Let's not forget she was researching the Barrow journal, and the last time I checked, that made her a possible enemy. She could be working for the Brotherhood of the Blood Moon. Or worse . . ." His brother frowned. "She could be working for the Drakors. Better be careful with this one, Grigori. After losing Mikhail, we cannot take any chances."

"I know," Grigori replied, not admitting he was planning more than one night with Madelyn. The last thing he needed was his little brother lecturing him on relationships and not sleeping with the enemy.

Their middle brother, Mikhail . . . The mere thought of his name struck Grigori like a dagger to his heart. His brother was in exile. They didn't know if he was even still alive. The last time he'd seen Mikhail had been two hundred years ago, the year he had returned home and brought James Barrow with him.

We were the fools who spilled our secrets. Barrow had never intended his diary to be their potential downfall, but over the years it simply became a font of knowledge that no one expected to survive the ravages of time.

"Grigori, I know you. You hide in your office, running the family business and playing the part of a mortal, but you are not. You are the eldest Barinov dragon. You cannot lose yourself to some human female. Even assuming she's not helping to bring us down and destroy our family, she will make you soft and when she's gone . . . It will weaken you. You're acting like she's a possible true mate. Father warned us about mortals," Rurik said.

The mention of their father brought back ancient memories. It was strange to think that their father had only died only two decades ago. It felt as though he'd been gone for a lifetime.

"I remember." He shut his eyes for a brief moment and almost saw his father's face, the stern but loving countenance as he told Grigori and his brothers the rules of dragons. *"Never mate a mortal. When dragons lose their mates, they grieve deeply and don't live much past the moment their mate dies."*

"She isn't my true mate, it's simply her scent that's caught me. But I do plan to seduce her."

Rurik chuckled. "Father said that about mother, you know. He only wanted to seduce her and thought he could resist her being his true mate. They ended up mated for three thousand years."

"But Mother was a Dragoness, not a mortal," Grigori reminded him. He walked over to his stainless steel wine fridge and retrieved a fifty-year-old bottle of Bordeaux and a glass. He reached for second one but his brother interrupted him.

"None for me. I have to head back. The club needs me. Call if the little mortal gives you any trouble."

"She won't." He listened to the sound of his brother's laughter, scowling until he heard the door to his penthouse close.

Then he poured himself a glass of wine, retrieved a book of German poetry by Rainer Maria Rilke, and sat in his favorite chair by the fire place in the center of the room. His fireplace was a circular stone structure two feet tall and was full of glass crystals with flames powered by gas. The sight was intoxicating, like diamonds on fire. Two of his *favorite* things. He tried to lose himself in the poetry and not think about Madelyn asleep in the other room. The scent of her filled his head and made his body throb with an almost violent need, but he kept control. *Barely* . . .

THANK YOU FOR READING! I HOPE YOU ENJOYED RURIK! BE sure to turn the page to see a sneak peek of the cover of *The Lost Barinov Dragon*, the 4th upcoming book in the series!

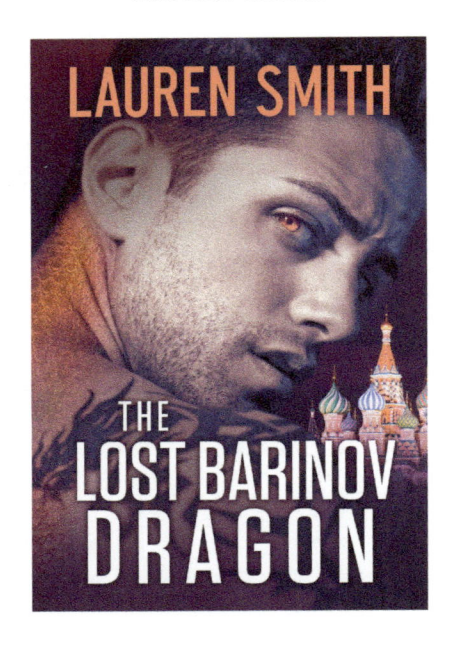

LAUREN SMITH

THE LOST BARINOV DRAGON

OTHER TITLES BY LAUREN SMITH

Historical
The League of Rogues Series
Wicked Designs
His Wicked Seduction
Her Wicked Proposal
Wicked Rivals
Her Wicked Longing
His Wicked Embrace (coming March 2018)
The Earl of Pembroke (coming March 2018)
His Wicked Secret (coming soon)
The Seduction Series
The Duelist's Seduction
The Rakehell's Seduction
The Rogue's Seduction (coming March 2018)
Standalone Stories
Tempted by A Rogue
Sins and Scandals
An Earl By Any Other Name
A Gentleman Never Surrenders
A Scottish Lord for Christmas

Contemporary
The Surrender Series
The Gilded Cuff
The Gilded Cage
The Gilded Chain
Her British Stepbrother
Forbidden: Her British Stepbrother
Seduction: Her British Stepbrother
Climax: Her British Stepbrother

Paranormal
Dark Seductions Series
The Shadows of Stormclyffe Hall
The Love Bites Series
The Bite of Winter
Brotherhood of the Blood Moon Series
Blood Moon on the Rise (coming soon)
Brothers of Ash and Fire
Grigori: A Royal Dragon Romance
Mikhail: A Royal Dragon Romance
Rurik: A Royal Dragon Romance

Sci-Fi Romance
Cyborg Genesis Series
Across the Stars (coming soon)

ABOUT THE AUTHOR

Lauren Smith is an Oklahoma attorney by day, author by night who pens adventurous and edgy romance stories by the light of her smart phone flashlight app. She knew she was destined to be a romance writer when she attempted to re-write the entire *Titanic* movie just to save Jack from drowning. Connecting with readers by writing emotionally moving, realistic and sexy romances no matter what time period is her passion. She's won multiple awards in several romance subgenres including: New England Reader's Choice Awards, Greater Detroit BookSeller's Best

Awards, and a Semi-Finalist award for the Mary Wollstonecraft Shelley Award.

To Connect with Lauren, visit her at:
www.laurensmithbooks.com
lauren@laurensmithbooks.com

 facebook.com/LaurenDianaSmith
 twitter.com/LSmithAuthor
 instagram.com/Laurensmithbooks

CPSIA information can be obtained
at www.ICGtesting.com
Printed in the USA
LVHW071551090119
603249LV00027B/69/P

9 781947 206236